NO REST FOR THE DEAD

A NOVEL

BY

JEFF ABBOTT • LORI ARMSTRONG • SANDRA BROWN
THOMAS COOK • JEFFERY DEAVER • DIANA GABALDON
TESS GERRITSEN • ANDREW F. GULLI • PETER JAMES
J.A. JANCE • FAYE KELLERMAN • RAYMOND KHOURY
JOHN LESCROART • JEFF LINDSAY • GAYLE LYNDS
PHILLIP MARGOLIN • ALEXANDER McCALL SMITH
MICHAEL PALMER • T. JEFFERSON PARKER
MATTHEW PEARL • KATHY REICHS • MARCUS SAKEY
JONATHAN SANTLOFER • LISA SCOTTOLINE
R. L. STINE • MARCIA TALLEY

EDITED BY ANDREW F. GULLI AND LAMIA J. GULLI

WITH AN INTRODUCTION BY DAVID BALDACCI

A TOUCHSTONE BOOK
PUBLISHED BY SIMON & SCHUSTER
NEW YORK   LONDON   TORONTO   SYDNEY

Touchstone
A Division of Simon & Schuster, Inc.
1230 Avenue of the Americas
New York, NY 10020

First Touchstone hardcover edition July 2011

TOUCHSTONE and colophon are registered trademarks of Simon & Schuster, Inc.

For information about special discounts for bulk purchases, please contact Simon & Schuster Special Sales at 1-866-506-1949 or business@simonandschuster.com.

The Simon & Schuster Speakers Bureau can bring authors to your live event. For more information or to book an event contact the Simon & Schuster Speakers Bureau at 1-866-248-3049 or visit our website at www.simonspeakers.com.

Designed by Akasha Archer

Manufactured in the United States of America

10 9 8 7 6 5 4 3 2 1

Library of Congress Cataloging-in-Publication Data
    No rest for the dead : a novel / by Sandra Brown . . . [et al.] ; with an introduction by David Baldacci.
        p.   cm.
    I. Brown, Sandra.
    PS3600.A1N62 1011
    813'.6—dc22   2010050146

ISBN 978-1-4516-0737-6
ISBN 978-1-4516-0739-0 (ebook)

For Mom and Dad

Contents

CONTENTS

The three transitional passages on pages 101, 109 and 158 were written by Jonathan Santlofer.

Introduction

DAVID BALDACCI

With the typical mystery story, readers are enthralled by the talents and imagination of only one writer. However, with this crime caper, the reader will enjoy the skillful spoils of *twenty-six* esteemed wordsmiths who craft plots, wield poisons, and toggle the life-death switch with the best of them. This is a rare thing indeed because mystery writers are notoriously reclusive, paranoid, and unfriendly folks when it comes to their work. They like calling the final shots on their novels; such absolute power is intoxicating if only for its rarity, particularly if they've sold their work to Hollywood and find that their power has withered to less than zero. However, outside the realm of stories and with drink in hand, they are interesting and convivial people who always have a crowd around them at parties, as all good storytellers do. That so many have agreed to craft chapters in the tale you're about to plunge into is as much a testament to the persuasive powers of the editors at *The Strand Magazine* as it is to the graciousness of the creators assembled here.

Mysteries are the guilty cheats of the book world. Some highbrow critics and reviewers look down on them in public and then eagerly read them on the subway hidden behind an absolutely pristine copy of *Ulysses,* bubbling with the pleasure of the child who has just discovered Sherlock Holmes. It is also perhaps the sole arena on processed paper where the reader can match wits with the creator. If you're really good, you can sometimes arrive at the answer before the creator wants you to. You may also cry, as you do with love-story weepies; or laugh as you may at the pratfalls of comic characters; or be horrified as only horror stories can induce. Yet with the unique class of the whodunit you may enjoy all of those emotional swings and still be primed and poised to reveal the answer prematurely! And if you do succeed in besting the creator, you of course have de facto license to race to Amazon or Barnes andnoble.com, or else your personal blog, and crow about your victory to the digital heavens.

However, here I believe you will have met your match. The lineup of writers who have contributed to this mystery is akin to the Murderers' Row of the 1927 New York Yankees. There is not a weak spot in the bunch. You will be enthralled as much by the charming quirks provided by individual voices as the story passes from one creator's mind to the next as you will by the quality of the tale. While they each deliver their own signature brand of storytelling to the novel, it is startling how these writers, several of whom are friends of mine, have woven a yarn that seems to be the product of one mind, one imagination (albeit schizophrenic), and one on steroids of such strength that even Major League Baseball would ban them, and that is indeed saying something.

The story kicks off with a bang. A murderess was executed ten years ago. Rosemary Thomas brutally killed her husband, Christopher Thomas, stuffing his body inside an iron maiden and shipping it to the German Historical Museum of Berlin. Everyone knows she did it, though a few doubts linger, which led to the detective in charge losing his bearings and his wife. Then a stunner comes along. A memorial service is planned for Rosemary on the tenth anniversary of her execution. All the usual suspects, and several folks with passable motives to have done the deed, are invited. The scene is set. I won't give away any more than that because it would be unfair to the creators who have worked hard to put this all together.

Yet I will add that if you were expecting an Agatha Christie ending where Poirot or Marple stands up, calmly lays out the case, and reveals the true murderer, you're in for a shock. The creators have, collectively, another denouement in mind. And in my humble opinion it's a twist that is so original you won't have to concern yourself with bragging on your blog about how you figured it all out long before the conclusion. Well, I guess you still can, but you'd be lying.

If this were a peer-review process, I'd give everyone involved a glowing report. A vigilant reader can certainly tell when a writer is operating at a high level. But it really takes another writer to delve into the nuances of a story, break it down like game film, and truly see the effort that has gone into the product. We can well appreciate what it takes because we aspire to do it with every book. Being merely human, sometimes we triumph and sometimes we don't.

Yet there's nothing like drilling a line just right, honing a plot twist to perfection, or tooling a character arc until it gleams with the shine of genius. All of which originates with the sweat on the writer's brow. It's hard, what these writers have done. Give them their due. When you've finished with the story, tell your friends to read it. Let them in on the fun. Tell them it's a brain twister for sure. And, okay, you can tell them you figured it out in the last three pages and therefore found it a bit predictable, but they won't. Which will make you look like a person who is several pay grades above the FBI's best. And everyone will have a good time enjoying the simple (and complex) experience of tearing through a great mystery.

Read on!

Diary of Jon Nunn

ANDREW F. GULLI

August 2010

There is always that case, the one that keeps me awake at night, the one that got away. It'll always be there, gnawing at the edges of my mind. It doesn't matter that ten years have passed, it doesn't matter that the case is officially closed. An innocent woman was executed, I was the one who helped make it happen, and on the sad night when the needle was inserted into her arm, injecting her with death, part of my life ended too.

Back then, I thought I was working a straightforward case, but every action I was taking was a step closer to ending it for Rosemary—destroying her life and mine. I thought I had the facts—the physical evidence: the bloodstained blouse, the missing button, her fingerprints; her contradictory answers during the investigation; the public argument she'd had with her husband after he demanded a divorce; her trip to Mexico the week he went missing when she'd told friends that she doubted Christopher would ever come back. Of course she was right. He never did come back, not alive.

Christopher Thomas's badly decayed body was found inside an iron maiden in the German Historical Museum of Berlin several weeks later. It seemed like a simple case, crazy, but simple: in a fit of rage Rosemary Thomas killed her husband, then dragged his body inside the maiden because she knew that it was going to be shipped back to Germany.

It didn't take long for the jury to convict her.

An open-and-shut case.

And yet . . .

It never felt right, never made sense. Sure, there was motive and opportunity, there was the physical evidence, but if you met her, if you knew her the way I got to know her . . .

But it wasn't until later, after I'd taken a step back from the case, that I realized it had angles I hadn't seen, layers I hadn't uncovered, back when it mattered, back when I could have saved her. Back when I was too busy making sure not to let any personal feelings for the suspect interfere with my duty. Back when I was standing too close to see anything clearly. Maybe some of you have seen the movie *Vertigo*. Well, picture me as the guy who is manipulated like a puppet and whose life unravels as a result.

Luckily, I had a friend.

When I was lost and close to suicide after Sarah left, Tony Olsen picked me up and never let me feel that I was a burden, or that he was doing me any favors. When I was drinking myself into oblivion, it was Tony who brought me to his home, made sure I stayed away from drink, and gave me a job handling security for his firm. The crazy thing is he'd also been a friend of Rosemary's . . . you'd think after what I had done he'd want me dead.

I gave up drinking but the ghosts remained, and for years, both drunk and sober, I've fantasized about getting all the suspects together, all those I'd mistakenly ruled out, getting at the facts and exacting justice, for Rosemary, for her kids, for my own life.

It took me a long time, but I managed to convince Tony to help me. I needed closure, and it could only come from a second bite of that poisoned apple. It's why now, all these years later, I need to get the principals together in one place. I need to confront the people who might have done it.

But Tony was right—we couldn't just *ask* them to come together to give me another crack at solving the case.

We talked a lot about it, how we could get them all together, but the answer was there all the time—the memorial that Rosemary had requested in her last will and testament, to commemorate the tenth anniversary of her death. The innocent would pay their respects. The guilty would attend to avoid rousing suspicion. And why worry? Rosemary had been found guilty and executed. No DA in his right mind was going to reopen the case. They would all come, I was sure of it, some of them wearing innocence like a mask.

I've been an agnostic all my life. I've never believed in anything. I can't imagine the phoenix rising from the ashes. From what I've seen, ashes always remain ashes, and sooner or later everything rots and decays. But with this idea of bringing them together, of finally uncovering the guilty party, I was going to resurrect myself.

You're probably thinking I'm just a policeman obsessed with a case he couldn't crack. But you're wrong. It's more than that. I have to know the truth: the truth about Rosemary and the truth about who really killed Christopher Thomas. You see, I have to find out who destroyed my life, who slept well the night Rosemary Thomas knew she'd never again see the bright morning through her cold prison bars.

Prologue

JONATHAN SANTLOFER

August 23, 2000
Valley State Prison for Women
Chowchilla, California

I *am already a ghost.*

Rosemary Thomas stared at her long fingers painted with stripes, the cell's bars casting shadows. She raised her hand and studied it as if it were a newly discovered specimen, noting the pale blue veins under translucent flesh.

Yes, she thought, *I am disappearing.* She traced fingertips across her cheeks like a blind woman touching a stranger's face, could barely feel them, barely take in the reality of her situation: *I have less than an hour to live.*

"How did this happen?" she whispered to no one, yet it was real and she knew it, knew that her husband, Christopher, had been murdered, knew that he had absurdly been sealed into an eighteenth-century torture device on loan to *her* department of the museum, knew that all of the evidence somehow pointed to her.

WIFE'S FINGERPRINTS ON IRON MAIDEN

Just one of the many headlines in the many newspapers that detailed the crime, *her* crime, or so the district attorney had proved.

Rosemary pictured him, an aging peacock in a three-piece suit, how he'd lobbied loudly and publicly for equality—*No deals for the rich!* his motto throughout the trial—and with his reelection only weeks away not something he was going to trade for the life of *one rich woman*. He'd gone for blood on day one, asking a surprised judge and jury for the death penalty and "nothing less."

Her case had become a cause célèbre, pro-life versus pro-death forces having a field day. Funny, thought Rosemary, that it had taken a murder to finally get her some attention.

Had it not been an election year with the DA, the judge, *and* the governor up for reelection, her lawyer insisted she would have gotten a reduced sentence.

But it *was* an election year. And she *was* going to die.

When had it happened, when had she finally given up hope? When her brother's words condemned her, or when the cop, Jon Nunn, whom she'd trusted, had given his damning testimony?

She thought of the burly cop on the stand, hair a mess, three days' growth of beard, the dark circles under his eyes. And how, when he'd finished testifying, he'd glanced over at her with eyes so sad that she'd nodded in spite of her anger, as if to say she understood he was doing his job, even as she realized that the prosecution now had all they needed, and the absolute certainty of her fate washed over her.

Rosemary sighed, took in the bare walls of the special security cell where she'd been moved after she'd lost her last appeal. She had lived with two weeks of hourly checks, the "death watch" as it was known, a guard taking notes as if there were something to report: the inmate moved from bed to chair; the inmate did not eat her dinner; the inmate wrote in her diary; the inmate is crying.

Yes, she had cried. But not anymore. She was past tears. That's what she'd told the psychiatrist and the chaplain and the caseworker, all of them well-meaning but useless. What could they do for her?

She was sane.

She'd been born a Christian but was now an agnostic.

She was charitable.

She'd actually said that to the caseworker, and the absurdity of the statement had made them both laugh.

Was it the last time she would ever laugh?

Rosemary paced across the tiny cell, back and forth, hand tapping her side, adrenaline coursing through her veins. She hadn't slept but wasn't tired, the evidence against her replaying on automatic—the blouse, the button, her strands of hair, the fight, the fingerprints—but none of it mattered now. She was going to die.

Today, her last twenty-four hours, she'd felt almost resigned to her fate. That was how she'd described her state of mind to her friend and only visitor, Belle McGuire.

Loyal, dependable Belle. She had given Belle something to safe-guard until the children were older. But would it even matter in ten years time? It would to Ben and Leila; it always would to them. Rosemary squeezed her eyes shut at the thought of her children. She'd refused the nanny who offered to bring them to say good-bye. How do you say good-bye forever to your children? How do you explain this to them?

She sagged onto her cot, played with a loose thread at the cuff of her orange jumpsuit, wrapped it so tightly around her finger the tip turned white, until the picture of another finger—Christopher's finger—flashed in her mind along with other crime scene photos of her dead husband's decomposed body.

Rosemary pushed herself up from the cot, six steps to the bars, pressed her cheek against cold steel, squinted to read the clock at the far end of the hall. But why? To tell her that the minutes of what was left of her life were ticking away?

She turned away and stared at the tray on the edge of her bed, stains blooming through the napkin. Her last meal—a cheeseburger and fries—ordered when the sad, smiling guard said she could have any-thing she wanted.

Anything? A new trial? Freedom? Her life?

She'd returned the woman's sad smile. "I don't care," she'd said. And when the cheeseburger had arrived oozing blood, with fat french fries lapping up the liquid like leeches, she'd covered it with a napkin, the thought of eating impossible.

She hadn't been able to eat in weeks, living on tea and crackers and last night a few cherries Belle had brought from her garden, which had stained her fingers like blood.

A shadow fell across the bars and Rosemary looked up—the war-den, three guards, and the prison chaplain.

"It's time," said the guard, the one with the sad, kind face, a heavyset woman whom Rosemary had come to know during the time she'd spent behind bars. Images fluttered through her mind like a series of snap-shots: standing beside her father, his stern face turned away from hers as it always was; an awkward debutante at her coming-out party, tall and gangly; and in white lace on her wedding day, Christopher Thomas beside her.

Christopher, her beautiful shining knight.

Christopher, who had betrayed her.

"Are you ready?" the guard asked, unable to meet Rosemary's eyes.

An absurd question, thought Rosemary. *What if I say,* No, I'm not ready? *What then?* She imagined herself tearing down the hall, the guards running after her, inmates cheering and jeering. But she said, "Yes, I'm ready."

There were no handcuffs, no chains, just guards on either side of her, the prison chaplain carrying an open Bible, the warden leading the way.

How odd, thought Rosemary, *that I feel . . . nothing.*

The sad, kind guard held her arm, and the hallway stretched out in front of her. A fluorescent light flickered. The walk seemed to take forever.

They led her through an oval-shaped door into an octagonal room, and Rosemary saw the gurney that filled half the space and a table with tourniquets and needles laid out and windows all around, and she realized it was a show and that she was the main attraction.

She gasped, breath caught in her throat. She felt her legs go weak, sagged, and might have fallen if the guard did not have a firm grip on her arm.

"Are you okay?" the woman asked.

Rosemary said, "I'm . . . fine," thinking, *I will be dead soon.*

They were led, like mourners, through a side door that opened into a circular passageway that surrounded the execution chamber.

Jon Nunn watched as the witnesses assumed positions, like sentries, at each of the five windows, curtains drawn. They stared at the glass, at faint, distorted reflections of themselves. He looked from one to another: the district attorney, for once quiet; the judge, a woman who'd played tough along with the DA, nervously wringing her hands; Rosemary's brother, Peter, who had practically banged into him only moments earlier, booze on his breath; the reporter Hank Zacharius. There were other reporters too, guards and state officials, everyone somber and stony except for Belle McGuire, Rosemary's friend, face flushed and crying, the only one seemingly overcome by emotion.

Nunn thought of Rosemary the first time he'd met her, how tough she'd pretended to be, and hoped she could muster some of that toughness today, though his own reserve was empty.

Earlier this evening, he and Sarah had argued, not for the first time, about the trial, the crime, Sarah saying that the case had become his obsession and he could no longer answer her accusations or deny them, and he had stormed out—as he had on so many other nights—leaving her behind, fuming. He'd hung out in a bar till it closed, then found another that stayed open all night. Peter Heusen was not the only one with booze on his breath.

The "tie-down team" had strapped her to the gurney, five big men to tie down one small woman—a man at her head, one on each arm, one for each leg. Now there were straps across her chest, wrists, abdomen, the sound of Velcro remaining opening and closing still playing in Rosemary's ears.

"Rest your head on the pillow," one said.

Rest my head? Are they kidding? But she did, even said, "Thank you"—always the well-brought-up girl. She thought of her mother and for once was glad her parents were dead.

She stared at the ceiling, the walls, counted gray tiles versus white ones, anything to keep her mind occupied, spotted the camera, and thought, *They are recording my death,* and prayed she would be dignified, that she would not scream and that her body would not betray her with spasms. She couldn't bear the thought of that.

"Okay," said the man at her head, and the one at her leg touched her ankle so gently, so tenderly, she fought to control her tears.

The tie-down crew was replaced by a medical team, technicians wrapping tubes around her arms, flicking at her flesh to find veins.

She caught sight of the catheters and shivered.

"Can you make a fist?" one asked, and she did, pretending they were just taking blood, and thought of the blood test she'd taken before she was married and how excited she'd been to become *Mrs.* Christopher Thomas: how much she'd hoped for and how little had come true. She thought of the nights she lay awake, humiliated, waiting for him, knowing he was in another woman's bed, wishing him dead, wanting to kill him.

One of the technicians missed the vein and Rosemary flinched, tears automatically springing to her eyes.

No, don't cry. She squeezed her eyes shut.

Again and again the technicians tried and failed, until one of them finally said, "There, that's one," while the other continued to stab her arm over and over. "The veins have gone totally flat," he said.

Not *her* veins. *The* veins.

She wanted to scream, *I'm still alive.*

"Lemme help," said the other one, the two of them poking at her arm, dark shadows looming over her, and an image came to her, in the vet's office years ago, having her cocker spaniel put to sleep, the old dog riddled with cancer. How merciful it had seemed, the dog nestled peacefully in her arms while the vet got the IV going. "You're just going to sleep," she'd said, tears in her eyes, and had believed that until the creature let out a deep, guttural yelp, something she'd never heard before, and Rosemary had to steady his soft, old body, pet him, and whisper assurances, "There, there," until the drug got into his bloodstream and he went limp. She came back to the moment, looked at the group of people in the chamber and wondered, *Where are* my *assurances?*

"Okay," said the technician, taping the second IV to her arm, "we finally got it."

Please, God, let it be over quickly, thought Rosemary.

The technicians left and the warden and the chaplain came in.

The warden raised his hand and the curtains opened and she saw them.

Her heart pounding, Rosemary thought, *My audience. Some are witnesses to my death, some are participants.*

Her brother, Peter Heusen. Drunk already, she could tell, from the bleary eyes. She'd refused to see Peter this morning. She knew he'd simply been trying to cleanse his conscience.

There were other faces too, people she didn't know. And there was Belle, crying, watching Rosemary through the glass.

And Jon Nunn, who had tried to visit, but she'd refused him as she had every other time he'd requested. They locked eyes and he smoothed his shirt, then brushed absently at his stubble, as if suddenly upset at his rumpled appearance.

Rosemary scanned the crowd and her eyes stopped on Hank Zacharius, the journalist . . . her friend. He'd argued in article after article that they were executing an innocent woman, a woman who had been railroaded by an avid prosecutor and judge. She could still remember his attempts to question the evidence.

Hank Zacharius tried to convince himself that he'd come strictly as a witness and reporter—not as a friend—that he'd write one last piece detailing the horrors of capital punishment and that the writing would distance him from the event, but his heart was beating fast and his mouth had gone dry. He stared through the glass at Rosemary and took several deep breaths. He could not help but notice how thin she had grown, the once delicate bone structure of her face now skull-like, her bony arms bruised where the technicians had made their clumsy attempts to insert the fourteen-gauge catheters, the largest commercially available needles, that would deliver the mix of anesthetic and poison to stop Rosemary's heart. He thought about how hard he'd tried to prevent this from happening. His mind kept going back to the articles he'd written about the case.

> *Christopher Thomas's body was found in an advanced state of decomposition due to its incarceration in a contraption known as an iron maiden, which acted as a kind of pressure cooker. The device also crushed the deceased's teeth, though an identifiable fragment was discovered in the iron maiden itself.*
>
> *This reporter has argued that it would have been impossible for the accused, a 130-pound woman, to have lifted a man of more than six feet and 180 pounds into the iron maiden by herself. The state has put forth the idea that she had help from a known drug runner, who had been seen at the McFall Art Museum and who has subsequently and conveniently disappeared from sight.*
>
> *If Rosemary Thomas is executed on evidence that could have been planted, it will be the result of a witch hunt, of politicos saving their jobs, of trying to prove the wealthy can be treated as badly as the poor.*

But Zacharius's writings were tainted by his having known Rosemary since college, by their having been friends, and their relationship was used to discredit him: *He is partial. He is a friend. He is distorting the evidence.* And it didn't help that he'd written a series of anti-capital-punishment articles for *Rolling Stone* just a few months earlier, which made it look as if he were simply taking up his cause once again.

Zacharius stared past Rosemary and through the glass opposite saw Peter Heusen, weaving slightly, as if he might fall.

He's drunk, thought Zacharius. *Rosemary's goddamn brother is drunk.*

Peter Heusen was having trouble keeping down his breakfast of eggs Benedict chased by two tumblers of bourbon. His stomach roiled and his head ached. He swallowed hard and worried he might be sick. He saw himself in the witness box, stating how his sister had, more than once, said she'd wanted her husband dead. Of course he'd added that he was certain it was just a figure of speech, "though one could hardly blame my sister if she *did* kill that philandering scoundrel; I mean, who wouldn't?"

Peter Heusen swallowed again. What he wouldn't do for another glass of bourbon. He licked his lips and thought of Rosemary's young children, Leila and Ben, at home with their nanny, and what he would say to them later . . . *Oh, your poor dear mother.* He glanced at his older sister and thought how she'd always taken care of him. Rosemary the Responsible, that's what he'd called her, and he felt a tremor through his body. Even now she looked responsible, in control. *Always the opposite of me,* he thought, and swallowed again, and caught her eyes.

The warden took up his position at Rosemary's head.

The chaplain by her side asked, "Do you have anything to say?"

She looked again at the people on the other side of the windows and saw the district attorney and the judge . . . those who stopped at nothing to see that justice was done.

Justice? . . .

Oh, do I have some things to say. . . .

And she must have nodded because a boom mike descended from the ceiling.

But instead Rosemary shut her eyes and pictured her childhood bedroom, she and her mother kneeling beside her bed.

"Now I lay me down to sleep . . ."

She heard her words amplified through the mike and felt a hand on her arm, imagined it was her mother, though she knew it was the chaplain.

". . . if I should die before I—"

But the words suddenly made no sense—there was no *if*.

Rosemary tried to make her mind a blank, but images of her children bloomed like developing photographs, beautiful, innocent faces, and she could not stop herself from thinking that she would never see them again, never see them grow older, would miss their teenage years and college and marriages and grandchildren. And though she tried not to, a strangled sob burst out of her.

Melissa Franklin Forrest heard the cry and flinched. She had been staring at a spot above Rosemary's head—anything to avoid the woman's eyes—but now, hearing that sound and seeing the tears on Rosemary's face, she felt her own tears gathering.

She'd spent more than half her life as a judge and was considered a fair one. She had fought for reelection more than once, but right now it felt as if all of the good work she'd done was behind her—that this was the one act she would be remembered for, the one that would haunt her for the remainder of her life.

She had not wanted to be here, had not wanted to be a witness, but the state had insisted. She twisted a plain gold band around her finger, tried to breathe normally though her heart raced and her head felt light.

Had she not been easy on that rapist; had she not set him free to rape again; had it not been the case that preceded this one . . .

But she *had* let a rapist go free, and it *had* been the case just before Rosemary's.

Judge Forrest forced herself to look at Rosemary, at the straps that held her like a trapped animal, at the needles in her arms that would deliver the poison, and she thought, *Now I am guilty of murder too.*

Rosemary felt the cool saline solution rushing into her veins.

Then the warden removed his glasses, tilted his head toward a mirror, and Rosemary knew it was a signal, *the* signal, for the execution to begin.

Behind the mirrored glass, the executioner started the process.

First the sodium thiopental, a fast-acting barbiturate that was the anesthetic. Then fifty milligrams of Pavulon, a muscle relaxer that would paralyze the diaphragm and arrest the breathing. Last, the potassium chloride, which would stop the heart.

The chaplain asked again if she had anything to say, and Rosemary shook her head no as words tumbled from her mouth: ". . . though I walk through the valley of the shadow of death, I will fear no—"

Then she swallowed and tasted something bitter on the back of her tongue, and the words caught in her throat and the slight burning she'd felt in her arms became fire and her body was shaking, writhing, and she could not stop gasping and gagging.

"My God! My God!" Belle McGuire covered her face with her hands. "What's happening?"

The curtains were quickly drawn. But Belle, the others, could hear moans and cries even through the glass.

"It's worse than being stoned to death," Zacharius said, pale, glaring at Nunn.

Jon Nunn squeezed his eyes shut. He had to control himself from pounding on the glass and smashing it.

The medical team and the tie-down crew burst into the death chamber.

"Shit!" A large black man tried to restrain Rosemary's convulsing body.

One of the technicians yelled, "It's her arm! Look at the swelling. Jesus!"

"The straps are too tight," the warden said, "Only a fraction of the chemical is getting through. You're killing her—slowly! Get it off— *now*!"

One of the tie-down team tugged the strap off Rosemary's arm so fast it snagged the IV and the needle whipped through the air like a snake spitting poison.

"What is *wrong* with you people?" the warden bellowed, his face red. "There are state officials out there—*and* reporters—watching this! Jesus Christ!" He backed away to avoid a face full of paralyzing Pavulon.

Rosemary's heart was beating normally again and she watched all the drama around her as if it were some black comedy. Her joints ached and her muscles burned. But her mind was surprisingly clear.

"You okay?" the technician asked, and she nodded.

The chaplain was back, his hand on Rosemary's forehead. "It's okay, dear. It's okay." Then he started to pray as the technician got the catheters in place and Rosemary lay back against the pillow.

Belle McGuire turned to Nunn. She was still crying. "Make them stop. Please make them stop!"

"Not the first time I've seen something go wrong," one of the reporters said, shaking his head. "It'll get back on track in a few minutes."

Belle's face twisted with pain.

But Jon Nunn couldn't wait a few minutes. He pounded his fist on the glass. "Stop this! Stop it now!"

A guard was beside him in seconds. "Sir, you will have to leave if you don't—"

Nunn took one last half swing at the glass, then let his hand drop, and stared at the floor, taking fast, hard breaths.

The curtains opened and once again Rosemary looked at the witnesses. She tried to smile at Belle, then, scanning the windows, she found Jon Nunn, who leaned forward and pressed his hands against the glass—something he was not supposed to do, but this time no one stopped him.

It was not at all as she'd imagined, some drug-induced stupor followed by sleep. Instead, Rosemary Thomas had become hyperaware of her body, air going in and out of her lungs, bubbles of oxygen traveling along veins and arteries, heart pumping loud and clear, images sparking in her brain—her father laid up in bed; her mother smoking a cigarette at his funeral; her children, Ben and Leila, calling to her; the iron maiden; a blood-soaked blouse; Christopher's face, his finger; words, colors, everything whirling and mixing. She saw the district attorney looking solemn and the pain on the judge's face and the guards and the doctor and the reporters staring but not really looking.

Now she knew what was happening. Her breathing had become labored and a sudden coldness surrounded her heart. Just before her eyes closed, she saw Belle McGuire crying and Jon Nunn's face, his fingertips pressed against the glass like white, fluttering moths. It was as if his hand were on her arm.

She wanted to call out, but it was impossible: she couldn't speak. A noise, like air going out of a balloon, filled Rosemary's ears, and she knew it was her last breath, and then her heart turned to ice and cracked and broke apart and the world went bright white and she was flying.

1998

1

JEFF LINDSAY

The McFall Art Museum was closed for the night. Down in the main galleries the security lights were on, throwing bright, ugly puddles of light on the doors and hallways. It was very different from the careful track lighting of the day, lovingly trained on the paintings and sculptures that lined the rooms to show them at their best, without glare or shadow. The illumination from these nighttime lights was harsh, hard-edged. The garish pools of light they threw made the museum seem darker somehow, more strange and threatening than a building filled with great art should have been.

It was not a big museum, but it had made a name for itself in San Francisco, "the gem of the Bay Area," people called it, "an undiscovered treasure trove of art from nearly every era."

Near the marble staircase that led to the second floor, the sharply outlined shadow of a statue fell across the floor, the figure of a nude athlete holding half a javelin. The athlete had been dead for almost twenty-five hundred years, and his javelin had been broken for seventeen hundred, but still he stood poised for his throw. With the glare of the security light on his marble skin, that throw seemed imminent, adding to the strange sense of foreboding.

From the far end of the back gallery an eerie sound fluttered across the spotless tile floors. It echoed off the hard surfaces of the floor and walls until it was almost impossible to recognize it for what it was—the sound of a cheap radio playing a ball game. Moments later, the sound was joined by the scuffle of the night guard's feet as he walked back to the security station at the front door, where he put the radio down beside a bank of video monitors. The guard settled into his chair, just in time for the louder gabble of a tire commercial.

The sound echoed up to the first landing of the marble staircase but somehow failed to turn the corner and make it to the second floor. At the top of the stairs greater darkness waited to join the sudden silence. The pools of shadow were swept aside by one security light halfway down a hallway lined with office doors. The entire length of the hallway stood prey to the shadows, half dim and half lit by the small and ugly light from that one bare lamp.

All the way down at the far end of the hall, one additional pool of light spilled out into the hallway from the half-open door of the corner office. It was a much warmer light, though not terribly bright. Then, quite suddenly, the light went out. For several moments nothing else happened: no sound, no sign of any living thing moving anywhere near the corner office—but the careful observer might have noticed a strange, dark blue-purple glow coming from inside the room. Without really lighting anything properly, the glow somehow caused the lettering on the office door to jump out in almost three-dimensional clarity:

CHRISTOPHER THOMAS
Curator

From the doorway, there was almost nothing to see in the darkness of the curator's office. The walls reflected a faint texture that had to be books, hundreds of them, lining the room from the floor all the way up beyond the reach of a normal human being. They seemed to loom above the room, holding in and magnifying the tense emptiness that gripped this museum tonight. And faintly visible in the dim blue-purple glow was one end of a large leather couch.

At the other end of the room was a large draftsman's table with a lamp suspended above it on a gooseneck, and from this lamp came the glow. It shone down on a canvas stretched out on the table, and it reflected strangely off the thick, square glasses worn by the man who leaned over the canvas. When the young woman beside him opened her mouth to take a ragged breath, it lit up her teeth with a brilliant and otherworldly sheen.

"It's quite clear under the ultraviolet light," the man said. Something about the way he said his words made them sound stilted, as if he were reading from a script, but the young woman didn't notice. She was staring at his hands as they hovered just above the canvas. Like the rest of the man, his hands were long and angular and strong. "Here," he said, "and again, here." He moved his hand in a choppy half circle over the lower corner of the canvas.

The young woman ran her tongue out and across her full lower lip. She looked closely at him, the light casting strange shadows into the angles of a face not classically handsome—the slightly hooked nose, the too thin lips—yet something about him was beautiful, beautiful and dangerous.

"Are you listening?" he barked at her, her normally copper-colored skin edging toward purple in the light.

"Yes, yes, of course."

"Look," he commanded. He made a patting motion over the canvas. "It's very good. The artist used old linen and real Prussian-blue pigment, very expensive, but fugitive, so it's turned to black, a nice touch." The hand turned over, and the young woman watched with fascination.

So expressive, she thought, staring at the fingertips as they fluttered.

"But," he said. Quite suddenly, one of the hands moved away and switched on the conventional light. "Your Soutine is a fake. You've spent a great deal of the museum's money on a *fake*."

As that statement hit home, she snapped her eyes away from those hands and onto the man's face. "Fake," she said, shaking her head dazedly. "But that's—I have the provenance. And it was a good one, proving where the painting has been every moment since it left Soutine's studio in France in 1939."

The man straightened up—he was quite tall—and he inched closer to her. His movements, like his words, gave the impression of a bad actor, not quite sure how to act the part of human being. "I read your provenance," he said. "It doesn't add up."

"But I talked to the family."

"You talked to con men."

"What?" she gasped.

"The whole provenance is fake. Like the painting."

"Oh, my God." For a long moment she thought about a promising career, now smoldering in ruins. The years of graduate school, the overwhelming student loans she could barely pay, even with this prestigious job. And now—it was all over. She would be fired, disgraced, permanently unemployed. All she had worked for her entire adult life slipping away into shambles; the embarrassment she would share with her family, who had been so proud of her; the museum's first African-American curator, a symbol of sorts to her community, something she'd never wanted but had become.

"I'm afraid there's no doubt at all," the man said, putting those long hands of his together in front of him.

"Oh, dear God."

"A bit of a career-killer, isn't it, *Justine*?" He used her name as if it were in quotation marks.

"I—there must be something. . . ."

He smiled. His teeth were large but white and strong looking. "Something . . . we can do?" he said mockingly. "To make it all go away like it never happened?"

The young woman just shook her head.

"Or did you mean something *I* can do—to save your career, hide your mistake, keep your life from sliding down the drain?"

"Is there?" she blurted out.

He stared at her for what seemed like a long time. Then he straightened and took another half step toward her. "There might be something. But . . ." He shook his head.

"But what?" Justine asked, barely breathing.

"It's a huge risk for me. Personally and professionally. I would have to know that I can trust you completely."

"You can trust me. You're holding my career in your hands."

"Of course, but that's not enough." He fluttered one of those big hands, as if to say, *What's in it for me?* and she could not look away from it for several seconds. When she finally did and their eyes met, there was really only one thing to say.

"I'll lock the door," she said.

Later, after Justine was gone, Christopher Thomas sat up on the large leather couch and straightened his clothing. He felt rather pleased with himself, refreshed, and ready to get on with the night's real work. He stood up and stretched, then moved over to his desk. Justine had provided a pleasant interlude, but a great deal was still left to do tonight.

The desk telephone stood beside a five-by-seven picture frame that held a shot of his wife, Rosemary, and their two children. A pleasant-looking family group, and Thomas felt mild affection for the three of them: nothing that would prevent him from gratifying his frequent urges for other women, of course. He seldom seemed to have any time to spend on his little family, what with his work as curator and his other less public projects. Still, it was nice to have a family in the background. It made him feel so much more . . . authentic and irreproachable. Especially with Rosemary's pedigree—a child of wealth and privilege. Marrying her had been one of the smartest moves he had ever made. He gave the picture a brief, synthetic smile, pure reflex, and picked up the telephone, dialed a number from memory, and, after hearing a curt "Yes?" on the other end, spoke.

"I have three paintings you will be interested in." Again the corners of Thomas's mouth twitched upward in a mechanical smile. "Including a rather rare Soutine."

A moment of silence on the other end was followed by a harsh breath—an exhalation of cigarette smoke?—then the voice said, "Describe it to me."

Thomas did: the wild, almost otherworldly exuberance of the brushwork, the sense of immediacy that jumped off the canvas and into the viewer's heart—assuming the viewer had a heart, which Thomas did not. But it didn't prevent him from gauging the effect this painting would have on others.

Another long pause on the other end of the line was punctuated by two harsh breaths. Finally, the man said, in a soft and raspy voice, "All right."

Thomas smiled again. This time it looked a bit more like a real smile because he was about to get a great deal of money, and Christopher Thomas needed money. In spite of his rich wife and high-profile job, Christopher Thomas needed money badly, and quickly.

"I'm sending three canvases to your restoration company tomorrow afternoon at three thirty," he said. "They will travel in a white panel truck with the museum's name and logo on the side. All right?"

After one more long, harsh exhalation, the voice said softly, "Good," then the line went dead.

Christopher Thomas hung up the phone, feeling pleased with himself. Tomorrow afternoon, the three paintings would disappear from the truck taking them to be cleaned. Naturally, the museum would be upset, but they would also get a large check from the insurance company. And a collector somewhere would get three nice works of art, and Thomas would get a hefty chunk of cash. As an added bonus, the young woman who had recently left his couch would certainly be grateful that he had allowed her to keep her job. A return bout on the reliable leather couch was clearly in his future.

So a self-satisfied Christopher Thomas locked his office and went down the hall to the marble staircase. Things were looking up, and just in time. He mentally counted the money he would get as he headed down the stairs. He hit the landing and circled around, continuing down to the main floor of the museum. The sound of the guard's radio reached him, a roaring crowd that echoed into a confused blur and muffled the noise of his steps on the marble stairs. For just a moment he allowed himself to pretend that the crowd was cheering for him; he had done it. Payday. *Hooray for me,* he thought.

Thomas walked past the marble javelin thrower to the security station by the front door. "Good night, Artie," he said to the guard.

The man looked up, his face lit with an eerie glow from the half dozen video screens that surrounded him. "Hey, Mr. Thomas. You going to call it a night?"

"Yes. We all have to go home sometime." Thomas had arranged for Artie Ruby to get this job in security at the museum despite Artie's checkered past. The way Thomas saw it, didn't hurt having a crooked ex-cop working for you in security—it even came in handy sometimes.

Artie smiled. "Ain't it the truth. All right, you have a good night, Mr. Thomas."

Thomas nodded and moved to the front door, waiting for just a second before the guard pushed the security buzzer, then he was out through the glass double doors and into the night.

Thomas walked through the bright orange glare of the security lights on the front of the building and circled around back to the staff parking area. The long walk was annoying, particularly at the end of a hard day, but the insurance company insisted that the back door remain locked. Not that it would do them any good this time, he thought, wondering again just how much the Soutine might bring.

The parking lot was a great deal darker than the front of the building. It was normally lit by two large lights, one at each end, but Thomas saw that one of them, the one nearest his car, was out. He frowned and shook his head. Maintenance was supposed to check the lights regularly—again, as dictated by the insurance company—and someone had neglected the job. He made a mental note to scold the maintenance people in the morning. He certainly didn't need trouble with the insurance company, not right now when they were about to write the museum a hefty check.

Still shaking his head at this carelessness, he fished out the car keys from his pocket and stepped over to his car, a two-year-old BMW. As he unlocked the car and reached down to open the door, he felt more than saw a shape slip out of the shadows by the building's Dumpster and come up behind him. Before he could turn around or even straighten up, something cold and hard pressed into the back of his neck and a voice said, "Get in the car."

Thomas froze. For a moment he could not think, or even breathe,
The cold spot jabbed harder into his neck. "In the car. Now."

Thomas unfroze, jerked the door open, and got in behind the wheel. The shadow slipped behind him into the backseat and closed the door, quickly and soundlessly, then the cold spot was back on his neck again.

"How are you doing, Chris?" the voice said, the words friendly, but the voice that spoke them was cold and empty.

"Who are you?"

"A friend of a friend. Somebody who asked me to stop by and say hello."

"I don't—what *friend*? What do you want from me?"

"Oh, I think we both know what I want," the voice said with reptilian amusement. "You've been ignoring our mutual friend, and he hates to be ignored. Hates it like hell." For emphasis, the man jabbed at Thomas's neck with the gun barrel. It hurt. "Is that how you treat a good friend? Somebody who lends you that much money, from the goodness of his heart?"

Thomas now knew who had sent this man. He had known on some level since the man came at him out of the shadows, but now he was quite sure. He had half expected something like this ever since he had borrowed the money. It had been a truly stupid move, one of the few really dumb things he had ever done, but he had needed the money. And now he was paying for it.

"I can get the money," Thomas said.

"That's very good news, Chris. Why don't you do that."

"I just—I need time."

"We *all* need time, Chris. But we don't all get it."

"No, listen," Thomas said. "I really do—I have a very large piece of money coming to me, very soon."

"I'm very happy for you. But I need something now."

"I don't have it now. But I will—I'll have all of it, very soon."

Nothing in the soft laughter that came from the man in the backseat was funny. "You know how often I hear that?"

"It's true," Thomas insisted. Reluctantly, he told the man about the canvases that would soon disappear, and the large bag of cash that would take their place.

Silence, a long and uncomfortable silence, came from the backseat. Then: "And this happens when?"

"Tomorrow. I should have the money within the week. All the money."

Another long silence followed, and Thomas felt a slow drop of sweat crawl down his neck, in spite of the chill in the car.

Finally the man spoke. "I would hate to think you're yanking my chain, Chris."

"I swear to you."

"Because you are really pissing off some very serious people."

"I swear," Thomas repeated.

"Give me your hand."

Thomas blinked at the strange request. "Wh—what?"

"Your *hand*. Gimme it."

Slowly, awkwardly, Thomas extended his hand into the backseat. The man took it and held it, and for a moment the small, hard circle of steel at Thomas's neck disappeared.

"I am going to believe you just this once. And I hope this isn't stupid of me."

"No, I really—" Thomas said, but the man took hold of Thomas's little finger and interrupted him.

"Don't disappoint me." The man pulled upward, hard, and the sound of the little finger's snapping filled the car.

"Aaaggaaahhh," Thomas cried out. The pain was intense, and he tried to pull away his injured hand, but the man held on.

"Do you understand what I'm saying?" the man said, wiggling the broken finger.

"I—I—aagahhh—yes, yes, I understand."

"You *sure*?" the man said with an extravigorous tweak of the finger.

"Yes, ah, I'm—ow—positive."

"One week." The man dropped the finger, opened the back door of the car, and disappeared into the night.

Christopher Thomas watched him go, cradling his savaged finger. The whole hand throbbed, all the way to the wrist, and for quite a while he could do nothing except hold it to his chest and bite his lip. But the pain did not die down, and finally Thomas fumbled the keys into the ignition, started the car, and drove carefully away.

2

Such a generous host."

Justine said that, and he thought, *Naïve*. She had been in Europe twice before, as she'd made a point of telling him just before the plane took off. A month in London in her sophomore year at that place near Austin—he could never remember its name—and then four months in Amsterdam at the Rijksmuseum on some sort of internship. That was where she'd learned about painting, or claimed to have learned; he had his doubts about that, but he had never openly expressed them. Not that open expression was necessary— raising an eyebrow was often quite sufficient in the art world.

Christopher Thomas looked at her over the café table. He smiled. "But the rich always are," he said. "I can't recall a single occasion, not one, where I've been entertained—how should I put it?—*parsimoniously* by people with money. Can you?"

She did not reply. And the reason, thought Christopher, was that she had never really been there. She met these people through the museum, but meeting was one thing; social acceptance was another. It was different for him. Not only had he married Rosemary, but he had worked his way up through the art world. He had come from nowhere, but that was no disadvantage if you were a chameleon. Take on the local color. Think the local thoughts. It was easy. People in the art world listened to him, deferred to him.

Justine reached for the bottle of Chablis that the café proprietor had placed on the table. She filled his glass, then poured a small amount into her own.

"Well, I guess I'm not used to this," she said, feeling slightly out of step, slightly apart from this literal ivory tower, nothing new. It was the way she'd felt in graduate school and just about every other institution. "But I must say I like it."

He took a sip of the wine. "Of course. Who wouldn't?"

"It sure beats work."

He shook his hand with the bandaged finger at her in mock admonition. "Listen, this *is* work. Remember, this is a conference and we're here on behalf of the museum—not because we want to spend five days in France. Not because we want to stay in the Château Bellepierce. Not because we want to sit in cafés like this and drink Chablis. We can go to Napa for all *that*."

She laughed nervously. "Of course. It's just I forget sometimes."

"Don't."

"Tell me again what happened to your hand?"

"I never told you the first time you asked."

They lapsed into silence. She looked over his shoulder, blurring him out for a moment, to the small line of pollarded trees on the other side of the square. Under the trees, on a small rectangle of raked white earth, a group of men in flat caps were playing *boules*. Somebody was winning, she saw, and was being slapped on the back in congratulation; a small triumph, a little thing. Beyond the *boules* players and the trees, in the church on the corner, a stout woman dressed in black was standing at the open doorway, looking in her direction.

Christopher looked at his watch. "We'd better get back to the château. It's four o'clock. There's a lecture at five. I think we should be there."

Everybody would be there—every one of the eight connoisseurs invited by their host and all twelve experts. They would listen, ask a few questions, then break up until drinks before dinner. It was hardly demanding.

Justine drained her glass. At home she would never have drunk wine at four in the afternoon, but this was France and it seemed a perfectly natural thing to do. She felt . . . almost happy. When Christopher had suggested that she come on this trip, she had at first been reluctant. She had not been away with him before, and she was not sure whether she wanted to. He was her boss, and although they had crossed the line on several occasions, he was married—and she knew Rosemary. She would never have initiated something like this herself; he had done it, he had pushed her into it at a vulnerable moment and she had acceded. What else could she do?

But inviting her to come on this trip seemed to be upping the stakes, flaunting their affair. Well, if he was ready for that, then perhaps she was too. She had nobody else in her life at the moment. Of course he had girlfriends—everybody knew that, including Rosemary, or so people said.

She thought back to their conversation about this trip. . . .

"You've heard of Carl Porter?" he'd asked. "The Porter Foundation?"

"Yes," she'd said. Though she hadn't, not until she'd googled him.

"Sometimes people forget that there are real people behind these foundations. Carl lives in France and has for years. The money comes from cosmetics—lipstick or something like that. Cheap stuff. Anyway, Carl and his wife got bored with Palm Beach and decided to move to France. He was a big collector. And he knew what he was doing. It's a great collection now and he likes to share it."

It started to make sense to her. "Share it? You mean he might give us—the museum—something?"

Christopher shook his head. "No. Carl is tight. He's looking for ways of taking it with him."

"So, this invitation?"

He explained it to her. "Carl's idea of sharing is to invite people to come and tell him what great paintings he has. He has what he calls *conferences*. They last five days or so, sometimes a whole week. He invites other collectors and a bunch of people he calls experts from the museums and galleries. That's *us*."

"And we sing for our supper?"

Christopher smiled. "Exactly. You won't have to do anything. It's just that the invitation is for two people from the museum. Of course, if you'd rather I took someone else . . ."

"I'll come."

Justine came back to the moment, staring at Christopher Thomas, his angular face, the permanent sneer on his lips.

Christopher seemed pleased. For her part, she was under no illusions as to why he had asked her. He would need entertainment. He had actually used that word before when he referred to what was between them. She was *entertainment*. She could have been angered, but rather to her surprise she found that she was not. In a way she was even flattered that he—the great Christopher Thomas—should find her entertaining. And what else did she have? She had long ago had the insight—which sometimes people did not get until much later on—that this was no dress rehearsal. You had one chance at life and you had to grab what was offered you. She had worked her way up from circumstances few if any in the rarefied world of art even knew about, and she had no intention of going back. She'd kept her job because of him; certain invitations came her way because he felt fit to pass them on; she was in France because Christopher Thomas liked her enough to ask her. If that meant that they shared a room, then that was not too much of a price to pay. She was a willing participant, something she had been telling herself for several weeks.

Christopher drove back to the château in the rented Peugeot. It was not a long drive as the château was barely five miles from the village. It was good land: the wide landscape of Charente stretched under the high Poitou-Charentes sky, here and there a major town, but for the most part a place of small villages surrounded by sunflower and wheat fields, vineyards, stretches of forest. The château had been virtually derelict before Carl acquired it from its last owner, an almost blind French colonel, the last vestige of a distinguished family that had lived there for five centuries. He had left much of the furniture simply because he could not bear to sell it and had wept as he had shown Carl and his wife, Terry, round each room.

Christopher had been there before on several occasions after Carl had moved the collection from the secure warehouse near Philadelphia where it had spent the previous eighteen months. Carl had wanted his advice, not only on the paintings he had but on works he intended to acquire. Christopher was happy to give his opinions and had even persuaded Carl to sell several paintings of doubtful merit or questionable provenance. This advice had been rewarded with a fee—a remarkably generous one in view of Carl's reputation for meanness—or occasionally with a gift of a small painting. Christopher had a Vuillard pastel—admittedly an undistinguished one—that Carl had given him in gratitude for brokering the acquisition of something that Carl had long been looking for.

Christopher had held on to the Vuillard for a year before discreetly selling it to a dealer in Paris who assured him that it would be sold to a private client and not appear in the auction rooms. He knew that Carl looked at all the catalogs—Christie's, Sotheby's, Phillips—and if the Vuillard came onto the open market, he would see it and would not be pleased.

Christopher and Justine had arrived the day before, taking the high-speed train down from Charles de Gaulle and picking up the rental car at Angoulême. Justine had been fascinated by the château and somewhat relieved she had her own room. But that night, after dinner, Christopher had knocked on her door and she had let him in.

"It's a very old house," he had whispered. "And I get *so* lonely."

The main conference started the next day with a discussion of two of Carl's latest acquisitions—a Dürer and an early Hopper. The Dürer was introduced by a woman from Berlin, who talked at great length. "Look at the face, the way it leaps out of the background, caught by the light. Everything else is in shadow, only the face is illuminated."

Christopher nudged Justine. "He was using a camera obscura. You read Hockney on that?"

A man sitting nearby looked disapprovingly in his direction; Christopher acknowledged the look with a nod. Justine suppressed a smile. She remembered a friend saying to her, "Look, Justine, that man is using you. It's so obvious." And she knew that her friend was right but said, "But he's so amusing. He makes it fun. Don't you understand that?"

The Hopper was more exciting. It was not well-known and had languished in an obscure private collection for thirty years before Carl had the chance to buy it for a mere $4 million. A hotel room at night with a curtain moved by the wind: classic Hopper territory, with its air of something about to happen. Carl gave the talk himself—his main performance of the week—and his audience listened with all the attentiveness of those who were being paid to listen or, if not actually being paid, were the recipients of a week of hospitality from a man who had $4 million to spend on a painting of an empty room in which something indefinable was going to take place.

Christopher's attention wandered, and he found himself looking at the back of the neck of the German woman who had talked to them about Dürer. German. Precise. A bit superior. Scholarly. She'd be fussy and out of place in San Francisco; too stiff. Yet women like that were a challenge, attainable but not available, which made her all the more interesting. This German woman, who now, for no reason, turned her head slightly and met his glance, crossed her legs this way then that— shapely legs—and smiled at him.

He returned the smile.

"I'm not sitting next to you at dinner," Justine said to Christopher.

"But we'll see one another later?"

She touched him lightly on the forearm. "Yes. Why not?"

He could think of several reasons why not. All of them good reasons—none to be revealed, of course. There were his appetites to be satisfied, and for now the lovely Justine would adequately fulfill them.

He glanced at the German woman as they moved through to the dining room, a long room with a chambered, painted ceiling portraying an apotheosis.

He was seated next to the German woman—a coup—and Carl was on her other side; they were clearly in favor.

"Carl," he said, pointing to the ceiling, "you've told me before, but I've forgotten. The apotheosis above our heads. Who?"

"Who's being carried up to heaven? Or who painted it?"

"Who's being carried up?"

"The great-grandfather of the man I bought it from. The colonel."

The German woman craned her neck. "And did he deserve it?"

"In his view, yes," said Carl.

They laughed. Then the German woman turned to Christopher and said, "I was hoping to be able to talk to you."

He raised an eyebrow. She was more attractive up close, and the accent intrigued him. She sounded more Swedish than German.

It was a request—or the intimation of a request. They were planning an exhibition in Berlin of a Flemish artist whose work was represented in Christopher's museum. Could he oblige? And they would reciprocate, of course, when the occasion permitted.

The German woman spoke precisely. "I could come and fetch it if you can't spare anybody."

"Sure. And I could show you San Francisco."

"That would be very kind."

He noticed her skin, which had the sort of tan that some northern-European types get so easily, that soft golden color that he found irresistible. She was a few years younger than him, he thought; and he looked at the left hand, pure reflex—a ring, a garnet, but on the wrong finger, just ornament.

They slipped into an easy, friendly conversation. Carl was engaged to his left, and so they spoke through the first course and into the second. She was flirting with him; the signals were unmistakable. He felt intrigued, slightly flattered too.

"Where are you staying?" he asked. "I mean, here. I'm at the back. I've got this great view—the river and a sort of folly at the end of the lawn."

"I'm on that side too," she said. "I believe that I'm a few doors down the corridor. Yes, *two* doors, to be exact."

He thought that he understood perfectly. He was surprised, but happy, and he found her room easily.

He did not see Justine at breakfast the next morning. There was a lecture at ten, when a man from the National Gallery in London was going to discuss Carl's collection of old-master drawings. She would be there and he could talk to her—and sort it out. *She has no* claim *on me,* he told himself. *No claim at all.*

But where was Justine? He felt slightly irritated; this was work—they had discussed that—and he did not want her to give offense to Carl by not turning up at his carefully orchestrated events. Then he half turned and saw her, sitting at the far end of the back row, her eyes fixed on the lecturer. She did not catch his eye, although he thought that she must have seen him looking at her.

After the talk was finished, after some questions and some fidgeting among the guests, Carl looked pointedly at his watch. Then it was time for morning coffee, which was served on the terrace.

The light outside was bright, and Christopher slipped on a pair of sunglasses while he sipped his coffee. Justine came out and looked around quickly—again she must have seen him, he thought, but she made a point of going to speak to somebody else. He put his coffee cup down on the stone parapet that ran along the side of the terrace and walked over to intercept her.

"Good morning."

She looked at him coolly. "Good morning."

He looked about him; the other guests were busy chatting to one another; he would not be overheard. "You're ignoring me."

She feigned surprise. "What made you think that?"

"Don't be disingenuous. You looked right through me back there."

She hesitated, as if assessing how quickly, and how far, to ratchet up the tension. "You're the one who's doing the ignoring."

She held his gaze, although she was looking into sunglasses and he into her eyes. He had the advantage.

"How is your German friend?" she asked.

"What?"

"Your German friend. Your new friend. I spoke to her this morning. Just before the talk."

"You—what?"

"She was surprised," Justine said. "She was surprised to hear that you were here with *me*. She thought—"

Christopher turned and walked away.

Justine followed him and grabbed hold of his arm. Her grip was surprisingly firm; he felt her nails, digging into him. He tried to shrug her off, but her grip was tight.

"What do you think you're doing? Not in front of everybody," he hissed.

"Nobody's looking," she whispered. "Listen, Christopher, have you ever thought of this: One day one of the people you use will do something to hurt you? I mean, really hurt you?"

He kept his voice down. "I don't know what you're talking about."

"Oh, don't you?"

"No."

Justine left him, and he rubbed his arm where she had seized him. He would make her answer for this.

That evening, Carl said to him after dinner: "Chris, come look at something really interesting, upstairs. Just you."

"Of course, Carl. Now?"

Carl nodded and led the way up to the second floor, to a room that Christopher had never before been in. The small, private salon was hexagonal for the shape of the tower space it occupied. The overall feeling was one of intimacy: a large bookcase, small paintings on the wall, a tapestry above the fireplace.

"Poussin," said Carl, pointing at a picture of a man sitting in an arcadian landscape. "A lovely little picture. Blunt wrote about it, you know. He drew my attention to it."

Carl closed the door behind them so that they were away from the eyes of anybody who might be in the corridor outside. "Can't be too careful. Look at this." He opened a drawer in a small chest near the window and took out a painting about the size of a large book in a narrow gilt frame.

"Lovely," said Christopher. He bent over to peer at the painting. There was a woman and two youths, angels; the angels' faces were unmistakable. It could only be one particular artist. He stood up again. "*Very* lovely."

Carl was looking at him. "You know what it . . ."

Christopher spoke quietly. "I can see what it is." He paused. "And what do you want me to say? Do you want me to say, 'Yes, this is it'?"

Carl shrugged. "I don't want you to say anything about what this is. What I do want you to say is that you'll take it to San Francisco for me and hand it over to that restorer friend you have out there—you know the one. He'll do what's necessary."

Christopher frowned. "Why get me to take it? Can't you take it yourself?"

Carl laid the painting down on a table and looked at it fondly. "I can't do that. I can't risk its being . . . intercepted. You know I can't." He looked up at Christopher and held his gaze.

Christopher did know. He knew that this painting, from the studio of Sandro Botticelli, and probably from the artist's hand, could not fall into the hands of customs.

"So," Carl went on. "You're perfect. Did anyone ever tell you that your face, Christopher, is the quintessential honest face? Successful museum director on his way back from a meeting in France. Nobody's going to stop you and say, 'Do you mind telling us something about that little painting you have concealed in your suitcase, Mr. Thomas?'"

Christopher looked at Carl, who was studying him intently, a bemused expression on his face.

"Sorry to have to say this, Christopher, to an old friend, but those who have been party to my confidences and then . . . and then have forgotten to keep them, have become unwell. Quite unwell."

Christopher couldn't believe Carl was threatening him. He moved back toward the door.

"Well?" asked Carl.

"I have to say yes, don't I?" said Christopher.

Carl slipped the painting into a velvet sack and handed it to him.

Christopher stashed the painting in his room, then went to the drawing room, where the other guests were seated, enjoying conversation over late-night cups of coffee. He sat down. Neither Justine nor the German woman was there. After a few minutes he excused himself. His encounter with Carl had left him feeling raw.

The following morning he knocked on Justine's door, and when she opened it, he leaned forward and kissed her.

She turned her cheek and looked away.

"Please. Let's not be children." He took her hand. "There's something I need to ask you to do. Can you be discreet?"

"Of course I can. You *know* that."

"We need to get a painting back into the States. Can you take it in your cabin baggage? The painting is not large."

"Why me?"

He used Carl's line. "Didn't anyone ever tell you how innocent your face is—and how lovely?"

"What sort of painting?"

"You'll know when you see it." He paused. "So you'll do it?"

Justine thought a moment. "Yes. I'll do it."

3

RAYMOND KHOURY

I'm seeing him this morning," Christopher Thomas said into his cell phone as he stared out the glass wall of his office at the marina below. "I'm going there at six."

"Call me when you're done," the voice on the other end said.

The curator demurred. "It'll be late for you. I'll call you in the morning—your morning—and let you know how it went."

A small smile curled up the edge of his mouth as he listened to the silent acquiescence on the other end of the line. He wasn't being unreasonable. Carl Porter was in France; Christopher was in San Francisco. There was a nine-hour time difference between them, and Christopher knew full well that 3:00 or 4:00 a.m. conversations with anyone were best avoided, especially when they were about something as sensitive as what they were discussing. But it wasn't just about being reasonable. It was more than that. It was about keeping the upper hand. Keeping control. And if there was one thing Christopher Thomas was good at, it was staying in control. Even in situations that he'd been forced into, such as this one.

"I'll expect your call at seven," Porter grumbled back, clearly unhappy with being dictated to.

"Count on it," Christopher replied before hanging up, his pulse racing with mixed emotions.

He'd hadn't liked being forced—even threatened—by Porter into smuggling the Botticelli into the United States. Christopher Thomas wasn't used to being forced to do anything for anyone. But his anger had gradually been superseded by greedy exhilaration at the potential outcome of it all. He stood to make a lot of money from the sale of the painting, and that was nothing to be angry about, especially now, when he needed it.

His eyes lingered on the view outside his office. It was a prestigious view, one that spoke of status, one that only a man who had attained a certain level of success in his line of work could ever hope to have. It was the view of a man who had arrived.

The McFall Art Museum had a prestigious location too, on the northern waterfront of the city, right on Marina Boulevard, and as its star curator, Christopher had a corner office. He stood at the floor-to-ceiling glass wall behind his desk and took in a gleaming white gin palace that was gliding out of the marina down below, his gaze eschewing the magnificent Golden Gate Bridge that stretched beyond and locking instead on two tanned, bikini-clad playthings cavorting on the yacht's rear deck. The sight stirred something within him, a hunger that had driven him for as long as he could remember, a hunger for bigger and better things. A hunger that, if anything, his conversation with Carl Porter was about to help nourish if he played his cards right.

He watched the yacht drift away, checked his watch, then turned and sat at his desk, taking in the sumptuous world he'd created for himself in his office. Suddenly, it seemed to pale by comparison, despite the cosseting it offered and the wealth of character it presented. It had never failed to impress those who had been invited into its hallowed ground: exquisite chairs and side tables by Frank Lloyd Wright and Michael Graves spread out around his sleek Ross Lovegrove glass-and-steel desk; a grandiose B&B Italia shelving system, housing his perfectly arranged collection of hardcover art books, many of them signed and inscribed for Christopher by the artists whose works they contained; posters of past exhibitions Christopher had put together over the years showcasing the works of some of the biggest names in contemporary art; and the space for rotating works of art borrowed from the museum's collection—currently a huge self-portrait of Chuck Close that dazzled in its intricate patterns of color—adding to the splendor of the office. It was a splendid place to work, but it wasn't enough. He wanted more.

Much more.

He checked his watch again and let out a deep breath. Four hours to go.

He hated to wait, but he didn't have a choice. He leaned back in his plush Eames desk chair, shut his eyes, and focused on the money that would soon be in his hands.

He arrived early at the restorer's premises and, as a precaution, parked a block away before walking briskly to the workshop's entrance, a black leather portfolio held firmly in his hand. The restorer answered the buzzer himself and let him in, the studio's heavy steel door clanging shut behind him.

"Always a pleasure to see you, my friend," Nico Bandini said as he shook his hand heartily, "and just in time for a nice little shot of grappa to kick off the evening, yes?"

"Perfetto," Christopher answered with a smile. "Who am I to break with tradition?"

He followed the gregarious art restorer through the high-ceilinged studio. All around them, a small army of craftsmen in white overcoats sat hunched at their workplaces, toiling away like monks in a medieval scriptorium, peering with supreme concentration through their magnifying lenses, painstakingly cleaning and repairing valuable works of art, seemingly unaffected by the heady smell of paints, oils, and varnishes that smothered the loftlike space.

"Busy?" Christopher said, more an observation than a question.

"I'm doing all right," Bandini replied. "There is always a demand for fine arts, especially when the economy is this good."

"That's true, you can always find a buyer when it comes to the arts." Christopher noted, consciously positioning himself for what was to come.

"If you can even call some of it art," Bandini scoffed. "People are willing to pay through the nose for some ridiculous polka dots printed up by one of Damien Hirst's minions." He shook his head. "The world's gone crazy, hasn't it?"

"In more ways than one. But, hey, I'm not complaining. Nor will you when you see what I have here."

Bandini smiled, then led Christopher into his office, closing the door behind him.

"Hit that lock too, would you?" Christopher asked.

"Of course." The restorer clicked the lock into place. "I know this isn't a social call. So what have you got for me this time?"

Christopher set the portfolio on the restorer's cluttered desk. "Have a look."

Bandini unzipped the black leather case and pulled out the small package. It was the size of a coffee-table book, wrapped in a sack of dark brown velvet. He reached in and pulled the framed canvas out and held it in both hands, studying it with pursed lips.

Christopher suppressed a smile as he watched the man's eyebrows rise and heard him let out an admiring whistle.

"Provenance?"

"Blue-chip," Christopher replied confidently. "Private seller. I've got all the relevant paperwork."

"Ah," Bandini observed curiously, "so whoever buys this can actually hang it in his living room."

Christopher smiled. Most of what he brought to Bandini were works he'd "borrowed" from the museum's collection. He'd chosen ones that wouldn't be missed or replaced the ones that might be with forged copies created by Bandini's own craftsmen. The Botticelli was different. "They can hang it on their front porch for all I care. As long as they pay enough for the pleasure."

"What do you think that pleasure's worth?" the restorer asked.

"It's a great piece, and it's unquestionably from the master's own hand, not from some acolyte in his studio—as I'm sure you can see."

The man frowned. "Don't sell me, Christopher. I know what it is."

The curator shrugged. "Three is easily fair, I think. Might get more at auction. But given the circumstances and in the interest of getting it done quickly, I'll take two-eight for it."

Christopher studied the restorer's face, gauging any microreactions that rippled across his features, looking for confirmation that he'd pitched it at the right price but not really expecting to get it. As expected, the restorer didn't even bat an eyelid. They'd both done this many times before, and like consummate poker players, they both knew how the game was played.

Bandini stayed silent, his face locked in concentration.

"Doable?" Christopher pressed, his mind processing the cut he'd be getting. "Anything above two point five is yours," Porter had said. At $2.8 million, Christopher stood to clear $300,000. Tax free.

Not bad for an afternoon's work.

The restorer pondered the question for a moment, his gaze not moving off the painting he was still studying, then his face relaxed. "Possibly. Actually, more than possible. Probable. I think I have the perfect buyer for it." Bandini grinned at the curator. "A gentleman from the home country."

"Botticelli would be pleased."

The restorer set the painting back down onto the portfolio. "I'll call him tonight." His expression turned curious. "So you're in a bit of a rush to get this done. Any reason I should know about?"

"It's not me. It's my seller. He's got time issues."

"Ah."

"So . . . you seem reasonably confident you can get this done, right?"

"I think so," Bandini said, his tone now noticeably drier.

"So you wouldn't mind giving me an advance?"

The restorer's face curdled. "I thought you weren't in a rush to get paid?"

"I'm not, but . . ." Christopher hesitated, brushing the man's question away while feeling droplets of sweat popping out across his forehead. "You know how it is—"

"Are you having money problems, Christopher?" Bandini asked, dead flat, and eyed Christopher's bandaged finger.

Christopher slid his hand behind his back. "No, I told you, I'm not," the curator shot back, slightly too strongly, he thought, a second too late. He dredged up a carefree smile. "Look, it's not a big deal, okay? I just thought that since we both know you won't have too much trouble offloading it, a small advance wouldn't be an issue."

The restorer studied Christopher quietly for a moment. "I don't do advances, my friend. You should know better than to ask. And you know why I don't do advances?"

Christopher felt his temples heat up. "Why?"

"Because people who need advances have money problems. And people with money problems tend to get desperate, and when people get desperate, they get careless. And that worries me. It worries me a lot." Bandini's eyes narrowed. "We've done a lot of business together over the years, Christopher. Should I start worrying about you?"

"No, no, no," the curator insisted. "Don't be ridiculous. It's fine. Pay me when you sell it, it's not a problem. All right?" Christopher flashed a radiant, magnetic smile that had played no small role in getting him what he'd wanted throughout his life.

The restorer studied him coldly for a long beat, then his face relaxed as if the strings pulling it taut had snapped. "Of course," he said, patting Christopher on the shoulder. "It shouldn't take long. Now, how about that shot of grappa?"

Bandini was deep in thought as he made his way back into his office after seeing Christopher Thomas out.

The painting was good, there was no doubt about it. He knew he'd be able to get more than $3 million for it. He might even orchestrate a mini bidding war for it, he mused. A Botticelli of that quality didn't come up for sale too often. But something else was worrying him.

The curator. He seemed edgier than normal. Bandini could sense it. And edginess, he knew, was a reliable harbinger of trouble ahead. Trouble that was best avoided—or eliminated.

He called his two favored clients, one after the other, describing the work to them and arranging to drive it around and show it to them in the morning. Then he made another call, this one to a man who was definitely not a client and who wouldn't know a Botticelli canvas from a Banksy print.

"I need you to keep an eye on someone for me," he told the man. "My . . . supplier. You know the one I mean."

"How close?" the man asked.

"Microscopic," Bandini replied, before filling him in on what he was worried about.

On the way back to his office, Christopher Thomas was buzzing with nervous energy. He tried to focus on the positives. Bandini hadn't flinched at the price he was asking. Christopher was pretty certain that the restorer would deliver, and soon. He usually did. But the man had also spooked him with his insistent questioning and his probing stare. Bandini, he knew, was no softie. He may have been supremely talented as a craftsman and as a forger, but he was also as tough as nails and worryingly unforgiving. Christopher had witnessed that firsthand.

The museum's offices were mostly empty now, with only a few of his staff still around, notably those dealing with the Far East and working around the daunting time difference. He stepped into his sanctum and crossed to the small array of bottles sitting on a gleaming art deco tray, where he poured three fingers of Tyrconnell single malt into a fat crystal tumbler. He raised the glass and watched the light dance across the amber nectar within its chiseled edges, then brought it up to his lips, the spicy bouquet of vanilla and oak tickling his nostrils before the liquid slid down his throat—then he heard her voice. In his office, coming from behind him, by the door.

"Where'd you go? I saw you walk out with a portfolio."

He turned. Justine was standing there.

Uninvited.

"Most people knock," he said as he turned away, then took another sip of whiskey. "No, actually, scratch that. Not most people. All people. Everybody."

He heard the door click shut, then she said, "Most people wouldn't help you smuggle a small fifteenth-century masterpiece past customs

He turned again, in time to see a small, self-satisfied grin spread across her pretty face.

"Actually, scratch that. No one would. So I guess that buys me some dispensation from the protocol, don't you think?"

He exhaled slowly, then said, "What do you want, Justine?"

"You've been avoiding me. I'm getting worried that our little partnership is going off its tracks."

His eyes narrowed. "Our 'partnership'?"

"Hey, I carried the damn thing in," she said as she stepped closer. "I was the one holding the bag. Literally. You made me risk everything for that damn painting."

"What risk?" he said, scoffing at the idea. "You saw how easy it was. Just like I said it would be. Besides," he pressed on, his voice taking on a sharper, angrier note, "I don't remember forcing you to do anything."

The flash of doubt in her eyes found an echo in his satisfaction.

"Where is it?" she asked.

"It's none of your business."

"None of my business? It couldn't be more my business if I'd painted the damn thing myself. We're partners in this, Chris. Remember that. And like it or not, you're going to give me my fair share."

"Or what?" he rasped, feeling his pulse quicken as he set his glass down on the table and looked at her with eyes that sizzled with menace.

Justine felt a surge of paralyzing fear. She'd never seen this side of him before and she gasped as he got up from his chair and came at her with lightning speed, crossing the room in four quick strides and taking her by surprise. Grabbing her with both hands, he pushed her backward until they both came to a slamming halt against the inside wall of his office, by the door.

One of his hands tightened against her neck.

"Before you threaten me, darling," he hissed, "you need to make sure you've got what it takes to see it through."

She froze as his face hovered inches from hers, his breath heating up her cheeks, his teeth bared at her like those of some kind of Gothic beast, his eyes narrowing as they drilled into hers.

Her lips were quivering. "You don't know what I'm capable of, Christopher," she whispered, trying to keep a tough edge to her voice but knowing she wasn't pulling it off.

She felt his fingers tighten even more around her neck, heightening the fear coursing through her. A vein in his temple was throbbing with mad fury, and his gaze was still locked on her as he edged in closer, his lips now brushing against her earlobe, the prickle of his stubble teasing her neck. "Oh, we both know you're capable of some very surprising things, don't we?"

4

JONATHAN SANTLOFER

The main gallery of the McFaul Art Museum was buzzing. The art world was out in force, curators and collectors, artists and dealers, in high-end designer clothes, tattoos—the latest fad, etched across backs, creeping up the arms of young and not-so-young men and women—no one looking at the art, everyone busy reciting his or her résumé, affecting ennui, eyes flitting like hummingbirds seeking someone, anyone, more important to talk to.

Rosemary Thomas stopped a moment to catch her breath, leaned against the wall to survey the blur of mostly black-clad cool cats and sophisticates, many of whom she had known for years, but whom among them could she trust? Did they know? Were they laughing at her?

Poor Rosemary, that husband of hers, well, you know . . .

The thought of it, that she was a joke, someone to be pitied, unbearable.

Ironic, she thought, fixing on the dazzling and disjunctive centerpiece of tonight's reception—a ten-foot-long, 1947 Jackson Pollock "drip" painting, the artist at the height of his manic creative powers—the kind of painting that rarely, if ever, became available, a gift that she helped Christopher acquire for the museum.

Their museum as Christopher liked to call it. What a joke. Christopher, a hotshot senior curator of twentieth-century art while she remained a mere associate in Arms and Armor, a musty room that attracted even mustier old men and unwashed teenage boys.

But wasn't that the way they'd planned it, Christopher's career to be the one that mattered?

I couldn't make it without you, babe.

How many times had he said that? And she'd believed him, content to play the quiet, supportive wife with the right pedigree—Shaker Heights family, coming-out party, Wellesley undergrad, New York's prestigious Institute of Fine Arts.

The museum owed much of its reputation to her. It was because of her family's long-standing social connections that she'd easily made contact with old European families and had them donate rare pieces to her museum rather than the bigger, glitzier California institutions. And now, Christopher was building the contemporary collection, the cool stuff that brought in a public who didn't care much for armor and Gothic goblets, hermetic stuff, old and dry, exactly how Rosemary was feeling these days, like a relic, old and uninteresting, once the backbone of the museum, now ignored, ready to be discarded.

We've outgrown each other.

You mean you've outgrown me.

I want a divorce.

After all she had put up with—the women, the humiliation—and now *he* wanted a divorce.

I won't let you divorce me.

How can you stop me?

Christopher's face, the sneer on his lips, burning in her mind as another man's face came into focus.

"Oh—" A quick intake of breath. "Tony."

"Are you okay?"

"Me? Oh, yes. Yes. Of course." *Can he see it, the shame on my face?*

"You look flushed."

"No, I'm . . . I'm fine. It's just these events—you know."

"Yes, hard work for a curator, but it's surely fun for me to see the museum acquire such a spectacular piece."

"Thanks to you." *That's it, the right thing to say.*

"Well, not me entirely." Tony Olsen shrugged, modest, or trying to be. As a generous donor and chairman of the board for the past four years, he had shaped the museum's direction, and during that time he and Rosemary had become good friends. "Christopher had a lot to do with it. You must be very proud of him."

"Yes . . . of course." She swallowed hard, felt the blood rush to her head, nausea rising.

"Are you sure you're all right, Rosemary?" Tony laid a hand on her shoulder.

She tried to smile, Christopher's face still looming in her mind, his words like acid in her gut.

But the children . . .

They'll get over it.

"Let me get you a drink."

"That's the last thing I need, Tony. We were so busy I skipped dinner, not a good idea, but I'm fine, really I am."

He looked into her eyes, "Rosemary, we all know how much you helped with this acquisition—it's not even your department—and Christopher getting all the credit. It isn't quite fair."

"Oh, it's   I'm better at writing grant proposals and soliciting donations than socializing."

"You're a lot more than that. You're the anchor around here."

The image struck her as unflattering: a weight that dragged things under.

She touched his arm, felt the plush cashmere under her fingertips. "You should mingle, it's your duty."

Tony Olsen gave her cheek a peck and smiled warmly before he moved into the crowd with the kind of ease Rosemary admired but could never muster.

An anchor, that's what I am, a dead weight.

But she'd been a good wife to Christopher, encouraging, willing to take a backseat, allowing him to shine, to be the star. She'd always known that was what he wanted.

She stared at the crowd; at least half the art lovers had their backs to the Pollock masterpiece.

"My God, you look awful." Peter Heusen eyed his sister over the rim of his champagne glass. "You're as white as a ghost. What's the matter?"

"Nothing."

"Was it something that oily billionaire Olsen just said?"

"No, of course not." Rosemary tracked Tony Olsen, watched him expertly chatting up half a dozen people at once.

"You know he made his first million in munitions."

"I don't believe that."

"Your naïveté is a continual source of amazement." Peter sniffed. "Well, I don't like him."

"You don't like anyone who has more money than you."

"That makes everyone, doesn't it?"

"Oh, please, Peter, we have the same trust, so I know exactly what sort of income you have, and it's plenty. You should be grateful."

"My dear sister, you play grateful so much better than I."

"Let's not get into this, not here." Rosemary sighed.

"Into . . . *what*? You mean the loan I asked you for—the one you refused?"

Rosemary tried to whisper, but it came out a hiss. "We get the same monthly money, Peter. I just don't spend mine the way you do."

"That's obvious." Peter gave his sister the once-over, top to bottom. "Aren't you expected to dress for these events?"

"Very funny." Rosemary smoothed imaginary wrinkles from her plain beige dress.

"Not funny at all." Peter angled his chin toward the center of the room. "Look at your husband all decked out in his designer tux. Clearly he has no problem spending your money. Why aren't you on his arm?"

"He's got a lot of people to juggle."

"Yes, Christopher's specialty is *juggling,* isn't it? He should have been in the circus."

"*Not now,* Peter."

"My God, Rosemary, you play the martyr even better than grateful, defending that lout while he makes a fool of you."

"Keep your voice down, Peter." Rosemary scanned the nearby crowd to see if anyone was listening, but they were all too wrapped up in themselves to notice.

"Why? Everyone knows. He's not exactly hiding his affairs."

Rosemary's legs felt weak, her face on fire, but she said nothing.

"Well, if you're just going to stand on the sidelines and pout, I'm off."

"That's a good idea," she said, her voice going strident. She took a few steps back. She wanted to turn and run, but she was frozen, her mind like an old record stuck on repeat.

Is there someone else, Christopher?

That's not the issue.

It is. For me.

It's not about you.

I'm entitled to know.

It's my business, not yours.

I won't let you humiliate me like this. I won't!

And what will you do?

She saw his face again as he'd said that, the cold sneer twisting his lip, the arrogance.

Rosemary felt cold, then hot, the spotlights blinding, the room suffocating. *I have to get out of here.*

A manicured hand on hers, nails ticking her flesh.

"You're Chris's wife, aren't you?"

The young woman who said this reminded Rosemary of a ferret, sleek and mean looking, shadowed eyes narrowed, a tight, insincere smile.

"Yes." Rosemary nodded.

"You don't know me. Haile Patchett, I used to work at the Natural History Museum in Los Angeles?" She flipped her long red hair to the side.

Rosemary took in the skintight dress, six-inch heels, a dozen silver and gold bracelets at her wrist, the kind of woman she could never compete with; the kind of woman she never met back in Shaker Heights, who seemed to be standard-issue in New York or L.A. or San Francisco; the kind of woman that Christopher always fell for.

Rosemary just stared at her, had to control herself from lashing out. "Oh, but I do know you, and not from anything you do at the museum." She sucked in a deep breath. "How dare you come here?"

"Whatever do you mean?" Haile held on to her smile.

"I think you should leave."

"Oh, I don't think so." Haile arched one perfectly penciled brow and peered past Rosemary into the crowd—a crowd that was ripe for the picking, she thought, but not tonight. She was looking for someone specific. She looked Rosemary up and down, barked a laugh, then turned away.

Rosemary's face burned as she watched Haile Patchett wiggle through the crowd like a snake. Then she caught sight of Christopher, at the center of the throng, expertly juggling six or seven people at once, his pretty associate, Justine Olegard, standing beside him dutifully.

He was sleeping with Justine too, she knew it.

My God, is there any woman here he hasn't . . .

Rosemary watched Christopher laughing, brushing the blond hair away from his forehead, still playing the golden boy, and felt an ache in her chest that caused her to gasp. And then that redhead, Haile Patchett, joined the group, her hand on Christopher's arm.

Rosemary wished she could disappear, become invisible. But isn't that what she'd always been?

It's my time, Rosemary, and I don't need any baggage.

Was that what she was, baggage?

I've done plenty for you, Rosemary, but it's over.

Done for me? What have you done for me?

The room was thrumming, the noise, the lights, the small Jackson Pollock studies—wild splashes of brush and ink—pulsating on the white walls.

Then it all seemed to stop, the clamor reduced to the slightest hum, the crowd disappearing, and it was just the three of them: Christopher and that horrid redhead spotlighted in front of the Pollock—two figures performing against a backdrop of shimmering paint—and Rosemary, watching. She couldn't hear what they were saying but read their body language, the woman pitched forward, hip thrust out, Christopher whispering in her ear, her hand gripping his arm.

But when the woman reached up to touch Christopher's hair—here, in the museum, with Rosemary watching, with *everyone* watching—that was it.

The room was spinning around her like those Jackson Pollock drips. Rosemary knew she was moving, could hear herself mutter, "Excuse me, excuse me," as she cut through the crowd, the sound of her own breath loud in her ears, heart pounding as Christopher and that woman grew larger and clearer, the individual strands of Christopher's blond hair and the woman's black-red nail polish standing out in high relief while everything around them blurred.

Christopher Thomas beamed at the small coterie of fans gathered around him, then looked past them, and there she was: his wife, hovering at the periphery of the crowd like a pathetic waif.

He took in the light brown hair hanging limply to her shoulders, her shapeless beige dress. He'd long ago stopped seeing the pretty woman behind the plain packaging. He tried to locate his feelings for her but could not.

"Hey, juggler." Peter Heusen slapped his brother-in-law on the back.

"What?"

"Juggler, you know." Peter mimed the act.

Christopher Thomas regarded him with disdain. *Peter, the blow-hard. Peter, the freeloader. Peter, who had his uses.* Christopher patted his brother-in-law on the back and turned away.

"So, how does the Pollock look to you?" Christopher asked Tony Olsen.

"Shimmering. Brilliant. Expensive."

"What about s-sloppy?" said Peter Heusen, insinuating himself between the two men, slurring his words.

Christopher sighed loudly. "My brother-in-law fails to notice the internal structure that Pollock is working with, the choreography of the drips, the interweaving skeins of paint almost like a dance."

Peter made a noise through his nose and Christopher snagged him by the elbow, turned him around fast, and hissed in his ear. "Go away, Peter, *now*. You're not even supposed to be here."

"Oh, fuck off, Thomas, I know you," Peter said, his boozy breath hitting Christopher's face like a damp sponge.

"Chris—"

Christopher let go of his brother-in-law and turned to the familiar voice.

"I've left over a dozen messages for you," she said.

Haile Patchett.

Christopher could feel the crowd closing around him, collectors and artists, his staff, even the chief curator, his boss, Alex Hultgren, a man devoid of humor, and the chairman of the board, Tony Olsen.

"I can't speak now," he whispered to Haile. "I'll call you."

"That's what you keep saying but you never do."

"Who's this, Chris?" Justine Olegard took a step in front of Haile Patchett.

"I could ask you the same question," said Haile, eyeing Justine, lips pursed.

Christopher looked from one to the other. "I can't do this, Haile, not here," he whispered close to her ear.

"Oh, you remember my name, what a surprise." She trilled a fake laugh and Christopher tightened a grip on her arm.

"Oh, relax," she said, "I'm not going to cause a scene."

"You already have." He looked around, saw the chief curator, Tony Olsen, Justine, all watching him.

Christopher painted on a smile, trying to defuse the moment, as Haile Patchett reached up to smooth his hair, an old habit, something she'd seen in a movie no doubt; everything about Haile was theatrical. And he would have stopped her, the act totally inappropriate for the setting, his hand already up reaching for hers when he saw Rosemary cutting through the crowd toward him, her features distorted with anger.

"Enough!"

Rosemary Thomas was surprised to hear her voice, so much louder than she expected. She swatted Haile Patchett's arm away from her husband.

"What on earth—?" Haile glared at her, mouth open.

"What *you've* done for *me?*" Rosemary shouted at Christopher. "For *me?*" She was trembling but it didn't matter; nothing seemed to matter. "To think what I gave up for *you*—the years, my *life*!—and for *what?*"

"Rosemary, please." Christopher made tamping-down motions with his large hands, a smile frozen on his lips.

Everyone around them had gone quiet, a ripple effect in motion, the crowd quieting in successive rings until the only people left talking were those on the outer fringe, a throbbing chorus at the museum's perimeter.

Christopher reached for Rosemary, but she slapped his hand away and pulled back.

"Rosemary—"

"You bastard! I gave you all this. And now—"

"Rosemary, *please*. You've had too much to drink, darling, you're not yourself." He managed an arm around her shoulder, but she shook him off.

"I've had nothing to drink. I've never been more sober." The sound of her voice, her words, still shocked her, but she couldn't stop. "You want a divorce, Christopher? We'll see about that!" Then the room was spinning, the ceiling slanting on an oblique angle, the floor coming to meet it, and she saw Justine's eyes narrowing and Haile Patchett smiling and Tony Olsen frowning and all the artists and dealers and curators like grotesque caricatures out of a Daumier print staring at her, and then, in a moment, as if someone had thrown a switch, the room came back to life, everyone chattering but looking away, embarrassed, pretending nothing had happened. But it was too late; the reality of what she had done in the middle of the exhibition, in the middle of the museum with everyone watching, rippled through her. Tears in her eyes, cheeks burning, she pushed her way through the crowd and ran out of the room.

5

SANDRA BROWN

Mom?"

The day was only five seconds old, and already Rosemary dreaded the remainder of it. She rolled onto her back and pried her eyes open. Her daughter was standing beside the bed, still in her pajamas, a Barbie tucked beneath her arm.

"Are you awake, Mom?"

"Yes, honey."

"Where's Daddy?"

Chris's side of the bed was conspicuously empty. Rosemary cleared her throat. "He had to go into work early today."

It was an obvious lie, even to a child. One Rosemary had used too often.

Leila looked at Rosemary with sulky reproach. "Your eyes are puffy."

"Are they?" Rosemary could tell by feel that they were. "I slept . . . hard." She tried to muster a smile.

"Was it a nice party, Mommy?"

Rosemary avoided answering. "Is your brother up?"

"He's downstairs. We're hungry."

"Ask Elsie to fix your breakfast."

"We like *your* pancakes better, Mom."

Her daughter stood there waiting for her. Rosemary pushed off the covers and got out of bed. The events of last night would catch up with her sooner or later, but in the meantime she must act as though this were an ordinary day.

For the children's sake.

For her own sanity.

The first indication that this might not be a normal day in the life of Rosemary Heusen Thomas came at eleven o'clock after the pancake breakfast. Her children had eaten. She had pretended to. She'd sorted dry cleaning with her maid, Elsie, asked her to schedule the window washer for one day next week, and, having received a reminder post-card from the dentist, called to make appointments for her and the children.

Normalcy.

Getting on with the routine things of life.

But then just as she was on her way out to the garden to cut roses, Elsie approached her with the cordless house phone. "It's the museum, asking for Mr. Thomas."

Rosemary waited until Elsie was out of earshot. "Hello?"

"Good morning, Mrs. Thomas." It was Chris's secretary. "I hate to bother Mr. Thomas at home," she cooed. "But something's come up that needs his immediate attention. May I speak with him, please?"

"He's not here."

"Oh."

The single syllable was heavy on inflection, causing it to vibrate with implication. Rosemary's cheeks flamed with anger and resentment, but the newfound audacity she'd exhibited last night was made shier by caution this morning. She decided she should volunteer nothing, say as little as possible.

With all the composure she could muster, she asked, "Have you tried his cell phone?"

"Numerous times. Mr. Olsen is quite anxious to speak with him. Do you have any idea where I might reach him?"

"I'm sorry, no."

"Or when he might be available?"

"No."

"Will *you* be coming in today, Mrs. Thomas?"

The busybody was really rubbing it in, wasn't she? The department of the museum in which Rosemary worked wasn't any business of hers. She was fishing for information—about Chris—that was all.

"Not today, no. Now if you'll excuse—"

"You have no idea where I can find your husband?"

Rosemary pretended not to have heard the question and discon-nected before anything more could be said.

Rosemary didn't hear the door open or even his footsteps.

Her brother, the last person she needed or wanted to entertain today, breezed in uninvited. Since their childhood, he'd had a knack for tormenting her when she could least withstand it. He'd shown up just in time for "cocktails, wouldn't that be nice?" and her lack of enthusiasm for the idea hadn't deterred him from asking Elsie to roll out the liquor cart.

Having little choice, Rosemary left Elsie in charge of seeing that the children were given their supper and joined Peter, who had made himself right at home and poured himself a drink.

"Wild horses couldn't have kept me away. I couldn't wait to see what you have planned for an encore. Throwing china at Chris's head, maybe? Driving his car into the swimming pool? I hope it's something fabulously dramatic. A drink for you, Rosie? Forgive my candor, but you look like you need a little pick-me-up."

"No, thank you. I'm surprised you're not hungover. You were well into your cups last night."

"But not so drunk that I didn't appreciate the full impact of your performance. My God, Rosie." He raised his glass in a mock salute. "You made me proud. Standing up to Chris, with past and present lovers hanging on every accusatory word. And the museum muckety-mucks, looking on with their mouths agape. It was too, too much. Honestly, I didn't know you had it in you." He winked. "Makes me wonder what else you're capable of."

"Shut up, Peter," she snapped.

He grinned at her over the rim of his highball glass as he sipped from it. "Will the cheating bastard be joining us for drinks?"

"I wouldn't count on it."

Peter laughed. "What did he have to say for himself today, now that his sins have been exposed? Has he repented? Brought you flowers? An expensive piece of jewelry?"

"I haven't seen him today."

Peter set his glass on the table and leaned forward. "Really?"

"He . . . he didn't come home last night."

"Hmm. Interesting. I wouldn't peg him as the tuck-tail type." Peter looked at her archly. "Of course, who could really blame him for staying away after the public dressing-down you gave him? I suppose he's playing the injured party."

"Which would be like him, wouldn't it?"

Peter reached for his drink again and sipped it while watching her thoughtfully. "It's unlike you to speak ill of Chris. Even knowing what a fornicating, lying, opportunistic bastard he is, you've always defended him. Until now. Why the switch?"

"He asked me for a divorce." The secret was out. Everyone had heard her; there was no point in hiding it now. "He *insisted* on a divorce."

"And you lost it. Or so I gather by last night's scene."

"Maybe I will have a drink." She poured herself a glass of white wine and sipped from it, aware of her brother's amused gaze. She wondered if he noticed that her hands were trembling.

"Imagine Chris showing up at the museum this morning," he said around a chuckle. "How did he face the staff? Your friend Tony Olsen looked ready to kill him. He's probably called an emergency meeting of the board of directors, but I'll bet he was there to greet Chris—"

"Chris didn't go to work today. At least he wasn't there this morning." She told Peter about the call she'd received.

"Where do you suppose he spent the day?"

"Honestly, I don't care."

"Bunking with one of his lovers?"

Rosemary acted as though she hadn't heard.

"Perhaps making cozy with the beautiful Justine?"

Justine. Rosemary's blood turned hot when she thought of Chris's latest conquest. Everyone at the museum knew he had taken Justine on his most recent trip to France. She was the latest in a long line of pretty curators singled out for special attention by him.

Peter continued with his speculation. "Or maybe he's with that red-headed bitch, the one with the long fingernails who was draping herself over him last night when you made your move?"

"They deserve each other," Rosemary mumbled. Then, rousing herself, she said, "I don't know where he is, only that I haven't seen him since I left the museum last night."

"As for the state of your marriage . . . ?"

Tears filled her eyes. "My children," she said hoarsely. "This will be awful for them."

Peter linked his hands and turned them inside out high above his head, stretching luxuriantly. "Ah, well," he said on a sigh, "maybe you won't have to worry about the messiness of a divorce. Maybe Chris's other sins have also caught up with him."

She wiped her eyes. "What other sins?"

"Come now, Rosemary. You can't be *that* naïve. If he breaks his wedding vows, do you really believe he would be true blue to other covenants?"

"What are you talking about?"

Peter brushed a nonexistent piece of lint off the leg of his trousers. "It's not for me to say. Maybe you should ask Stan."

Stan Ballard, their lawyer and estate manager.

"What would he know that I don't?"

Rosemary could tell by her brother's sly grin that he was itching to tell. "Remember Chris's recently broken finger?"

She nodded.

"He didn't get it by slamming the car door on it as he claimed." Peter's gaze wandered to the Golden Gate Bridge, which was shrouded in fog. He smirked. "If Chris doesn't turn up soon, maybe someone should drag the bay for his body."

At the San Francisco Police Department, Detective Jon Nunn's cell phone rang. It was Tony Olsen.

"Mr. Olsen. What—"

"I thought we were past that 'Mr. Olsen' business."

They'd known each other for a few years now, but for some reason Jon Nunn could only think of Tony Olsen as *Mr. Olsen*. But he humored him now. "All right, *Tony*. It's been a while. What's up?"

"Do you remember the McFall Art Museum?"

"Of course," Nunn said, remembering all too well the awkward hours he'd spent there like a fish out of water. Olsen had enlisted Nunn and his wife, Sarah, for a charity event at the McFall—the museum's feeble attempt to give back to the community by establishing summer programs to keep kids likely to commit crimes off the streets. Olsen said the exposure would be great PR for Nunn's career, and he felt safer having Nunn and a couple of other cops in attendance while inviting a shady element indoors. Sarah jumped at the chance and enjoyed every minute of it.

"Well, you know I'm on the museum's board. Chairman in fact." Olsen paused. "Something's come up that I was hoping you could help me with."

"Sure, Tony." Nunn was thinking the theft of a valuable painting, vandalism maybe.

"It concerns Christopher Thomas, one of our curators."

Nunn remembered the name—how could he forget with the way Thomas had ogled his wife and every other attractive woman at the fund-raiser.

"He hasn't been seen in a week. It seems he's gone missing."

Recognizing the seriousness in the older man's voice, Nunn stepped into his cubicle to help block out the ambient noise in the Violent Crimes Unit, where detectives who weren't actively detecting were talking on their phones or bullshitting with each other.

Nunn listened as Tony Olsen described an ugly scene that had taken place between Christopher and Rosemary Thomas at a black-tie museum function a week earlier.

"According to the staff, he didn't report to work the following day, which was understandable," Olsen said. "Everyone in the hall had overheard the confrontation. It was believed he was embarrassed and needed some time to sort things out with Rosemary."

"That's the wife?"

"Yes. She's a dear friend of mine. She also works at the museum. A valued employee, a very knowledgeable woman."

"But they had issues."

"Well, his affairs have been no secret," Olsen said scornfully. "He's not a particularly nice guy, Jon. He and I have had our differences."

"Then why are you concerned?"

"He's disappeared. He hasn't been seen since that night. Rosemary had her say, then ran from the hall. Chris excused himself and followed her out. That's the last anyone saw of him."

Nunn thought a moment. "Has she reported him missing?"

"She's gone to Mexico."

"What?"

"No, it's not what you're thinking. She went on behalf of the museum. There's an exhibit in Mexico City, Spanish armaments from the conquest. She oversees the Arms and Armor department of the museum, so she went to check it out."

"Just like that?"

"She's been in conversation with the museum down there for some time. But, yes, her decision to go seemed rather sudden, though I encouraged it. She was still very upset over what she called 'making a fool of myself at the Pollock event.' If you ask me, the SOB had it coming to him, and more, for a long time. I told her a few days away would do her good."

"Is she aware that no one's seen her husband since she told him off?"

"She acknowledged that he didn't come home the night of the incident, but she wasn't that worried about it. I'm assuming it wasn't unusual for Chris to spend a night out. Certainly since she had brought his philandering into the open, it wasn't surprising that he didn't go home."

Nunn mulled it over. "So no one's actually reported him missing.'"

"No."

"I'm in homicide, Tony."

"I realize that. But I hoped to get your read on it before getting the police officially involved. There's no love lost between Chris Thomas and me, but I'd hate for Rosemary's heartache to be made public. More so than it's already been. Not to mention the museum's reputation. The board's concern is safeguarding that."

"I get it. Donors wouldn't appreciate a scandal involving museum personnel. But marital problems are marital problems, Tony. Common and not that scandalous."

After a slight hesitation Tony said, "I suspect that Chris's extracurricular activities may have extended beyond unfaithfulness to his wife."

"Care to expand on that?"

There was a pause, then Olsen said, "Not until I have to."

"Well, can you venture a guess where he might be?"

"After five days, when he still hadn't come to work, the museum staff came to me. Things were stacking up. Issues needed his attention. Beyond that, they were concerned for his well-being. I called Rosemary at her hotel in Mexico. She still hadn't had any contact with him. She said if I wanted to find him, I should talk to one of his girlfriends."

"What exactly is it you're asking me to do, Tony?"

"To look into it, his disappearance. You're the only policeman I know personally, and I know I can trust you to be discreet."

"I understand, but if he doesn't turn up soon . . ."

"I know."

They talked a few more minutes. Nunn promised to be back in touch soon.

He would put out feelers, interview the girlfriends, do some snooping, and it would probably result in his locating Christopher Thomas sunning himself on a private beach with one of his babes, her ass in one hand, a tropical drink in the other.

But a week after Nunn's initial conversation with Tony Olsen—there'd been numerous conversations since—he was waiting outside customs when Rosemary Thomas reentered the United States.

She looked bedraggled as she pulled her suitcase behind her. Nunn placed himself in her path. "Rosemary Thomas?"

"Yes."

"My name's Jon Nunn." He presented her his badge. "I'd like to talk to you about the disappearance of your husband, Christopher Thomas."

6

FAYE KELLERMAN

If anything had taught her patience, it had been the past couple of weeks. Ostensibly, the trip to Mexico was a chance for her to eye a magnificent collection of colonial Spanish armor, but the real reason for the sudden departure was to give Rosemary something that she had sorely been lacking for years.

Perspective.

She gave the intruder a quick once-over with a cool eye. His jacket was a size too small and a couple of years out of fashion. His hair appeared as if it had been styled by a nearsighted barber, and he was in need of a shave. His mouth was thin, his nose too long, but he was attractive and looked intelligent. "Who are you?"

Again, Nunn presented his shield, but she shrugged. "I know a dozen artisans who could forge that for five dollars or less." She started walking, her suitcase in tow. *Act tough,* she told herself. "Leave me the hell alone."

Nunn had to do a two-step to keep pace with her. "Could I talk to you for a minute?"

"Not for a second." She stopped and glared at him. "How dare you come to me with your badge and your insinuations?"

"I don't remember any insinuation, ma'am."

Rosemary kept walking but Nunn dogged her heels. She slung a large purse over her shoulder, almost clipping his face.

"Your husband's missing."

"Oh?"

"That doesn't concern you?"

Rosemary swallowed. "My husband's business is not *my* business."

"Really?" Nunn tried to look her in the eye; impossible.

"Two weeks ago, it might have been, but not now. Christopher told me in no uncertain terms that I was a blight on him both professionally and personally, so why should I give a damn about him?" Rosemary took a deep breath, then another. "I don't know where he is—and I don't care." She reached the automatic doors, and when they opened, she stepped outside. The traffic was thick and the noise deafening. She debated jaywalking to get rid of the cop, but decided it wasn't worth the risk. She found the crosswalk and waited for the light to turn green. "Please, just . . . go away."

"I hear you two fought. What else?"

Rosemary kept up the false bravado, though her head was starting to pound. "If you're a detective, you should know."

"Okay, let me tell you what I *do* know. Your husband had demanded a divorce, and that night you had a meltdown."

"And . . . ?"

"And then you fought, publicly."

"Silly ninny that I was. I made a complete ass out of myself." She tried to smile. The light changed to green, and suitcase in tow, she started across the four-lane roadway. "And for what? For some pompous, adulterous, priggish twit who has been using me—or more to the point, my money—for umpteen years? God, I detest that man!" she said, though a part of her ached when she said it.

When she got to the other side of the street, she ducked into the parking structure, took a deep breath, and picked up her pace, and Nunn had no choice but to follow.

"And you have no idea where he is?"

"No, nor am I concerned that he is missing. If God is half as benevolent as the preachers claim He is, He'll make good and sure he stays missing." Rosemary stopped and turned on Nunn until they were almost nose to nose. She wanted to run, but she stood fast. "Have I made myself clear, Officer?"

"Like it or not, Mrs. Thomas, you're going to have to deal with the situation."

"I *told* you, Christopher Thomas is no longer my business."

"I'm afraid he is." Nunn looked into the woman's eyes, which were pale blue and sad. He didn't buy her tough-gal act. "How about we go for a cup of coffee and discuss this?"

"Look, mister, I—"

"It's *Detective* Jon Nunn. SFPD—homicide."

She eyed him once again. "Why in the world would I want to talk to you?"

"I'm here because I had my arm twisted by a friend of mine—and *yours*."

"Whose name is . . . ?"

"Tony Olsen." He studied her face as her eyes widened. "And he's worried about your husband."

"Well . . . I'm not."

"You're not the least bit concerned that your husband has vanished?"

"*Vanished* is a rather strong word."

"It's an applicable word, Mrs. Thomas. No one has heard from him in two weeks. He's hasn't shown up at work. He isn't answering his calls. His cell phone mailbox is full. E-mails sent to him go unanswered."

Rosemary bit her lower lip. "I—I don't know where he is, Detective. I'm sorry but I can't help you."

"You were the last person to see him alive."

"Are you threatening me again?"

"Just stating an obvious fact, Mrs. Thomas. Everyone at the museum, at the Jackson Pollock event, saw you run out of the room. And everyone there also saw your husband run after you. And no one— and I mean no one—has heard from your husband since. And I know that because I've interviewed every one of them . . . except you." Nunn let that sink in. "Right now, you've got a chance to talk to me *unofficially*. How long that'll last . . ." He shrugged.

Rosemary swallowed hard. "How do you know Tony?"

"We go way back. It's complicated." He took the handle of her suitcase. "Where's your car?"

She grabbed her suitcase back from him. "This—this is none of your business."

"Last chance, Mrs. Thomas. Official or unofficial?"

Rosemary didn't speak for a moment. Then, finally, she said, "There's a coffee shop about five minutes away—ten blocks to the north. I'll meet you there."

The woman had been described to Nunn as mousy and meek, but from his first impression he'd have to say she was anything but. Still, he felt it was an act, a bruised woman acting tough. And she was good-looking, not exactly a knockout, but her sad blue eyes were beautiful, and she had a dynamite figure he hadn't missed, and a tan courtesy of her sojourn in Mexico. He liked that she looked him squarely in the face when she talked to him, her eyes trying not to betray her vulnerability.

She was nothing like the suspects he was used to dealing with.

Olsen, what did you get me into?

She arrived five minutes after he did and slid into the red Naugahyde bench seat opposite. She hid her face behind a plastic menu.

Nunn studied the list of food items. Typical coffee shop fare. The place was staffed with hairnetted waitresses in white, fluffy skirts and white aprons. He said, "What can I get you?"

"Peace and quiet."

Nunn laughed.

She put the menu down. "I'm not hungry and the greasy smell is making me ill. Just get your questions over with—please."

"Hey, you picked the place, not me."

"I'm noted for picking losers." Rosemary tried to smile but her eyes filled with tears. After a moment she said, "I'm usually not a bitch. Christopher was the nasty one. Now that he's gone, I suppose I've discovered the wicked side of myself."

"Now that he's *gone*?"

"*Gone* as in gone from my life, not gone for good." Rosemary dried her eyes on a paper napkin. "See, this is precisely why I didn't want to talk to you. I say one thing and you've warped it into an accusation."

"Look, Mrs. Thomas, I don't know what happened to your husband, but if something did happen, this little interview is only going to be a dress rehearsal. So in reality, I'm doing you a favor."

Rosemary stiffened again. "Am I supposed to be thankful?"

"You can continue with your snide comments or we can work together to figure out what's happened to your husband."

"You see, here is where we differ. I don't care. Christopher stepped out of my life that awful night and I'm *glad*." She straightened her shoulders to emphasize what she'd said.

"So what happened that *awful* night?"

"You're the one with the facts. You tell me."

"You stormed out of the gallery and Christopher followed you. People heard you argue, slinging accusations at one another."

Rosemary said, "I told him he was pathetic, and he told me I was frigid. But what really infuriated me was his calling me an albatross around his neck. As if I was a liability. It was *my* money and *my* devotion to his career that made him what he was."

"That must have really angered you."

"I already said that." She paused. "So now you're playing shrink?"

Nunn smiled as a waitress came over to take their order. Rosemary surprised him by ordering a hamburger with all the fixings, a double order of french fries, and a Coke. He ordered coffee, black.

"What happened after you argued?"

"I went home, Detective. I don't know what Christopher did—and I don't care."

Nunn gave her a chance to add to her story. When she didn't speak, he said, "Aren't you leaving something out?"

"Yes. I forgot to tell you that I absolutely loathe the bastard!"

Nunn dropped his voice. "Mrs. Thomas, I told you. I've talked to people. All sorts of people. I know you went home—eventually." He leaned back in the booth and saw the panic in her eyes. "I spoke to the guards. You two weren't very discreet. They heard the both of you arguing." He leaned forward and dropped his voice to a whisper. "Why don't you get it off your chest? Tell me about it."

Rosemary stared at a worn spot on the Formica tabletop. "There's nothing to tell."

"You did go back to the museum."

"I went back to my office to get some peace and quiet. I was ..." Her eyes watered again. "I was so ashamed of my behavior."

Nunn nodded sympathetically. In the back of his mind, he was cursing himself for not bringing her into the station house, for not formally Mirandizing her. But now that she was talking, he didn't want to interrupt.

"I couldn't believe how low I had sunk." She looked up at Nunn. "Why should I care if we divorced? We hadn't been a real couple in ages. I was angry, I was spiteful, I was sick. After arguing outside the event, I knew that if I didn't leave, I'd do something I really regretted. So I got in my car and drove away from him. I couldn't possibly go home—not in my condition—so I turned around."

"And went back to the museum, to your office?"

She nodded. "But Christopher, being Christopher, couldn't leave it alone. He had to torture me. He had to make sure that he had the last word."

"He followed you."

"He couldn't leave it alone," she said, a bit breathless.

"He came to your office?"

"My first mistake was thinking that we could actually have a civil conversation."

"He was mad."

"He was irate." She sighed. "My head had cleared . . . somewhat. I replayed that horrid scene in my head and decided that, above all, I wasn't going to stoop to his childish level of hurling barbs and insults. Our marriage was over and the sooner I accepted it, the happier I would be." She studied Nunn's face. "One of the reasons I went to Mexico. It was time to be good to myself. To discover the old Rosemary—the one who probably attracted Christopher in the first place."

"What happened when he followed you into your office?"

"We argued. I threw things. He threw things. It was loud and embarrassing. One of the guards came in to investigate. At that point, I was so flustered, I just picked up my purse and left."

She locked on his eyes. He now noticed flecks of silver amid the blue, like diamond dust. They were beautiful.

"That was the last time I saw him." She almost smiled. "And what an image it was—his beet-red, sweaty face . . . his snarled mouth . . . his shaking hands. He looked like a . . . gargoyle." A sad laugh. "I've carried that image with me. Every time I think about the upcoming divorce and I get scared, I just picture that face. It calms me down." She bit her lower lip. "And he was alive when I left him, Detective. Alive."

That might have been true, but Nunn had already caught her in a lie. Although the guard had gone in to investigate, he never said anything about her leaving. As a matter of fact, the guard distinctly remembered Rosemary smiling, telling him that they just had a little marital tiff. But Nunn didn't want to confront her—not yet.

Nunn looked at the woman sitting across from him. "I need a favor from you." Rosemary looked up but didn't speak. "I need you to come down to the station house and give a statement. It'll clear up everything and then I won't have to bother you again."

"Why should I do that?"

"But why *wouldn't* you want to do that?" Nunn asked. "Clear up this business and your name."

"I never realized that my name was sullied."

"It's just a simple statement."

"Once you put things in writing, it's never simple."

Nunn could see that she wasn't going to fold that easily. "Hey, you walked out of your office, so technically the guard was the last man to see Christopher alive."

"Exactly," Rosemary told him. "So talk to him."

Her hamburger came. Rosemary picked up a french fry but then let it fall on her plate. "I don't know why I ordered this." She pushed her plate aside. Her eyes darkened and she stood up. "I'm leaving."

Nunn dropped a twenty on the table and followed her outside. "Mrs. Thomas—wait!"

But she didn't stop. When she got to her car, she couldn't unlock the door. Her hands were shaking too hard. Tears streamed down her cheeks. She dropped her keys and buried her face in her hands. "Please . . . just go away."

Nunn tried to make his voice as soothing as he could. "I can go away, Mrs. Thomas. But what happened . . . is not going to go away. It's never going to go away until we find your husband."

"So go look for him and stop bothering me!"

She was sobbing by this point. Nunn picked up her car keys and placed them in his pocket. "You're way too upset to drive."

Her hands slowly peeled from her face. "Please, please leave me alone."

Nunn placed his hand on her shoulder. "Make it easy on yourself. Let me take you down to the station house so you can get all of this off your chest."

"I told you everything."

"I know you did," Nunn said calmly. "You were very forthright. And that's good. All I need from you is a written statement of what you told me. That's it. Simple."

"Nothing in life is simple," she said, her face suddenly older.

"Look, once I get a statement from you, I get Tony off my back, I get my superiors off my back, and that's that."

"I may be the jilted wife but I'm not a moron, Detective."

"I can see that. But it doesn't have to be complicated." Nunn's brain was obsessing on a single thought: how to get her voluntarily into the interview room. "Look, forget about the statement, don't write anything down. You come down to the station house and we'll *talk*. That's all. Just you and me. We'll talk. What do you say?"

Rosemary dried her tears on her shirtsleeve and took a deep breath.

Nunn waited for a response, but when she said nothing he gently took her elbow and guided her to his waiting car.

Diary of Jon Nunn

ANDREW F. GULLI

Once she stepped into the interview room, that look in her eyes warned to tell me how it was going to go.

Rosemary gave her statement. Unlike our talk in the coffee shop, her voice now shook. She second-guessed and contradicted herself even more than she had earlier. But any cop will tell you the innocent are never consistent; it's the ones who look you in the eye without blinking, say their piece as if they're reading from a script, they're the ones you have to watch out for.

I couldn't help liking her. She was nothing like the suspects I'd dealt with before. At times I wanted to help her along, help clarify things, but it was useless. The wheels were turning in one direction and I had to be an unwilling participant. God—yeah, God should bless those suckers who go against the tide and get crushed—I never did back then and look where I'm at now.

After she finished giving her statement, she got up from the gray institutional chair and smoothed out her skirt. She didn't belong in that dingy office. I drove her back to the coffee shop so that she could get her car and gave her the line about calling me if anything came up.

She called three days later asking if there were any leads. I used that as an excuse to see her. I told myself I was just doing police work . . . and I was.

But as I got deeper into the case, in the days and weeks that followed, I realized that I liked being around her even if her story didn't add up.

I'll never forget that day—bright and sunny—the kind of day when even as a cop you felt nothing bad could happen.

Sarah and I woke up at the same time. "Something bothering you?"

she asked. After ten years of marriage, she could tell by how I stirred when I was sleeping if I was struggling with something.

"No, just this museum case." I stretched out my arms. "No body or blood yet, but when he does turn up . . . he won't look pretty."

Sarah was surprised. I hardly ever talked about my cases and rarely expressed my opinions. I'd always prided myself on keeping my cool-cop distance. But something about the Thomas case had gotten to me. Sarah could see it had become personal even though I denied it.

"You sure you're not going to find this guy on the Riviera with a case of convenient amnesia?" she asked, getting out of bed.

"I don't think he's coming back alive."

"His wife must have done it." Sarah was never the judgmental type, so I was surprised. I watched her as she walked over to the window and pulled open the curtains.

"What makes you think that?" I sat up in bed.

She turned around to face me "The plain wife, married to the dashing, philandering husband who married her for her money and status, decides she's had enough one day and kills him."

"How do you know all that about him?"

She smiled. "You've only told me *all that* a million times." She walked back to the bed, got in, and snuggled up next to me. "This is your chance to shine, Jon. Our dreams may come true if a high-profile case you're working on goes to court. You can retire, write a book—the whole world will be yours."

I wished she had said something else.

On my way back home from work that day, I stopped at Rosemary's house. I wanted to see her, though I couldn't tell you why, or what I was planning to say. Part of me wanted her to crumble completely, admit everything, and that would be it. But I knew that if and when she did, I'd feel dirtied up by the whole thing. Even if she did kill him, I'd hate the part I'd played in bringing about her demise.

The maid showed me in, and as I was walking into that palatial living room of hers, I heard a man's voice: "It was only a matter of time before the big boys got him . . ."

It was some guy with long hair, a scraggly beard, and dark, intense eyes. He was sitting on the sofa, scotch in hand, very much at home. Rosemary turned, studying my face, looking for a sign that might betray why I was there. I didn't have much to say, so she smiled and said, "I'd like you to meet Hank Zacharius."

I had heard of Zacharius, the investigative reporter. He'd been a thorn in the side of the SFPD ever since he'd uncovered some kind of corruption involving higher-ups at the department.

"Jon Nunn," I said. He stared at me as if trying to assess what I was all about, then gave me a loose handshake, kissed Rosemary's cheek, and left.

I looked around the place—living room big enough to fit my apartment four times, the marble this and marble that, the cut-glass chandeliers, expensive art on the walls, the swimming pool I glimpsed through the French doors—the kind of place that would make Sarah happy. Although the woman to whom all this belonged was anything but. She sat back down on the couch after Zacharius left and was looking up at me, almost questioningly. Her face had grown thinner since our first meeting, and her eyes seemed to have grown larger, prettier.

"Who are the *big boys,* Rosemary?"

"Oh, you know Hank Zacharius, he's into that stuff . . . he has his theories." She paused. "So why are you here? Is there any news?"

"No, nothing." I suddenly felt awkward at being there. "I guess I just wanted to check up on you. . . ."

Her face reddened. "I've told you all I know, Detective."

I walked over to the window and looked down at the tree-lined valley. I thought of Christopher Thomas standing where I now stood. Nothing was enough for him, the money, the wife, the power—some people's appetites could never be satisfied. *What a bastard.* I wouldn't blame her if she did kill him. Something in me stirred, *the big boys . . .* Zacharius and his clichés . . .

I walked back to the sofa and sat down across from her. "Rosemary, you need to level with me."

"I have leveled with you." She looked steadily into my eyes.

"You have to tell me whatever you know about your husband's shady dealings."

She wouldn't budge. "You really need to leave right now; my lawyer told me that I shouldn't even be talking to you."

"Look, it's probably only going to get worse after this. You're the main suspect in his disappearance. The chance of him turning up alive is zero. You have to give me some information that'll point the police in another direction—take the spotlight away from you. This is no time to be worrying about protecting the family name."

She sighed. "I guess there were rumors about forgeries, about drugs. He knew about the rumors. He thought they were funny. I never took any of them seriously."

The sky had started to darken. "What was Zacharius—?"

Rosemary looked up behind me. I turned. The maid had come in; behind her were two guys I recognized from the department—Grygera and Swanson.

"What is it?" I asked. For some reason, I had thought they'd come to talk to me, but, no, it was Rosemary they were looking at. I turned to her. I'll never forget the look in her eyes.

Grygera said, "Rosemary Thomas, I have a warrant for your arrest."

7

JONATHAN SANTLOFER

Joseph Arthur Kroege hated the summer. Not just the heat, but the attitude it seemed to foster, the total lack of professionalism among his museum employees. As if the warm weather were not only an excuse to play, but justification to drop all responsibility. Each year he knew half his staff would be vacationing at one European shoreline or another, although he didn't know which and didn't care.

The German Historical Museum of Berlin was his only concern since taking over as director nearly two decades earlier. An academic by training—and some said by *nature*—Kroege believed in hard work and routine.

Today, as every other day, he'd left his flat in Mitte on upper Friedrichstrasse at exactly 8:12, had taken the U-Bahn to Museumsinsel, and had arrived at the museum at nine sharp. He'd spent only six minutes, rather than his usual ten, reviewing his daily calendar when he realized the crate from America was still languishing in a basement workroom and had been for a week. That was it. Enough. Infuriating. That one of his prized objects—and one of the most popular with the museum's visitors—should be sitting in a dank workroom galled him.

Kroege reached for his phone, then realized the museum installers were, like just about everyone else, on vacation.

The hallway leading to the basement storeroom was hot, the consequence of turning off the museum's air-conditioning at night, an energy-saving effort that Kroege disapproved of despite the board vote, and particularly irritating at the moment with his starched white shirt already sticking to his thick upper body.

He was sorry he'd loaned the iron maiden to the American museum in the first place and would not have if the curator hadn't persisted in a letter-writing campaign that culminated in her calling and pleading, insisting it would be the centerpiece of an exhibition devoted to savage-torture devices, and, in her polite-though-forthright manner, convincing him. Unlike most of the American curators Kroege dealt with, who acted as if they were entitled to anything and everything, Rosemary Thomas had been a velvet steamroller, as genteel as she was persuasive. And good to her word, her exhibition at the McFall Art Museum had garnered serious press, which had credited his museum with the loan, and so perhaps it had not been a bad idea, though right now he was anxious to get it back on display.

The workroom felt like a tomb, no sign or sense of a human presence among the multisized crates and art objects awaiting repair, tools strewn along a worktable, sawdust on the floor, more suspended in the hot, sticky air.

Kroege snorted with disgust. How dare his employees leave the room in such condition? He shook his head as he made his way toward the largest crate, taller than he by several feet and twice as wide.

Kroege circled the crate as if inspecting some object from outer space and stopped dead when he noticed a foot-long crack in the plywood. Had the maiden been damaged in shipping?

He plucked an electric drill from the worktable and quickly removed a dozen Sheetrock screws until one side of the panel fell open—and with that came the faint odor of rotten eggs or fruit.

Kroege, features screwed up, imagined some idiotic American workman accidentally packing his lunch along with the precious maiden.

He stared at the one exposed side. It looked fine. But he had to see if it had been damaged elsewhere.

More screws undone, more plywood tugged away, until the maiden stood in all her glory, a black iron monolith, forbidding and impressive.

Kroege pictured its insides, the iron prongs that closed on its living victims, a torture device from which the only escape was death.

He ran his hand over the hard, pebbly surface, ignoring the smell, which was stronger now, more like rotting meat than fruit or eggs, but the device itself looked fine, unscathed.

Just then he looked down and saw the liquid seeping out from the bottom.

"Was zum Teufel . . . ?"

Kroege bent over to swipe a finger through the puddle, but never reached it, the stench so strong, so repulsive, that he immediately straightened up, fighting the urge to gag.

He stared at the iron maiden, then slowly, and with much effort, began to pry her open.

He didn't get far.

The object inside, as big as Kroege, wrapped in heavy, opaque plastic and bound with tape and rope, tumbled out and hit the floor with a thud. Then, as its contents settled, the top of the plastic split open and a milky ooze, studded with lumps and streaked with lemony yellow and deep crimson, pooled around his shoes, while the stench filled his nose and caught in the back of his throat like burning acid and rot. When, as if hypnotized, he dared a closer look, he recognized a human skull and the black hole of a mouth that appeared to be moving.

Hand over his nose, Kroege looked closer, realizing too late that the movement was caused by a swarm of maggots.

Then he was spinning, flailing, shoes skidding in the primordial ooze, and slipped and fell, his face inches from the hideous skull, one murky, jellied eye socket staring at him as he frantically scampered away and somehow managed to right himself, the contents of his belly having finally worked their way up into his throat, vomit spewing forth as he raced from the workroom.

The Police Reports

KATHY REICHS

STATION	CODE	BERLIN POLICE DEPARTMENT (POLIZEIBERLIN)		CASE NUMBER 08443

Borough **Mitte**		Troop	Station	Case No.
Complainant—Last Name, First, Middle	C	**BSS**		98—234

Kroege, Joseph Arthur (German Historical Museum, Berlin)

~~Victim Last Name, First, Middle~~	~~Location of Case~~
Unknown deceased	Suspicious death

Property Involved	Value	Identifiable
Apparatus referred to as "iron maiden"	**more than 1 million DM**	

On 18 July 1998 at 0940 hours, Senior Investigator MAX REIMAR, Berlin Police Department, Investigation Unit, responded to a call from the German Historical Museum reporting a body inside an apparatus shipped from San Francisco, USA. On confirming the presence of decomposed human remains, photographs were taken of the exterior and interior of the museum workroom and of the exterior of the apparatus. A statement was taken from JOSEPH ARTHUR KROEGE, director of the museum. The area was secured and Medical Examiner DR. DAGMAR ZEPPER was notified. Dr. Zepper arrived on scene at 1150 hours. At 1310 hours the apparatus and remains were transported to the Institute of Legal Medicine, Berlin, for autopsy and identification.
Enclosures: Genl 1—Evidence Record
Genl 1—Witness Statement
Genl 34—Photo Record

Signature and Rank	Shield No.	Approved	Case Status	CA	C EC	Open	This Report
Inv. Max Reimar	2417	NAD					**18/7/1998**

Lab Use Only	Lab Use Only		Name of Station/ Agency **Berlin, PD**	Continuation Sheets 1/1
			Case Number 08443	Term, Message No. & File
	Date of Occurrence 18/7/1998	Laboratory Case Number	Borough of Occurrence **Mitte**	
	Investigating Member **Inv. Max Reimar**		Submitted by **Inv. Max Reimar**	
	Name only, (L,F,M) of Victim **Unknown**		Name of Complainant **Joseph Kroege, BNM**	

EVIDENCE

ITEM NO.	DESCRIPTION	EXAMINATION REQUESTED	ID	HOLD AT STATION	TO TROOP	TO LAB
	The following was item obtained at the German Historical Museum					
519	1—Iron maiden w/ human remains					X

TRANSFER RECORD

DATE & TIME	ITEMS INVOLVED	FROM	TO	SIGNATURE
18/7/1998 1310 hrs	519	Max Reimar	Dagmar Zepper, MD	Dagmar Zepper, MD

STATION	CODE	BERLIN POLICE DEPARTMENT (POLIZEIBERLIN)		CASE NUMBER 08443

Borough **Mitte**

WITNESS—LAST NAME, FIRST, MIDDLE	TROOP	STATION	FILE NO.
Kroege, Joseph Arthur	**C**	**BSS**	**98–234**

TITLE—LAST NAME, FIRST, MIDDLE	CHARACTER OF CASE
Unknown deceased	**Suspicious death**

Witness Statement: KROEGE, JOSEPH ARTHUR
On 18/7/1998, at 0940 hours, Senior Investigator MAX REIMAR, Berlin Police Department, Investigation Unit, spoke directly to Mr. Joseph Kroege, director of the German Historical Museum. Mr. Kroege reported that upon arriving at the museum at approximately 0900 hours he proceeded to his office, then to storage room 14-B, and opened a shipping crate. According to Mr. Kroege, the crate had been at the museum for approximately one week, having been returned from a museum in San Francisco, USA. Mr. Kroege attributed the delay in verifying the crate's contents to an unusually high level of absenteeism among museum employees due to summer vacation.

Mr. Kroege stated that upon opening the outer crate, he noticed fluid and an unusual odor. He continued to unwrap the inner packaging, wanting to verify the presence of a human-sized and -shaped apparatus known as an "iron maiden." Mr. Kroege stated that the specimen was an eighteenth-century torture device that had been on loan for an exhibit in San Francisco, USA.

Mr. Kroege stated that upon opening the iron maiden device itself, an object that appeared to be a body, wrapped in thick plastic, fell to the floor. He stopped all activity and phoned the Berlin Police Department emergency line.

SIGNATURE AND RANK	SHIELD NO.	APPROVED	CASE STATUS	CA	C	OPEN	THIS REPORT
Inv. Max Reimar	2417	NAD			**EC**		**18/7/1998**

Institute of Legal Medicine
REPORT OF AUTOPSY EXAMINATION
DECEDENT

Document Identifier: C1998073042

Autopsy Type: ME Autopsy

Name: Unknown (Presumed, Thomas, Christopher, DOB 19 09 52)

Age: 35 to 50 years

Race: White

Sex: M

Stature: 183 centimeters +/-

AUTHORIZATION

Authorized by: Dr. Dagmar Zepper

Received From: Berlin City Police, District 3

ENVIRONMENT

Date of Exam 20/7/1998   **Time of Exam** 0915 hours

Autopsy Facility Institute of Legal Medicine, Berlin

Persons Present. Adolph Munger, Mette Brinkman

CERTIFICATION

Cause of Death

Undetermined

Manner of Death

Homicide

The facts stated herein are correct to the best of my knowledge and belief.

Signed by

Bruno Muntz, MD 20/7/1998, 1429 hours

DIAGNOSES

Decomposed human adult

IDENTIFICATION

Body Identified By

Personal effects; partial print, left fifth finger

EXTERNAL DESCRIPTION

Body Condition Decomposed/skeletal

Hair Degraded, original color is undeterminable
Teeth Missing, save one fragment
Clothing was adult male-type trousers, jacket, shirt, and undergarments. A gold belt buckle bore the initials CT, surrounded by a circular diamond pattern. When removed from the apparatus, the remains weighed 60 kilograms. Organs were liquefied. Brain and soft tissue were putrefied. Some bones remained connected by ligamentous tissue. One digit was deeply embedded in the left femoroacetabular junction, preserving the tissue of the distal aspect. Insect specimens were collected and submitted for analysis. See separate entomology report.

INJURIES

Though sloughing, the skin of the torso and limbs showed multiple sharp-instrument perforations. Though putrefied, the muscles of the torso and limbs showed multiple sharp-instrument perforations. Fifty-three fractures and perforations were seen on the skull and postcranial skeleton. No associated hemorrhage was evident. All sharp- and blunt-instrument trauma was consistent with postmortem injury due to spikes projecting inward within the iron maiden apparatus.

DISPOSITION OF CLOTHING AND PERSONAL EFFECTS

Clothing discarded. Belt buckle returned to family along with remains.

PROCEDURES

Radiographs
Selected postmortem odontological and long-bone radiographs were obtained to aid in determining identity and cause of death. See separate radiology and odontology reports.

IDENTIFICATION

See separate fingerprint report.

INTERNAL EXAMINATION

Body Cavities

Organs liquefied. No samples retained.

SKELETAL EXAMINATION

Survey

The bones consisted of a complete adult skeleton. Fractures and perforations were noted at fifty-three locations. (See attached skeletal diagram.) Femoral measurements were taken to establish height. Following skeletal survey and measurement, radiographs were made of the maxilla and mandible, the torso, and the long bones of the lower and upper extremities. Blunt- and sharp-instrument trauma was evident at fifty-three sites. No associated hemorrhage was observed at any trauma site. Following the examination of radiographs by the radiologist and the odontologist, the bones were packaged for transport to the United States.

SUMMARY AND INTERPRETATION

At the time of discovery decedent's identity was unknown. The body had been wrapped in thick plastic and taped.

Officials at the San Francisco Police Department provided information of a missing person, Thomas, Christopher, last seen alive 20/06/1998. Dr. Dagmar Zepper, Berlin, medical examiner, assumed jurisdiction of the body and authorized autopsy. Review of Christopher Thomas's medical records showed that he was a white male, stature 180 centimeters, forty-five years old at the time of his disappearance.

Autopsy examination showed a skeletonized human adult with liquefied organs and putrefied brain and musculature. Long-bone measurements were consistent with a white male of stature of approximately 180 centimeters. Findings were consistent with enclosure of the body within the iron maiden apparatus following death.

Fingerprint analysis positively identified the decedent as Christopher Thomas. See fingerprint report.

Entomological analysis suggested a PMI greater than 18 days, a time period consistent with an LSA for Christopher Thomas of 20/06/1998 with discovery of the body on 18/07/1998. See entomology report.

In my opinion, the cause of death in this case is most appropriately certified as "undetermined." Examination of the skeletal remains does not allow differentiation of death from a natural disease process such as pneumonia, or from a nontraumatic external means, such as asphyxia.

The circumstances of body treatment require manner of death be classified as "homicide."

Bruno Muntz   *20 July 1998*

Bruno Muntz, MD   20 July 1998

DIAGRAMS

1. Skeleton (front/back)

ASSOCIATED REPORTS

Entomology
Fingerprint
Odontology
Radiology

THE PRESENT

8

JOHN LESCROART

The fog was in.

The forty-two-year-old estate lawyer Stan Ballard pulled his car into an open parking space at Ocean Beach about a hundred yards south of San Francisco's legendary tourist attraction the Cliff House, which was all but invisible through the gray cloud that enveloped the western half of the city.

For a long moment, cocooned in the warmth of his Lexus, Ballard simply sat behind the wheel and let the motor run, watching the mist settle onto the windshield, almost as if it were actually raining. But there was no real rain, only the damned perennial fog. On the dashboard, he noted the external temperature—forty-three degrees—and shook his head with disgust.

The first day of summer. Ridiculous.

Ballard wore a light charcoal suit with infinitesimally small, maroon pinstripes that had set him back $1,900 at Barcelino. He also sported a TAG Heuer watch, a $200 custom-made ivory dress shirt with his initials on the breast pocket, a Jerry Garcia tie (to balance out the ultra-conservative tone of the rest of his attire), a highly shined pair of Brioni loafers. Even his knee-length, black silk socks came dear—$18 a pair. But he knew that if you wanted to instill confidence in your clients, you simply had to dress the part, as though money were the last thing you, or they, ever had to worry about.

Even without the elegant threads, Ballard cut an impressive figure. He worked out in his converted basement for an hour and a half every morning, so his six-foot frame looked pretty much the way it had when he'd pitched for Cal back in the eighties. A few lines had begun to crop up around his hazel eyes, but his light brown hair was still thick, his skin ruddy and smooth. The prominent, slightly off-kilter nose only added to his aura of powerful manhood.

Finally, he couldn't put the inevitable off any longer, and he killed the ignition, took a steadying breath against the temperature shock, and opened the door.

There, out on the beach, where she said she'd be, by one of the boulder-bordered fire circles the hippies and/or the homeless used most nights, he could barely make out the huddled figure of his wife. He'd been with Sarah now for eight years, and though they'd had some difficult times in their marriage—their inability to conceive their own children had been a festering wound for half of those years together—it hadn't been until recently that Ballard had begun to consider the possibility, for no specific reason other than apathy and guilt, that their relationship might actually end in divorce.

But they weren't there yet—he hoped.

Now Stan was playing the role of the dutiful husband, coming down here to the ocean's edge, at Sarah's urging, because she had told him she needed him. And because she had so obviously still needed him, suddenly in the here and now, what he was doing didn't feel like playing a role at all. Some flame still burned among the embers at the mere thought that he might still have an important place in her life, in her heart. And the warmth of that flame both surprised and disoriented him.

The ocean's melancholy roar as waves broke at the offshore bar thrummed under the early evening's weight. The tide was out, the sea itself not visible through the fog.

Stan came up beside her. She was wearing jeans and hiking boots and her familiar cowled BAY TO BREAKERS sweatshirt, with the hood up over her shoulder-length hair. He cleared his throat and she looked up at him, her shoulders giving in relief.

"Is there any more room on that rock?"

She shifted over a few inches, patted where she'd been, and he lowered himself down beside her.

"I'm sorry about this," she said. "I don't mean to be melodramatic. I was trying to keep you out of this, but it's been a few days now and I don't see how I can."

"No, you can't," Stan said. "Out of what, though, exactly?"

She held her hands clasped tightly in front of her, her elbows resting on her knees. "Do you know what August twenty-third is this year?"

Stan considered for a long moment. "Should I?"

"You might. It might say something if you did."

"Which means it also says something that I don't?"

She turned to face him. With ice-blue eyes, finely pored, fair skin, and wide, perfectly defined cheekbones, Sarah was attractive from any angle, but from straight on, her face could be distracting in its beauty. "I don't know. I honestly don't know, Stan." After a pause, she said, "It's the tenth anniversary of Rosemary Thomas's execution."

Nodding, Stan remained silent for a beat. "I guess that's about right."

"It's right. I googled it and made sure. Though I didn't really doubt it."

"How did it come up?"

"That's what's gotten me so upset. I got a letter—not an e-mail, mind you, but a real letter— from Tony Olsen." She raised her eyes and looked out in front of her, as if she could see the breakers. "Actually, it was addressed to you."

"When was this?"

"I don't know. Monday, I think."

Stan strained to keep the note of anger out of his voice. "And you opened it?"

"I had to. I was afraid of . . . I was afraid."

"Of what?"

"What he'd do. Of why he could be writing to you, after all this time. Of what he wanted with you."

"Tony Olsen's got nothing to do with me, Sarah. He was connected to Rosemary and Chris Thomas, and so was I, and that's it."

"I know, but your testimony . . . I know he never forgave you for that, and he's a powerful man, Stan." Again she faced him with a pleading look.

"So what did he want?"

"I've got the letter, if you want to read it."

"In a minute, maybe, but what's the short version?"

"He wants to have a memorial service."

Stan barked out an outraged laugh. "For Rosemary? That's insane. Why would anybody want to do that? Okay, a memorial for Chris, maybe, but not for the woman who killed him." Stan remembered now that Rosemary had mentioned such an event in her will, though he'd never expected anyone to take it seriously.

"Except nobody liked Chris."

"I liked him all right. I've got to believe his mistress—what was her name, Haile—she liked him. And there were others."

"Girlfriends, yes. But, according to Jon, the guy was a thorough shit. Believe me. He dug up some crazy dirt on Christopher Thomas during his investigation. And Haile? She was just impressed with his money and power. For you the Thomases were just early clients who helped you get going. But Christopher wasn't anybody's idea of a nice guy. And maybe, in fact, Rosemary didn't kill him."

"Wrong. That's your ex-husband talking. There's no maybe on that score. She killed him all right. The jury had no problem with that. There wasn't ever any doubt about whether—" Suddenly he stopped and turned to his wife. "Ah. But this isn't really about Tony, is it?"

Sarah hunched down farther into her sweatshirt.

"Maybe I ought to take a look at the letter," Stan said.

"All right." She reached inside the sweatshirt and came out with an envelope. "But you'll see, he never mentions Jon."

"No. He wouldn't, would he? Especially to us. You're married to me now. That case is what got us together. No need to belabor the obvious, but Jon always thought he screwed up that case—everybody knows that—and that was what screwed him up. Terminally."

"Not terminally."

"No? Well enough to lose you over."

"I know. I just wish it could have been something else."

"There was something else, if you remember. Animal connection, if nothing else."

But the small attempt at humor got no rise from her. "I sometimes wonder if there was nothing else."

"Well, thanks very much, now, after all these years."

She reached over and took his hand. "Don't be mad, Stan. I didn't mean that the way it sounded. I just don't know if I'll ever get over the guilt."

"Guilt for what? Falling in love with someone else who adored you while your husband fell into the toilet and never came out? And you know what the true irony is? *He was right all along*. All this agonizing and hand-wringing over how he'd blown the investigation. Give me a break. Rosemary killed Chris. There wasn't any evidence that pointed to anybody else—not to me, not to anybody."

Sarah looked up at him. "Why on earth would it have pointed to *you?*"

Stan shrugged. "It was just . . . a figure of speech."

"All right, Stan, all right. As you say, we've been through it all a million times." In a small voice she sighed and added, "Maybe you ought to look at the letter."

"Maybe I should."

If for no other reason than to give himself time to calm down, Stan studied the envelope—Tony Olsen's personal stationery. The address handwritten with a fountain pen in Olsen's careful script. Postmarked in the superexclusive Seacliff neighborhood of San Francisco, where the well-known venture capitalist had lived for the past twenty-five years.

When he'd finished reading the letter, Stan stood up and walked several feet away from his wife toward the ocean. The beating of his heart threatened to drown out the roar of the surf. He stood, hands in his pockets, numb enough now that the chill of the fog failed to touch him. Finally, his breathing under control, he turned and walked back to where Sarah sat. "What does he hope to get out of this? Why would anybody go?"

"If you don't go, you might look like you didn't care."

This brought a smirk of dark mirth. "Sarah, this just in: I *don't* care. All of this happened more than ten years ago. The guilty person got convicted, sentenced, and executed. Now Olsen wants everybody who was there the night Chris went missing to show up and do what exactly? Mourn the loss of Rosemary? I don't think so."

"You think it's really about Jon?"

"What else could it be? He's still whipping himself for thinking he made such a huge mistake. Which, by the way, he didn't."

"Tony never says any of that."

"That's because if he did, his motive for this memorial or whatever he calls it would be clear even to the people he invited who aren't connected to Jon. In any event, I don't think it's going to make any real difference."

"Why not?"

"Because who's going to go?"

"What do you mean?"

"Just what I said. Who would go?"

"Everybody. You all would have to."

"Or what?"

"Or you'd look . . . I don't know. Maybe guilty?"

"Of what? There's no unsolved crime out there, darling. Unless Tony's taking this whole thing to the press . . ."

"Which he'd do in a heartbeat."

Stan held up a hand. "Even so, so what? I'm a busy guy. So are at least half the people who were there the night of the murder. We can't make the memorial. We'll send flowers. End of story, such story as there is. Which is slim and none anyway."

"So you're not going?"

"No chance."

"And what about me?"

"What about you?"

"I pushed Jon when he wasn't sure. It was . . . my fault."

"No. That made you a good wife to a cop, that's all. Not an accomplice."

"But I still feel guilty about it." Sarah stood up and put her hands on her husband's arms, looking him in the eye. "They *executed* her, Stan. And say whatever else you will about him, we both know Jon isn't stupid. He must have come to believe she didn't do it for a real reason."

"Okay, I'll concede that's what he came to believe. But that doesn't mean he's right. I think the rule is that evidence talks and bullshit walks, Sarah. And high up there under bullshit is wishful thinking and second-guessing. You want my opinion, I'll tell you that Jon got caught up in a little of both."

Peter Heusen lived full-time on a seventy-two-foot cabin cruiser named *Désirée* that he moored just off the St. Francis Yacht Club. On this Thursday morning, he had sent his first mate, Roger, over in the dinghy at a little after eleven o'clock to pick up Stan Ballard. The dark pall of the persistent June gloom hugged the headlands at the Golden Gate, but here on the back deck where they'd set out the lunch table, the sun shone unobstructed in a light breeze. It was warm enough for shirtsleeves for Peter, and even Ballard had been persuaded to remove his suit coat.

The two men were neither exact contemporaries nor close friends, but they had something of a financial and personal history, and as they took their seats and let Roger pour the wine, small talk flowed as effort-lessly as the pinot grigio.

But when the mate disappeared back into the hold, Heusen put his wineglass down and leveled his gaze across the white linen, the silver, the crystal. "So, this invitation. I'm afraid I don't see the urgency around it that you do, Stan. The whole idea strikes me as somewhat eccentric, granted, but Tony's always had that side of him. Look at how he essen-tially became Nunn's protector and savior after Nunn essentially put the noose around Rosemary's neck. Can you say 'conflict of interest'? But that kind of inconsistency never seemed to bother him. He was glad enough that somebody had killed Chris, I'm sure. He truly hated the guy. But on the other hand, he didn't want Chris's killer to have been Rosemary. Or didn't want her punished for it anyway." Peter shrugged. "The guy's a junkie for drama, that's all. And maybe things have been slow for him on that score lately."

Stan sat back from the table far enough that he could cross one leg over the other in a relaxed posture. He held his wineglass by its slender stem and slowly turned it, hoping to convey a casualness that couldn't have been more at odds with his actual state of mental turmoil. "So, you don't see Nunn's involvement here?"

The question seemed to surprise Heusen. "No sign of it. What does he have to do with this? He'd be pretty out of place at this memorial, wouldn't you think? Having been the one who pretty much made sure Rosemary got convicted."

Heusen sipped some wine. "I think I'd put Jon Nunn out of your mind. Of course, for you, being married to Sarah, that might be a little more difficult."

In spite of Stan's worries, this comment brought a small smile. "Not to put too fine a point on it," he said, then added, "She's pretty con-vinced it's all about him, wanting to get it right this time."

"He got it right last time." Heusen shook his head dismissively.

"That's what I told Sarah."

"But she doesn't believe that?"

Stan took a beat. "She thinks there are still some questions."

"After a trial and appeals and . . . ?" Peter gulped his wine and poured himself another glass. His forehead was dotted with perspira-tion.

"It was still the fastest execution in the state in forty years."

Heusen held up a hand, his mouth twisted in distaste. "Please. I remember, all right. But I've got to believe that even if they appealed for another twenty years, it still would have turned out the same way. And you know why? Because my dear departed sister was in fact her husband's killer—it was proved." Peter drank the second glass of wine and slammed the glass down.

The talk came to a halt while Roger appeared again, refilled their glasses, and laid their plates in front of them—sand dabs, coleslaw, baby carrots. When the mate had finished and gone back belowdecks, Stan asked, "So you'll be at the memorial?"

"Well, she was my sister. I couldn't very well not attend, could I?"

"You don't feel that, in view of our investments and . . . ?"

Heusen waved away the objection. "Our investments are immaterial. I don't see what you're implying. I was the estate's executor. You were my adviser. All we've done is make money. It's benefited the children and it's benefited us too. No one could find any fault with that."

"No." Ballard took a breath, treading softly. He sipped his wine. "But we also made a nice profit for ourselves, didn't we? I mean, with both Chris and Rosemary gone, all the Heusen money came to—"

"I know where it came. It came to me, Stan, with a good hunk to you as commission. And a goddamned good thing it did too. I refuse to feel any guilt about that." Peter cocked his head. "Is this why you wanted to come out and have this little chat today?"

"Yes. Mostly, I'd say so."

Peter's face darkened. "You think someone, after all these years, will see a motive for one of us to have killed Chris?"

"If someone's looking," Stan said, "and I believe Jon Nunn *is*."

"Then let him look. He didn't find anything back when it mattered. He won't find anything now."

"But back when it mattered, Rosemary and Chris's money was in escrow during the trial. It wasn't until she was executed that it came to you, Peter. That was almost two years after Chris's murder."

"Ah. The way you put it, you make it sound like the perfect crime for a patient man. But you can't think anybody would believe that I would have let my own sister be executed just so I could get access to her money, do you, Stan?"

"No!" Too quickly. Stan sat back, assayed a smile, came at it again. "No, of course not. Although you must admit you'd been in a bit of a skid financially. I'm just saying that Jon Nunn might—"

"Jon Nunn, Jon Nunn, Jon Nunn," Heusen exclaimed. "The man's a drunk and a nonentity. If it weren't for the fact that you're married to his ex-wife, he wouldn't even be on your radar, nor should he be." Peter came forward, eyes shining over the table. "We've done nothing wrong over these years, Stan. And quite a bit of good. Rosemary was a gullible woman who turned out to be a victim of her own weaknesses, her own softness, her own inability to make good decisions. She should never have been entrusted with any part of our family fortune. Now, I'm not saying she deserved to die, of course, but there seemed to be a certain karmic justice in having it all come back to me, just at the moment that you and I were becoming positioned to take full advantage of it. In fact"—Peter raised his glass, the alcohol taking effect—"I'd like to propose a toast to our collaboration and to our continued success."

Having no choice but to comply, Stan Ballard raised his own glass to chime it against that of his wealthiest client.

Justine Olegard, curator at the McFall Art Museum, reached for the envelope that she'd tucked under the side of the blotter on her desk. She'd had a premonition when the thing had arrived the other day in the mail, and though Tony Olsen had always been a large benefactor and player in the museum's ongoing development, something about this particular envelope had struck her as somehow ominous, and she'd put off opening the thing.

Now, at her lunchtime on this Thursday, she had locked her door and, using her Navajo dagger, cut open the envelope. Sitting back, she read the letter quickly, then set it down squarely in front of her and read it again.

It couldn't have been less welcome news.

Tony would be using the museum to hold some sort of a memorial to commemorate the death—by execution no less—of Rosemary Thomas. This was just the kind of distraction that Justine, now on the cusp of the museum's new season, did not need.

In fact, she never ever again wanted to hear the names Rosemary and Christopher Thomas.

Of course, the demise of both Thomases had been the prime reason for her ascendancy at the museum. Back then, she had been in her early thirties and still liked to believe she had the bloom of youth, that she could be attractive to a charismatic and powerful man such as Chris

Thomas for her body and face as well as for her brains, erudition, organizational skills.

She'd been his associate curator. And, yes, he'd been married. He made no secret of that. But he'd told her that his marriage to Rosemary was a sham. They were both working to settle the visitation of the children and some financial details and to move on with their divorce, but in the meanwhile he was virile and powerful, and then there'd been the issue of the fake Soutine painting she'd helped acquire for the museum. If it hadn't been for Chris, well . . .

Still, she felt the familiar flush rise in her cheeks at the shame of it.

Shaking her head to clear it of these awkward and painful memories, she cast her eyes back to the envelope. After a moment, a muscle working in her jaw, she picked up the telephone and punched in the numbers she knew by heart. "Hello, Tony," she said to Olsen's answering machine, "this is Justine. I know it's been a couple of days since I got your note about Rosemary Thomas's memorial, but I wanted you to know that I think it's a wonderful idea, and it will be terrific to have so many of the museum's sponsors back in one location again, where I'm sure they'll be impressed with all of our improvements over the years. I'm sure it will be a wonderful event."

Her hand shaking, she hung up the phone.

Stan Ballard walked through a small grove of eucalyptus and up a hill through a forest of tombstones to a lone marble crypt. Out in front of him, the Pacific glinted out to the horizon. Without really consciously planning to, he had driven out here to the cemetery in Colma and had parked way down in the lot. Wandering aimlessly at first, he had walked off most of the effects of his lunch with Peter Heusen by the time he arrived at Rosemary's burial plot, where her remains lay beside those of her parents, her grandparents, and—to the disgust and dismay of some—her husband.

Going down to one knee, he put a flat palm on the slab of marble that had been laid over the bones of Rosemary Heusen Thomas and looked out at the ocean.

Hidden among the tombstones, he crouches beside a crypt large enough to shield his body while providing a bird's-eye view of the man who kneels in front of Rosemary Thomas's grave.

Such a stupid move for a man who has made millions off a dead woman, he thinks.

He takes in the man's expensive suit, shiny shoes slightly dulled by the graveyard's dirt and dust.

What is he doing here?

He watches the man drag his hand across the marble slab as if cleaning it. And he's saying something, though his words are lost in the air.

He wouldn't be surprised if the man started scraping at the grave, digging through dirt and grass and stone in search of some valuable trinket—an earring, a necklace—that he could yank off the bones of the dead woman, something more he could take from her.

Oh, these parasites.

He is tempted to walk up to him and ask, "Tell me, why are you visiting the grave of a woman whose money you have filtered into your own account?"

He would like to hear the answer because he is genuinely surprised and interested to know why some people act so foolishly sentimental, so guilty, after acting so badly.

His knees are starting to ache. He's tired and needs to stand or stretch but doesn't dare.

Now the lawyer stands and brushes dust from his pin-striped suit. He smooths his hair. He looks past the grave as if searching for something, then turns, and it's as if he's staring directly at the spot from where he is being observed.

9

T. JEFFERSON PARKER

The letter came on the first day of summer, addressed to my wife. It was from billionaire Tony Olsen, a man I did not love. The envelope was ivory colored and square—an announcement or invitation maybe. I collected it with the rest of the mail from our box out on Laguna Canyon Road, and I jammed the whole fat handful into a book bag and walked back up the steep street to our house.

The afternoon was sunny and warm, with a stiff onshore breeze that brought the smell of the ocean up the canyon. A few wildflowers were still holding on with the sagebrush. Two hawks circled above. I wondered if that big halibut was still hanging out at Divers Cove and thought I might go down there that evening and have another go at him. A yard long, at least. I missed him yesterday but I don't usually miss.

As I walked up the road to our house, I passed the homes of the professional surfer, the history professor, the rock singer, the arborist, the patent lawyer. We've got a good little 'hood. The gardens are perfect, we get the trash cans off the street pronto. Belle and I are the poor people—the artist and the camera store owner and their two kids.

Belle was in her studio at the far end of our lot. It's a metal building that was once a machine shop, but it has skylights and plenty of space. She was standing at an easel, working on a painting. Her shorts and hiking boots were covered in paint, her flannel shirt was paint splattered, her blond hair was tied back in a ponytail. She looked a mess, a gorgeous mess.

"You've got mail," I said.

"Any checks?"

"No. And no Victoria's Secret catalog either."

"Tragic."

I fished the Tony letter out of the book bag and set it on a workbench covered with paints and solvents and gesso.

"Open it," said Belle.

I opened it. "We're invited to a memorial for Rosemary Thomas. On the tenth anniversary of her death."

Belle didn't look surprised, just continued painting for a minute, then looked at me and lowered her paintbrush hand. "Who was it said that the past doesn't just come back to haunt us, it never really leaves?"

"We can just say no."

"She was a beautiful person and she helped me. What they did to her is unforgivable. You know how I feel about all of that, Don."

Yes, I did. Rosemary Thomas had discovered Belle's paintings at the Laguna Festival of Arts thirteen years ago and had brought them to the attention of her curator husband, Christopher. He was running the shows at the McFall Art Museum in San Francisco. He and Rosemary flew down one summer and Belle spent two days with them, showing them her work and studio, letting them hang around the festival and observe the scene. I was there for some of it. We came back here after the second night and drank. And Rosemary kept talking admiringly about Belle's work, particularly *Waves 27,* a small oil on canvas, a ship at sea in big, black waves, both beautiful and terrifying. Ryder, updated—the best of a series. We had it hanging in our dining room until shortly after Rosemary's execution, when we learned of arrangements she'd made with Olsen to have the painting installed in the McFall as part of the permanent collection.

That evening while Rosemary talked enthusiastically about art, especially Belle's, Chris just sat there looking at her with a wry smile. Later, more booze, and Chris confessed his disdain for most of the Laguna artists. He said they were worse than he'd feared. He said they could learn a lot from Belle, and from Art 101. He would consider her for a group show. You can imagine what that meant to her—it would be a huge leap in her career.

Starting then, Christopher began flirting with Belle more openly, as if he'd purchased her attention. He continued to treat Rosemary like something stuck to his shoe. I observed and tolerated this. For a while.

A month later, Chris came down without Rosemary and arranged to take Belle to dinner at a hot new restaurant in Newport Beach. Hip to this play, Belle and I decided she should go anyway. She did. Dinner was good. After, he said they should have port at the Four Seasons because they had a good list, so she followed him across town in her car. Of course after the port he invited her to his suite. Belle said she was spoken for and I wasn't a half-bad guy, which, to tell the truth, was a higher opinion than I deserved. He blushed and smiled. After dessert he walked her across that nice lobby toward the valet and put an arm around her and whispered in her ear that her talent was nothing compared to her tits and ass, and she'd be better off selling trinket paintings to tourists in Laguna than having her work blown off the walls of the McFall by painters a thousand times better than she was, and he squeezed her butt and left her at the valet stand.

She told me all this when she came home that night, humiliated and furious.

I drove up to the Four Seasons and called Chris on the hotel phone, said I was Rudy the valet, and it looked as if somebody had keyed his Jag. Chris said, so what, it's just a fuckin' rental car, and I said, suit yourself, sir, but we either have to file a report with Newport Beach PD or get a sign-off from you so the rental agency won't—

So Christopher Thomas, a take-charge guy, slammed down the room phone in my ear.

I bet myself it would take him less than two minutes to make the concierge desk. It took him a minute and a half. By the time he saw me, it was too late—I snagged him by his ear like a five-year-old and dragged him outside. Must have looked funny, a guy in a $2,000 cream silk suit led by the ear through the Four Seasons lobby, bent over, hands waving, whining about lawyers and damages and having me put back in prison for the rest of my life.

Outside, past the valet stand, I tripped him onto his back and held him there with my foot while I got Belle on the cell. I could feel his heart beating through my boot. I gave Chris the phone and told him he might want to apologize to my wife. On impulse I grabbed one of his ankles and dragged him through the flower bed that runs along the Four Seasons entryway, through the peonies and Iceland poppies and ranunculus and God knows what else that was planted there that week, Chris bouncing along, babbling away to Belle. I could hear her pleading with me to stop, but I wouldn't. He made a fairly convincing apology. Security was there by then so I dropped his leg and grabbed my phone and backed away to my car with the rent-a-goon yapping on his walkie-talkie, his voice high and his eyes big, not much of an intimidator, and half an hour later I was home with Belle.

I should have felt a little bit better about the world but I didn't.

So, you can imagine that the cops had some questions for me a year later when Chris's body showed up in an iron maiden torture device housed in a Berlin museum.

Such as, where was I on the night he disappeared? (Twenty miles off the coast of San Francisco, coincidentally, hanging out with a friend.)

Such as, why had I assaulted Chris at the Four Seasons? (It seemed like the right thing to do.)

Such as, tell us about your time in Corcoran State Prison (a deuce for forgery and resisting arrest).

And who were my friends? And what about my job as a bouncer at a Laguna nightclub? And my relationship with Belle. That was the hardest thing for them to understand. How a con like me could win the heart of a woman like Belle—beautiful and kind and talented and hotly pursued. I told them the truth: I had no idea how.

That was true back then. Still is.

But Belle had a secret: a commitment she'd made to Rosemary. I knew that much. She told me it was better I didn't know, and I didn't push, I respected her wishes.

"It's up to you, Belle," I said. "You want to go to the memorial, pay your respects to Rosie, that's good. The downside is the art-world phonies. But I'll be your escort. I'll be your man. I'll mind my manners and dress real sharp. I'll throw my coat over the San Francisco mud holes for you, and I'll take you to good restaurants and I'll make love to you any chance I get."

"Business as usual." She tried to smile but I could see the worry in her eyes.

"I'd rather stay home and spearfish. I missed a thirty-six-inch halibut yesterday, but I'll go."

"You've been brooding over that fish for about twenty-four hours, Don." She smiled and shook her head. You look up *beautiful smile* in the dictionary, they show you a picture of Belle's. "I need to go," she said. "I made a promise. And I don't have any trouble at all with Tony Olsen."

I said nothing, tamping down my envy of a handsome billionaire my wife didn't have any trouble with at all. I'm a jealous husband and I admit it. There was no real reason for me to humiliate Chris Thomas all those years ago, other than to smooth my ego, which had commanded me to make things right for Belle, to get her art shown, to make this McFall thing happen. When Chris rejected her, he became my enemy. So I escalated. It's a prison thing. You escalate before you get escalated upon. My only regret when I got home that night from the Four Seasons was that I hadn't escalated *enough*.

"We'll take the truck," I said.

"So you can dive Morro Bay and Point Arena."

"That thought comes to mind."

"And the Farallons?"

"I did that for Rusty."

The Farallon Islands off San Francisco are the most dangerous place on earth to dive. They're crawling with white sharks, the water is cold, the visibility is poor. Death can get its teeth into you before you even know what's happening. If the sharks don't get you, the currents will. The rocks are sharp as razors and there's not even a place to moor a boat for landing. It reminded me of what I'd seen in the fucking art world— sharks and teeth.

Rusty was an old friend, a brave and sometimes crazy man who was still making his meager living diving for urchins in that lethal water. He saved my life at Corcoran, and I will do almost anything to save his. He is stuck with me for life, and I with him.

I went to the South Farallons with Rusty the day Christopher Thomas went missing. Rusty and I made the rugged crossing that night and dove for urchin in the morning. I was forty feet down when a white shark emerged from the unfathomable darkness, came at me, and veered back into the darkness. I remember his teeth, the swatch of underside white. I realized, again, that miracles happen daily. We got six hundred pounds that day, not too bad, better quality than the Japanese can find, top dollar for Rusty.

The cops found this story hard to believe. A felon's alibi is rarely considered airtight, especially when corroborated by another felon.

"If you can survive the art snobs," I said, "I can survive the Farallons."

She looked at me, then went back to work on the canvas, a troubled look clouding her beautiful face.

We ate dinner outside that night in honor of the first day of summer, even though the clouds had deepened and brought a chill to the night. We've got an old picnic table in the backyard, set up under a coral tree.

There's a barbecue and a hammock. The kids, Jimmy and Elsa, were already inside working on the dishes and feeding scraps to the dogs. They don't know about me yet. There will be a time for that. I could see them through the windows, standing in front of the kitchen sink in the yellow light, innocent, full of life and promise.

"You don't have to go to San Francisco, you know," said Belle. "Those aren't your people up there."

"They're not yours either."

"It's for Rosie. Only and purely. I made a promise."

"If you go, I go. I might get to punch somebody out, make a scene. Get thrown in jail."

Belle smiled and shook her head. "I'm giving you an out."

"I don't want an out."

"I don't mind if you see Rusty. I understand. But the Farallons spook me."

"They spook everybody, even Rusty."

"But he dives them anyway."

"Yes."

"And you do too, which spooks me even more."

I looked at my wife, then out toward Laguna. The town was hidden beyond the hills, but I could see the glow of the city lights rising into the pale cloud cover. Down below us, the cars moved along Laguna Canyon Road, sending up a distant hiss.

Belle went to the house and came back with two snifters of cognac.

We walked up the road to a flat spot in the hills and looked down on the city.

"I wish it had never happened," said Belle. "None of it. I wish it was over. But it isn't. It never ends."

"Then we'll stay away."

"We can't. It's cowardly. And I *have* to be there."

It was a long drive but he's found Laguna Canyon Road.

Now he follows the couple from a safe distance, watches as they cut across a large swath of land studded with wildflowers and sagebrush.

When they stop in front of a small outbuilding, he waits behind a tree, raises the binoculars to his eyes, turns and adjusts the lenses until everything snaps into focus—the woman's face in close-up, blond hair, blue eyes.

He turns his attention to the man, focuses on the muscular arms, a blurry prison-type tattoo of a snake on his biceps, and wonders when the hell he will get out of there.

Binoculars back on the woman, the one who interests him. She knows something, this pretty woman with the worried, innocent face.

10

LORI ARMSTRONG

I've never been a morning person. But this morning I couldn't wait for the muse to drag her lazy bum over here and sprinkle inspirational dust on me. The commission was due next week. I struggled with it but I absolutely could not miss the deadline. Despite assumptions associated with my chosen profession as an "artist," I'm not a go with the flow kind of gal. I plan. I fret. With bills to pay I have a timetable to keep. Inspiration is a luxury I can't afford.

In my younger years, I'd postulated that creativity didn't hold normal office hours, nor did it owe allegiance to a singular space. I'd painted some of my best works in the dead of night, in a crappy apartment, no eye on the clock. Just me, paint, and canvas, locked in battle, the potential of the piece in my mind's eye warring with reality— mis shapen forms, mismatched colors, misaligned borders—which fed my frustration with the process but fueled my creative spirit to hold something tangible in my hands at the end of the fight.

My youthful idealism had been worn to a nub over years of feast and famine in the art world. Now with two kids to wake, coddle, and send to school, two dogs to pet, feed, and walk, plus a husband to tend much in the same manner as dogs and children, my middle-of-the-night painting sessions are as much a memory as the cramped apartment, the shrill sounds of sirens blaring outside my window, and the sickly bluish green fluorescent lighting that used to glow over my workstation. Gone too are the days of having to scrounge up items to pawn in order to buy another tube of Sennelier.

These days I bask in natural light pouring from the skylights above my workstation. In this dedicated "creative" space the younger me would've scoffed at, I'm treated to humid, salty ocean breezes wafting through the windows, rolls of canvas stacked against the wall, stretched in frames, draped across every horizontal surface, and dozens of tubes of paint in every hue imaginable. Still, in deference to my eco-consciousness—the only conviction left from my youth—they are *environmentally friendly* paints. I've got space and light and time—the latter at least until the school bus pulls up.

But I don't have concord.

You think too much, Belle.

It made me smile to hear Don's voice resonating inside my head. Don understands my neuroses better than anyone else. But he rarely lets me give in to them.

Even after managing to make a living as an artist for the past fifteen years, I still suffer from no-confidence days, when I'm reminded of harsh words from a decade past, words that slice my thin strip of confidence into a single frayed thread. On those bad days, my retreat to prove my critics wrong seems more like hiding than working.

Squinting at the blobs of paint on the canvas, I harkened back to the time I slaved feverishly, hoping to create a masterpiece that'd put me on the map—or at least on the wall of a successful art gallery. Rosemary had tried to give me that chance, despite her husband's attempt to screw me over, in more ways than one.

The irony isn't lost on me, trying to duplicate *Waves 27* for this new commission, a moody piece that was perfectly suited to the tragedy, secrets, and lies surrounding the Thomases. Working on the painting brought back a coterie of memories, most painfully, my final visit with Rosemary in prison when we'd last spoken of *Waves 27*. And with the shadowy underpainting in front of me, and the implications of Tony Olsen's invitation whirling in my head—knowing that the time had finally come, knowing what I was going to have to do—I was filled with a strange sense of foreboding.

Bang-bang-bang-bang ricocheted throughout the metal building as loud as gunshots. I jumped and whirled around, terrified I'd see something more menacing than spray cans of paint rolling across the floor after they'd been blown from the windowsill. A window I'd left open.

God. Spooked much, Belle?

Once I'd calmed down, a tiny bit of resentment arose. If I gave in to fear, I'd never accomplish anything—not what I'd promised Rosemary, not even the commission. So I propped the side door open to harness the lovely cross-breeze and took a deep breath.

Ha. There. Take that. I'm not afraid.

Leaving the cans where they fell, I gathered cleaning cloths soaked with linseed oil, wadded-up paper towels smeared with paint, and the spent, capless tubes of manganese blue and cinnabar green on my way to the garbage.

I lingered before the canvas, unhappy with the images, unhappy with myself. I was so lost in self-reproach that I didn't sense the intruder until air whooshed past my cheek, followed a split second later by metal flashing in front of my face. I recognized my palette knife—oddly sharp due to Don's whetstone skills—an instant before the edge was pressed into my neck. Then my left arm was chicken-winged behind my back, sending an excruciating shaft of pain from my wrist to my shoulders, which made me cry out.

"Don't make another sound," he said.

The man's voice was choked with a deep rasp, soft as a whisper, but as deadly as the steel against my throat.

"Put your right hand all the way into the front pocket of your jeans. Slowly."

I complied. I may have grown up on a ranch but I'm not exactly a scrapping tough girl. My mouth was bone-dry. My heart was jackhammering. My eyes watered like crazy. I could not pull enough air into my lungs.

He thickly whispered, "Good girl, Belle."

He knows my name.

Oh, God. He knows my name.

I wondered if he could be one of Don's former associates. I knew Don was an ex-con when I married him. As much as Don claims to be on the straight and narrow, I've suspected he's stepped off the path a time or ten. Like any woman in love, I've overlooked his lapses.

The idea that he could be looking for Don made me blurt out, "Don's not here." Then it hit me what a stupid thing I'd done, admitting I was alone. "What do you want?"

"Answers." He moved in behind me, so there was no chance I'd see his face. His body brushed mine in a way that caused my flesh to crawl.

"I know you went to see her."

At first, I couldn't understand whom he meant.

"Rosemary Thomas. You visited her the night before her execution."

My mind frantically tried to make sense of what he was saying.

"You aren't denying it," he whispered.

When I swallowed, the metal of the blade seemed to move in closer to my throat. I croaked, "Yes, I met with her."

His breath stirred my hair and his nose brushed the upper shell of my ear. "What did you talk about?"

"Nothing important."

"Liar." He jammed my arm higher up my back and I cried from the pain. "Try again."

"We . . . ah . . . talked about children."

"I don't believe you. Tell me the truth."

"I am. I'm telling you the truth."

"You sure? So you and Rosemary just . . . talked."

My "Yes" came out a frustrated hiss, similar to the whisper he used.

"You sure she didn't give you something that night?"

God. How would he know? "Just advice."

Evidently he wasn't satisfied with my answer. He abruptly released my arm and with his free hand grabbed a handful of my hair as he jerked my head aside, brandishing the knife in front of my eyes. "You lie."

"No. Please—"

He pressed the blade and my skin finally gave way. I gasped at the sharp sting.

"Tell me everything or the next one will hurt."

What if I told him what Rosemary had given me? Would he let me live?

He'd kill me for sure. Probably messily. The image flashed before me, my body sprawled on the ground, eyes staring vacantly at the skylights, my neck sliced. Don or the kids would find my body. Or the dogs. In my mind I could almost hear their barking as they tried to rouse me.

But the yips I heard weren't only in my mind. They were getting louder, which meant someone had let the dogs out of the house.

Despite the fear choking me, I managed to let out a scream, a scream so loud and long it hurt my own ears and turned my throat raw.

My attacker dropped back. The knife clattered to the floor and his footfalls faded as I fell to my knees, retching. I heard nothing but blood roaring in my ears and the furious pounding of my heart. I huddled against the ground and gripped the knife in my hand, just in case.

But it wasn't only my heart pounding—footsteps closed in, stopping next to my head. A hand landed on my back and I shrieked.

"Belle?"

Terrified, I looked up, expecting to see him again. "Don, thank God you—"

"What the hell happened? Who did this to you?" he demanded.

"I don't know. He ran out the door. But please don't—"

Then Don was gone, whistling for the dogs.

I should've saved my breath. Don wasn't the type to cocoon me when he had a chance to inflict damage on someone who'd dared attack me. Part of me feared what Don would do to the guy; part of me wished I could watch him do it.

I remained crouched on the floor, knife clutched in my hand. Too stunned to cry. Too scared to move.

When Don returned, huffing and puffing, anger contorting his face, slamming the door hard, I knew he hadn't caught the guy.

I launched myself at him. His strong arms encircled me and held me tight. "Oh, God. Don. If you hadn't—"

"Shhh. Baby, I've got you. I've always got you."

After years together and countless questions from people asking how we ended up together, I couldn't explain it. No one had ever looked out for me the way Don did. No one had ever loved me the way Don did. He'd do whatever it took to make me happy, and I'd learned firsthand how broad his definition of "whatever" was.

Once I stopped trembling, he eased back to look me over. His hard gaze zoomed to the cut on my neck. "You're bleeding."

"It's just a scratch."

His jaw tightened. "You calmed down enough to call the police?"

Don hated cops. Hated them. That he planned to dial 911 meant he was worried. I lifted my hand to touch him, to soothe him, and I'd forgotten I still held the knife. He didn't even flinch with the blade so close to his face, just kept his eyes on mine as he unwrapped my fingers from the handle and tossed the knife to the floor. "It's okay. We'll get the guy who did this to you."

"No cops."

"Belle. You're not thinking straight. We have to let the police know what happened."

"No, we don't."

"Jesus Christ. The fucker cut you! He could've killed you. I can't believe you'd let him go free. What if the kids'd been home, huh? Would you be as careless with their safety as you are with your own?"

I shook him, hoping it'd clear his brain. "Don. Listen to me. This wasn't a random attack."

He froze. "What?"

"The guy . . . knew me. He knew my name. He knew about my visit to Rosemary the night before the execution, and he somehow suspected that she gave me—"

"For Christ's sake, Belle," Don roared, "that's ten times worse. If this guy is gunning for you, then we definitely have to report this."

Silence.

We stared at each other. Measuring each other.

After a minute or so, Don threw up his hands in defeat. "Fine. No cops. But it proves I'm right. You can't go to the memorial, Belle. No way. This has gotten too goddamn dangerous."

The dogs barking and scratching at the door took his attention away from me.

We both knew his blustering was just that. I had no choice but to attend Rosemary's memorial service, even though I was pretty sure whoever attacked me would be there too.

11

MATTHEW PEARL

Waking up, sometimes you wonder whether you're really that god-awful person you were the day before. But sometimes nothing so profound finds a way into your head—dizzy, used up, in the morning you think, *What the—?* Then, nothing.

Jon Nunn, in these years since Rosemary's death, had to try to remember himself every single creaky morning of his life. For years, he'd alternate days filled by the righteous urge to save someone (typical for an ex-cop feeling out civilian life) and days darkened by the urge to strangle and bust up someone bad. Stan Ballard, who'd stolen his wife, was one imagined victim, sure, but sometimes just anyone would have done fine, anyone blamable for the happiness and freedom that came with not being him.

The hard guilt radiated from Rosemary's death (*No, her execution, jackass,* his unrested brain would nag him), but it had actually gone further by now. Having found no satisfaction on that score, it traveled back to Christopher Thomas's murder, as though Jon were responsible for that one too, for stuffing Thomas in an iron maiden, and responsible for all the chains of calamities in the world before and after the death of Rosemary. (*Execution, Jon boy, ex-e-cution.*)

It had started in small spurts, hardly noticeable a couple of years after . . . after all of it had settled in. All of it gone: his career, his wife, his balance. He'd begun to take walks where Christopher had been seen in the weeks before his murder. He'd stroll the streets around the museum where the art types would meet up with other art types for lunches, coffees, trysts. He'd drive to the grocery store where Rosemary did her shopping for the kids and sit in movie theaters where she had gone to cry in private and to get away from everything. Who would stop his meanderings? He wasn't flashing any guns or fake badges, he wasn't womanizing and manipulating the way Chris Thomas once did, he was just walking, talking, listening, looking. He was using up time between meetings. Better than drinking; anyone would have to admit that.

There were those parts of the city that the tourists pretended not to see on their way to the Golden Gate: the Tenderloin, the Mission, the dark corners of old Chinatown, where the city felt real and feral, like the New York City nobody remembered correctly from the 1970s. And sometimes the city didn't feel real at all—like *Night of the Living Dead*. It was as if the worst of the derelicts and addicts had some unspoken arrangement to stay in their zones, except sometimes they'd be seen roaming around downtown alongside shopping tourists, looking like lost zombies escaped from their pens.

Or was it Jon Nunn who was the escaped zombie?

Nunn saw a sign he tried to make sense of like a riddle of the meaning of life on one of the streets where small residences backed onto dangerously vacant lots. IF YOU DEFECATE ON MY HOUSE AGAIN, I WILL COME OUT AND SHOOT YOU WITH MY GUN.

What the—

Ex-detective Nunn was still learning to see San Francisco from a civilian side. San Fran was seen as a tolerant place, but inside it was a city with judging, searing eyes everywhere. The hordes of homeless, who took up whole city blocks in the zombie districts, even seemed to judge. Most of all, the police he once knew. They judged the harshest.

"Jon, you know I can't help you."

"I'm just taking a walk," Nunn had answered on that day, six years after turning in his badge, almost smiling. *Help me? No one can help me until I know.* "I'm just walking around," he told the other cop.

"Yeah, *here* you're walking," replied Todd Drainer, a vice cop Nunn had run two or three cases with fifteen years before. They both turned their eyes in unison to the worst of the run-down buildings lining the crumbling Chinatown block that Nunn had turned onto. A million miles, it seemed, from Jon Nunn's apartment. Yet, here gave him some hope for peace.

"I heard there's a fortune-cookie factory here," Nunn had said, as if he'd only just learned of its existence. "The tourists like it." He turned to face Drainer. "What're you doing here, Drainer?"

"Scaring up some cooperation for a case," Drainer said. "And unless you've become a crack addict instead of a raging drunk—" Nunn gave him a dark look. Maybe he was about to sock Drainer in the face, maybe not. "Sorry, Nunn. Didn't mean anything. My partner had a hard time after he retired, would wander around the red-light district like he was goddamn Batman and Robin. Fortune-cookie factory is that way, I think. I'd rather not ever see you back here."

"I'd rather not see you either, Todd."

Drainer had snickered and mumbled to himself as he walked away, and Nunn was sorry he hadn't socked him.

Nunn had gone through the back of the factory, stood in a dingy hallway watching a room filled with coughing and smoke, indistinct bodies in slow-motion decay. Nothing had changed from the last time he'd been here, years ago, looking for Christopher Thomas, who had been seen here several times in the months before his murder. *Why?* If he had a drug habit, that could have opened up all kinds of trouble for him. But the witness pool in this neck of the woods was too unreliable and high to make much out of this lead during the investigation or the trial.

In the meantime, a man known as Hong, the main drug dealer for this area, and a man not unknown to fencing anything—a television, a car, a piece of rare art—was arrested with a few of his men on drug charges. Nunn had pleaded with Drainer to hold off on the raid while he was investigating Thomas, but Drainer went ahead. Hong's coded ledgers noted payments to a scribbled name that looked like *Odd Body*. Two right before the date of Chris's disappearance. Nunn wondered if there was some connection. He wasn't sure what but had ideas. He had combed through the records of the museum and found that several pieces of art had gone missing in the years before Chris's death. If he had been in deep with Hong, was he keeping himself alive by paying him back in stolen artwork, or was Hong fencing it for him? Nunn couldn't find evidence that Chris had been anything more than a recreational drug user. Hong wouldn't say a word, then was stabbed in the neck in a holding cell by another prisoner with an old grievance and bled out. It had been a dead end then. It was still a dead end. For now.

Nunn had never turned up anyone named Odd Body either, though he'd looked.

Jon Nunn had felt the empty eyes of some of the habituals mark him and follow him out when he had passed through pretending he was looking for a lost drug-addled uncle.

When he got home one of those aimless days, something else had clicked in him. And Nunn had put a call in to Regina Cooper.

No, Jon Nunn wasn't running the case again—the case was running him, completely.

"I'm not buying," Regina said when she saw him there with that stubborn look on his face.

Nunn held up his seltzer with cranberry in a short glass. The favorite drink of the ex-drinker because it looked like something that could contain alcohol. Inconspicuous. "You won't return my calls."

"I should start changing up my haunt," said Regina, frowning a luminous, humorous frown as she took her usual place at the Mad Dog in the Fog, and her usual Jameson neat and a Bud were placed in front of her without her asking. "You remember something about real life, don't you? Imagine how much I'd get done if I tried to entertain every dying ex-cop." Regina Cooper had written several books about the big cases her office had helped crack during her time as chief medical examiner of San Francisco. They were considered masterworks in the field of forensic sciences, and she had become a staple on the cable crime show circuit before quickly tiring of it. During that time, a television network had bought the rights to her life and hired a former swimsuit model to play a funny and quirky version of her, though Regina was funnier, quirkier, and smarter in real life.

"What have you heard? I'm not dying," Nunn said, hearing himself laugh under the rumbling din of the Irish pub. It smelled like cardboard and old beer, the wood below his hand knotty and warped from slipshod cleaning.

"Yes, you are, of boredom, if you've called me. 'For a good time, call the chief medical examiner of the city of San Francisco.'"

"You know why I called," Nunn said soberly.

Regina closed her eyes shook her head. "Na-ah. No way, my friend."

"What does it hurt?"

"To look into a case that was closed ten years ago, with all the original examinations done in Germany? That hurts my head, Jon."

"Just noodle it a little before shooting me down."

"The thing about you, my friend, is you're timeless. You could have lived a hundred years ago, or a hundred years from now, and people would still know what you are."

"Which is what, Regina?"

"Lost."

"Don't you care that we might have had a part in sending an innocent woman to death?"

"You're looking for the TV version of me, I think." Regina stood and fished in her pocketbook for a few dollars.

"Wait!" Nunn put his hand on her wrist as an earnest Bob Dylan song came on. She froze.

"Everything all right, Regina?" Mick, the globular and imposing bartender, appeared, looming over Nunn.

"Yeah, fine," Regina said.

"Please," Nunn said to her when the bartender had warily scooted back to his spot. "You used to trust my instinct."

Nothing discomfited a woman who relied on humor in her personal interactions as much as seriousness.

"McGee."

"What?"

"Ignatius McGee," she said. "Forensic anthropologist. Nobody digs up the old bones like he does. But he's a tough one to get ahold of. He's based in Boston and booked up for years at a time. Plus, he doesn't really like living people."

Nunn went on, "I'm getting closer to ending all this. I need this, Regina. Can you at least get me a conversation with this McGee?"

Regina surrendered a little around her shoulders, returning to her stool and pushing her whiskey to the side.

The routine had solidified itself now. In San Francisco, the early morning was the kind of gray cold you feel in your bones. The late afternoon too. This left only a small window in the middle of the day that was clear and beautiful. Nunn would sleep most of the morning so that he could wake to the beautiful hours instead of to the painful fog. He knew it was temporary relief, but it was still something to help him to his feet.

Sometimes he'd tail Stan Ballard in the late afternoon. Stan must have thought his souped-up sports car put him above and beyond the reach of mortal men, but instead, it made him an easy target—he stood out like the arrogant bastard he was. Nunn would watch from afar his wine-and-cheese meet-ups with Peter Heusen on Peter's boat.

Nunn still couldn't think of Stan as Sarah's husband. It was just

Sarah and that . . . *bastard, sonuvabitch, scumbag*—these were all words that blocked out *husband*.

Nunn had followed the sonuvabitch bastard scum and wondered what the hell he'd been doing visiting Rosemary Thomas's grave, with that god-awful smirk across his face.

There. That proves it. It's not just that I hate him for stealing my wife. He's hiding who he really is. He's hiding it from my Sarah and from the world.

Peter, meanwhile, that two-bit snake, almost made Nunn equally angry with the dissipated life he had built on the foundation of his sole control of the old, drying family money.

More and more, Nunn would end up back at the old fortune-cookie factory, back in the rear encampment for heroin and methadone addicts that started as an informal needle exchange. The crack smokers poisoned the air. The smokers and shooters were supposed to stay in separate rooms along the corridor, but really, was anyone here going to complain? A filthy, scraggly dog desperately whined at Nunn—then choked and coughed. The mutt was attached to the wrist of a pierced, tattooed, formerly middle-class runaway who only used the dog to beg aggressively for money in the Haight and fed him the minimum to keep the dog alive.

When asked what he had to sell by one of the occupants, Nunn mumbled his stale story about looking for his confused uncle—what he used to say back when he was looking for Christopher Thomas years ago. Even though many of the shades in here had been there when he'd done this before, he didn't exactly worry about anyone putting one and one together.

"Tell me. Have you seen him here?" Nunn asked.

"Who?"

"My uncle," Nunn said, and showed a photo of Chris Thomas.

The shade went pale and shaky, looking over Nunn's shoulder to a new arrival. Dropping his head, the shade stumbled his way down the corridor.

Now two lean, tall, well-dressed young Asian men were standing at the entrance to the den. Their robust, healthy auras were all too conflicting with those of the place's occupants. They were the weakened leftovers from Hong's years of control.

"You lost, or are you a cop?" the more slender of the two asked.

"I could be neither," proposed Jon.

"Then you don't belong. That's a problem. And a problem here is a problem for me." He had a white scar across the length of his upper neck as if someone had tried to commit suicide for him.

"Maybe I'm just looking for a fortune cookie that finally gives me some good news," Nunn said, faking a laugh.

"You a cop?" the man repeated. The hulkier man had his hand inside his fatigue-colored jacket. Nunn could see by the way the arm was positioned it probably wasn't a gun he was reaching for—maybe a knife, or knuckles.

It would have been all the easier for these men if Jon were a cop. He could either be bribed or ignored, depending on what he was here for. Here was where Jon's anonymity came to good use. Without knowing who he was, any attack on him could be dangerous.

"Funny thing. I was looking for my uncle. You know him?" Jon held up the photo of Chris Thomas and watched their faces cautiously. Their eyes both flickered ever so slightly and they said nothing. They wouldn't talk, but still, the hornets were stirred by his visits. Jon hadn't felt this alive in ten years.

Rosemary, you watching this?

"No, I guess you don't. Oh, well. Long shot."

"Your uncle's not here, hasn't been any of the times you walked in here. You can see that. You should leave."

Jon stuck his hands deep in his pants pockets. "Here's the funniest part," Jon said, casting his glance around the filthy den. "I walk in here looking for my long-lost uncle, and see my dog, Max, that someone stole out of my yard. I was just about to call the police to help get him back from that freak over there with the tattoo of Jesus on his forehead."

"Don't bother," answered the interlocutor. He glanced at his companion, who took out a switchblade from his pocket and took a gigantic step toward Jon. Waiting to see if Jon would scream or run away—he did neither, just stood his ground—the muscle walked past to the unconscious addict and cut the rope off his wrist.

"Max, come here, old boy!" Jon called out. The desperate little dog ran over and jumped into Jon's arms, licking his hands. The dog would probably have run over to anyone who called his name in a friendly tone—but on top of that Jon had rubbed his hands in his pockets where he kept a stash of beef jerky for his long walks through the city, and the dog could have smelled it a mile away. Jon had a friend who was a former animal-control officer and now ran a rescue shelter—Max would have a new home within days.

"Now I feel better," Jon said, lowering the dog and taking up the leash. "Let's go for a walk, old boy."

12

MICHAEL PALMER

Hank Zacharius always knew when he was being followed, although he had never really gotten a good look at them and had only vague suspicions as to who they might be.

As a freelance investigative reporter, he was often working on as many as a dozen stories at one time. Corruption in Oakland city hall; union graft underlying the renovations of pier 41; the hedonistic society of young starlets that were catering to the wildest fantasies of selected studio executives and then using the resultant compromising photographs to blackmail their way into films. Years ago he'd been nominated for a Pulitzer for exposing the ties between higher-ups in the LAPD and the most powerful L.A. gangs.

No wonder his stories were so often blocked from publication by the crooked politicians and powermongers that were as much a part of the landscape as the Golden Gate Bridge in the City by the Bay. No wonder he was followed nearly every time he left his apartment. He knew things, lots of things, and there were always people who wanted to learn what he knew.

But tonight he needed to be certain he was alone.

Tonight he had scheduled a meeting with an informant—his best. It was hard enough to set anything up with a man who guarded his identity so closely that he'd never even given Zacharius his name. *Call me Calvin,* he'd say, *it's as good a name as any.* Calvin was a cop, or maybe a gang member, for all Zacharius knew. He had no idea. He had guesses, but he had never been able to nail down any of them, and that was probably good. Whatever he was, Calvin was, as they said in the business, plugged in. Ask a question, come up with the cash, and the man either knew the answer or knew how to find it.

Zacharius was aware that Calvin stood to make much more money by stringing information for some of the better-known reporters, the police, or even the feds. But the informant never said no to him, and when Zacharius's stories weren't selling, which at the moment was most of the time, Calvin often did what he could to help.

This night Zacharius was fearful not only of exposing his resourceful snitch but of putting himself in harm's way as well. Now after ten years, he was going to use any publicity surrounding Rosemary Thomas's memorial to show the world that she had not killed her husband, as he had always maintained in his initial investigation and reporting. His articles had largely been dismissed by his peers and the public, but Zacharius always knew there was more to the story, and not surprisingly he'd never been able to shake this one case.

He'd known Rosemary for twenty years. He'd even known Chris. Zacharius had been to their wedding, their children's christenings, birthday parties. Rosemary had cried on his shoulder after discovering the first of Chris's infidelities.

Altogether, he had written four articles about the highly publicized murder. One of them had centered on the physics of the crime itself, stressing Christopher Thomas's size and weight and the difficult logistics of getting his body into the eight-foot-tall, two-hundred-pound iron maiden. Then moving the corpse and torture device from the site of the actual murder to some sort of truck, to the Lufthansa flight that transported the body overseas. Another one traced Rosemary Thomas's movements throughout the week prior to her husband's murder, up to the widely heard verbal battle after Christopher had demanded a divorce. The timeline ended with her allegedly sedating him prior to killing him and laying him out in the museum's iron maiden.

The final article was speculative, but Zacharius considered it his best. It was an in-depth investigation of Christopher Thomas's life, focusing on his ever-changing finances, his overseas trips as gleaned from photocopies of his passport, and his relationship to an underworld thug, an art fencer, and possibly a Chinese drug lord named Roger Hong, another witness who had turned up dead.

But Zacharius was largely discredited—partly because of his friendship with the Thomases, particularly his friendship with Rosemary. It eventually got to the point where the news biggies wouldn't even read his stuff, let alone buy it or at least check the facts.

Now after ten years, he hoped to regain his credibility among his peers and the public.

The meeting place Calvin had chosen was number six on a list of ten locations Zacharius had provided in and around the Castro, Mission, and Haight districts. Zacharius would institute a meeting by taping a small piece of paper beneath the lip of a bar on Divisadero Street at precisely 4:00 p.m. Within a few hours, a piece of paper with a number from the list and a meeting time would be taped in the same place. This evening, the number directed the reporter to a trendy, always crowded coffee shop, just a few blocks off Golden Gate Park.

"Mr. Zacharius, I presume." They'd known one another for years, and Calvin greeted him the same way each time they met. The informant slipped into a seat directly behind him.

Zacharius turned to face him.

Calvin was a thin, African-American man in his fifties, physically unremarkable in almost every respect except for his eyes, which were dark and feral, probing one moment, scanning the room the next, always on red alert. But his averageness allowed him to maneuver in society, listening in on conversations as he passed, noting who was pausing to speak with whom.

"You look tired," Calvin said.

"I *am* tired. Sometimes it's hard—" Zacharius frowned. "I was the best, you know, the best."

"I know. You were damn good, Hank."

Zacharius sighed. "They tried to ruin me, Calvin. From the moment I claimed Rosemary Thomas was innocent. First they blocked the article I wrote detailing the facts of the case, and how she couldn't have killed him. Then they set about to discredit my theories about the posse of people who each had the big three—method, motive, and opportunity—by portraying me as some whack job."

"That's old hat, my man. Probably true but old hat just the same." Calvin leaned forward. "But you didn't seek me out to whine, did you, Hank?"

Zacharius worked some of the tension from his sloping shoulders. "I've got a hundred and a half I can give you right now, but it's been a little hard lately keeping the boat afloat these days."

"When I need the money, I'll send up a flare. What is it you want to know?"

"Thanks." Zacharius stared down at his hands, trying to get past his embarrassment.

"So, there've been developments, yes?".

Zacharius motioned the waitress over, ordered a coffee light.

He then slipped the invitation out of his jacket pocket and, after scanning the coffee shop once more, handed it to Calvin. "This arrived at my place today. There's a stamp on it, but it never was posted—just slid under the door of my apartment."

"*The* Tony Olsen?" Calvin raised an eyebrow.

"Yes. He was a friend of Rosemary's."

Calvin whistled. "Why do you think Tony Olsen wants to open up this old wound?"

"That's why I'm here. I was hoping you might have some theories."

The informant shook his head. "I don't, but it wouldn't take me too long to come up with some. Men don't go from obscurity to being as rich as Tony Olsen is without mucking about in a few compost heaps."

"And?"

The waitress arrived with the coffee. Zacharius drank half of it in a single gulp

"Maybe it's an owed favor to that cop who went nuts after the Thomas execution. Jon Nunn. Maybe this memorial is supposed to give that washout another chance—get all the principals together, see what happens."

"What's Olsen got with Nunn?"

"Don't play so naïve, my man," Calvin said "You know as well as I do what the cops are like in this city. A lot of them play both sides."

Zacharius remained silent.

"Speaking of cops who play both sides, ever hear of Artie Ruby?" Calvin asked.

"Artie who?"

"Artie Ruby, the cop who got into trouble for walking off with evidence years ago—white, powdery evidence from what I remember— and all of a sudden, just like that, he wasn't a cop anymore, and he was working security at the McFall Museum."

Zacharius felt a rush of adrenaline. "Why would a museum hire a rogue cop to provide security?"

Calvin chuckled. "You know Chris Thomas was crooked . . . drugs, forgeries, you've heard the rumors."

"And . . ."

"If you're so convinced Rosemary Thomas didn't kill her husband, you might want to talk to Ruby. I hear he's available for pretty small money."

"Any ideas where I can find him?"

Calvin shrugged. "Know a place named Steve's?"

"The Bogie rip-off by the Embarcadero?"

"I would start there."

Neon and black paint.

Zacharius felt that the attempt by the management of Steve's to create a noir ambience had failed miserably. Still, despite or perhaps because of the stench of stale booze, body odor, and cheap perfume, the place was busy. It took a twenty, but a heavily rouged barfly on the last stool pointed him to a back room that was hazy with cigarette smoke. He spotted Artie Ruby immediately—a skeletal, Runyonesque man with serious bags under his eyes, and the stub of a cigar poking out of the corner of his mouth. The worn leather easy chair next to the former cop was vacant. An ashtray on a stand next to the chair was filled to overflowing.

"So much for California's fearsome smoking ban," Zacharius said, moving the ashtray a few feet away and settling down in the chair.

"The cops are no more expensive than the fines," Ruby replied, staring straight ahead. "In fact, those two smoking over there are both detectives. Who are you by the way?

Zacharius introduced himself.

"Yeah. I've heard of you."

Zacharius rubbed at the stinging in his eyes. He had stopped smoking eighteen years ago and now was like a human bloodhound when it came to cigarettes, able to tell someone was a smoker ten feet away. Ruby had yet to make direct eye contact with him, but even at this angle, something about him was pathetic. *Small.* That was the word that popped into Zacharius's head. This was a small, limited man.

"I have three twenties in my pocket," Zacharius said. "They're yours if you'll come someplace away from this smoke and talk to me for a minute."

Zacharius wondered if he should have offered more, but something about Ruby said Zacharius could dole out what remained of his hundred and a half a bit at a time.

"You got any more than that?" the oddly pathetic man asked.

"If I like what you have to say, I do."

"Call me Artie," he said, pushing himself up abruptly and leading the way back down the hall.

They moved through the crowded nightclub to a small table in a black-lit corner that seemed to have been forgotten.

It was hard to believe that this twitchy, sad-eyed sack of a man was once a cop.

"You once worked in security at the McFall museum." Zacharius said. "You must have known the place pretty well, known Rosemary and Chris Thomas."

Artie continued staring off into the crowd. "You know, I never stole that cocaine from the evidence room. I was an honest cop. Oh, I cut a corner here and there, and maybe made a deal with a small-time crook to get at a bigger one. But I never deserved what came down on me."

"Who hired you to work at the museum?" Zacharius asked, trying to keep the conversation on topic.

"I ended up becoming a fucking pariah." The sadness in Artie's eyes had intensified, and for a moment Zacharius thought Artie was actually going to cry. Instead, he got Zacharius's assurance to cover his tab and ordered a boilermaker with Wild Turkey and a Heineken.

"Artie, tell me about Chris Thomas."

"I don't know anything. Thomas was a curator; I was a security guard—the two don't mix. I said good-night to him when he'd leave for the night. That's all."

The boilermaker arrived and the shot of Wild Turkey was gone before the waitress had turned away. Zacharius now sensed that Artie had been drinking before he arrived.

"You've heard the rumors about Thomas . . ."

"Yeah, so what, he used to screw around on his wife, lots of guys do that." Artie still wouldn't look Zacharius in the eye.

"No, I don't mean that. There was talk about drugs, forgery, theft . . ."

"I can't tell you anything about that. Like I said, I used to do my job and go home."

Zacharius knew that the window for getting any useful information was rapidly closing. The Heineken was gone and Artie's words were beginning to slur. Hesitatingly, Zacharius slipped all of his wad but a twenty under the table and stood to go.

"Pay for your drinks out of that," he said.

Zacharius had taken just a step when Artie Ruby cleared his throat, looked up at him, and spoke in a coarse whisper. "You should let sleeping dogs lie, Zacharius. You're messing around in a cesspool, and the whole mess is going to blow up in your face. Now, how's that for a fucking image?"

Diary of Jon Nunn

J.A. JANCE

After Chinatown, I went to a meeting, and when one didn't work, I went to a second one. The idea of seeing Sarah at the memorial, now that it was drawing closer, made my guts roil. I wanted to see her. I didn't want to see her. I wanted to smack Stan Ballard in the face. No, that's not true. I wanted to put a bullet through his heart. That way we'd match. We'd both have holes there.

I knew those scumbags would all come out to mark the occasion. They'd have to. Snakes can't hide under rocks all their lives. To give the appearance of having nothing to hide, they'd all be there; that's what I was counting on. Rosemary's good-for-nothing brother would come for sure. How could he stay away? He was in the witness room that night, and I noticed one thing about him that no one else seemed to catch. The other people there had the good grace to shed a tear or two, or at least they pretended to look sad. Not Peter Heusen. He had watched, grim faced and dry eyed, as they put the needle into his sister's arm. Maybe it was the drink. I don't know. He followed me out to the parking lot that warm, dark night. We had a few words. Rather, he did. Then I watched him drive away from his sister's execution in an older-model Lincoln. And after he left, I drove away too, fully intending to get drunk. Evidently I did that in spades. By the time I finally sobered up, well, Sarah was gone for good and my job was history. And Peter Heusen? As the legal guardian for both his niece and nephew and as the conservator of the Thomas estate, he had come up in the world. Way up. As far as Sarah and her new husband, Stan, were concerned, they seemed to be living in much improved circumstances as well. They had all moved on in Rosemary's unlamented absence, and as far as I could see, they had all prospered.

When the second AA meeting was over, I went to a third. It wasn't all about drinking either. I had managed to keep my craving for liquor in check. Nowadays my drug of choice was guilt—the hard stuff, pure and unadulterated. To quit that addiction, I'd need far more than ninety meetings in ninety days. There was only one cure and it hadn't changed: I needed to find the person who was really responsible for Rosemary's death. To do that, I had to find Christopher's killer, his real killer. And that's what I was doing. The ball had started rolling and there was no way to stop it now.

I thought about Rosemary and Christopher Thomas. How they had lived and died in a marriage of convenience. That was their hell, at least Rosemary's hell. But somehow I'd gotten sucked into it, had inadvertently become another one of Christopher Thomas's victims, right along with so many others.

13

GAYLE LYNDS

Haile Patchett didn't want to get caught by the police. She'd do whatever she could to avoid being locked up. But crime was in her blood. The danger, the fear, the cash—it always brought her a rush.

She put a smile on her face and kept her footsteps light as she walked toward the Ritz-Carlton, a sprawling, shingle-style resort commanding a bluff above the Pacific. The hotel was surrounded by emerald fairways, tidily winding cart paths, scattered cypress trees, and the endless sea.

When she stepped inside, she looked all around, nodding casually at the valets as if she belonged there. In her Vera Wang high-heel sandals and her Charles Chang-Lima sundress—short and sexy, just above the knees, to show her long, tanned legs—she could belong there. Should, even. But that was an old story.

Taking off her sunglasses, she entered the lobby, her shoulder bag clasped to her side. The men watched her, the clerks behind the registration desk and the aging husbands with glittering, hopeful eyes standing in line with their credit cards and forgotten wives. She was not truly beautiful, but she had something, something inside her that was like fire.

She passed hotel guests, lounging in padded wicker chairs before the sweeping views of bluff and bay, and stepped into the dark, wood-paneled bar. A slender woman of thirty-eight, with green eyes, red hair that flowed to her shoulders, and a nose so straight and true it could make Angelina Jolie jealous. Today was her birthday, but the only card in the mail this morning had been an invitation from Tony Olsen to celebrate Rosemary Thomas in a memorial service. *Jesus Christ.* Why was he honoring Rosemary's execution—not her birth? It seemed twisted, and the whole thing worried her.

She thought of Christopher Thomas and of all the promise that once came with being connected to him and of how none of it had panned out. Damn it, she'd played her part and played it well, helped him move the artworks he so carefully pilfered from the museum and sold overseas. She was supposed to have made real money, been living in splendor. Didn't she deserve better than this?

Haile turned away from the bar and shut her eyes.

She'd fled after Christopher's murder, had to lie low so she wouldn't be connected to the thefts she'd helped broker.

And now here she was, up to her old tricks, trying to scratch out a living as a cheap pickpocket, or worse.

She took a deep breath, checked her watch. It was only four o'clock, a little early. As she had expected, few drinkers sat at the small tables and no one was at the bar. Good. She headed toward it, her destination in any case. Behind the crescent-shaped cherrywood bar stood the barkeep in tidy black trousers, a neat short-sleeved, white shirt, and a knowing grin. He had seen it all, but he liked what he saw, so he allowed the grin to stay and deepen into something real as she approached. He was of medium height, about five foot ten, and athletic looking. She watched the muscles on his forearms cord as he grabbed glasses on the bar and efficiently arranged them.

She smiled back and settled onto a barstool and ordered a drink. She needed to steady herself for what lay ahead.

She downed the drink, stood up, and walked lightly away, back to the lobby, through the carefree tourists crowd returning from golf and sailing and shopping in the galleries and antique shops of Half Moon Bay. *Must breathe. Breathe.*

She laser-locked on the bulge in the front pocket of a man's pricey white tennis shirt, to her right. Pulling a copy of *People* magazine from her shoulder bag, she stumbled and fell into him, pressing the magazine flat against his fleshy chest with one hand while under it her other hand performed an expert dip.

"I'm so sorry!" She smiled sweetly, her hips pressed against him longer than necessary.

He grinned, enjoying it. "No problem . . ."

Still smiling, she let his wallet fall into her shoulder bag and moved on. She dipped a Rolex from an unzipped fanny pack, a stray iPhone from an end table, and another wallet, from a hip pocket. Not bad for a few minutes of work. But then, the scent of wealth was tactile here.

The men's eyes were avaricious. Once she would have reveled in all of this. She had not known any better, and that had given her tremendous power. But not now.

Haile was staying at the El Toro Motel, a two-story, red-tile-roof affair that looked more expensive than it was. She parked under a pepper tree and climbed the outdoor staircase—fake wrought iron that wobbled against the stucco building.

Sighing wearily, she unlocked the door to her room. She longed for a hot bath and her old jeans, Then she would decide what to do next. Cracking open the door, she watched the key-size receiver in her hand. It flashed hot red. She jerked up her head. Someone had been in her room. Maybe still was. Not the maid, because she had put a hold on housekeeping services. The flashing light was triggered by a pressure reader, thin as paper, the size of a dime, she had stuck low on the inside of the door where it would close against the jamb. The first time someone opened the door, there was no flash. There should be no flash now. So this was the second time, or third, or more.

Staying calm, she pocketed the reader and inched open the door, making no noise—she had oiled the hinges when she checked in. The long rays of the afternoon sun painted a golden rectangle into the room, leaving the rest in uneven shadows.

The closet was closest. A glass oval was in the door. She peered through. She had hung no clothes. The closet was empty. The door to the bathroom was closed.

14

ANDREW F. GULLI

I knew you were bound to turn up," the voice of a man said.

Her heart skipped a beat—there was no turning back now. She stood for a moment between the bathroom and the closet.

"Come in, Haile," the man's voice went on.

She stepped inside and saw a man seated at the desk. It took her a while to recognize him—Jon Nunn, the detective who'd questioned her years ago about Christopher's disappearance.

She was actually relieved. Nunn had gone off his rocker; he wasn't a danger to anyone but himself. "What're you doing in my room? I'm calling the police."

Nunn laughed. "Yeah, you do that, sweetheart, and while you're at it, you might want to tell them about that stolen Rolex in your handbag."

How would he know? Her mind was working furiously.

"What do you want?" She tried to keep her voice calm.

"Sit down, make yourself comfortable." He gestured to the bed.

She sat down and said nothing. She looked at his face and noticed how he'd aged since she'd seen him last. His eyes looked tired and puffy, and the lines between his eyebrows had grown deeper.

"I've been tracking you for a while," Nunn said. "Larceny, confidence games, all that good stuff you've been up to."

"What do you want with me?" Haile could hear her voice shaking.

"I still have some questions about your dead lover, Christopher Thomas."

"Are you crazy, it's been twelve years, that's over and done with. He's dead; she's dead. You can't resurrect ghosts, Nunn." Her mouth was dry with fear.

"It's not ghosts I'm trying to resurrect. Anyhow, if I were in your position, I'd humor any cop—even a discredited ex-cop—who had questions for me."

She gestured with her hands for him to continue.

"Listen," Nunn said. "Thomas was a womanizer, but he didn't pick just any women. They were always of a certain type—classy, well-educated girls who he could be sure would never blackmail him. Pardon the barb, but you never fit that mold. So why would he get involved with a crooked little tramp like *you?*"

"Was that a statement or a question?" she asked, opening a bottle of water that had now gone warm in her bag.

"Drugs?"

She didn't say a word.

"I know enough about you so that if you don't cooperate with me, I'll make sure you see prison, and by the time you get out, that pretty face of yours will look like a beaten-up old tire. I may be discredited, but I still have a few friends at the SFPD."

She tried to calm herself down. *He couldn't do anything to her. He was a washout. The case was closed.*

"You know, they probably have closed-circuit cameras at the Ritz . . ."

"What do want to know?"

15

J. A. JANCE

When Nunn left, Haile was standing in the middle of her room and looked up questioningly at her image reflected in a cheap mirror. She didn't like what she saw. She had walked away from that long-ago life. She had done everything she could to put it behind her, but here was Nunn reopening all of it, using any compromising information he'd been able to glean about her to get her to cooperate with him. She still wasn't sure how much he had managed to uncover about her life.

Had he been following her, watching what she did at the Ritz?

He must have. Anyhow, she couldn't be in this room anymore. She knew that he might be waiting for her outside, but she had to get out again.

Shielding herself from view, shoulders up, head down, she hurried along the path until she reached her car.

Once she was settled in the front seat, she started the engine and punched her foot down on the accelerator.

Hang on, she advised herself. She needed to concentrate on her driving as she raced through the neighborhood as if it were a Formula 1 course. She exited the immediate neighborhood with a series of maneuvers designed to smoke out and lose any tails. She couldn't afford to be followed.

At the moment, she was giving an excellent imitation of someone who hadn't a care in the world. She rolled down her window and let the damp, ocean-scented air wash through her long red hair, leaned back in her seat, and relaxed—or pretended to.

She thought, *Rosemary Thomas was executed for murdering her husband ten years ago. And now all these years later that detective is trying to use me to uncover facts about Chris's past, while Tony Olsen has invited me to this memorial even though I was never Rosemary's friend and I was screwing her husband.*

Why?

Haile stared at the road.

Who wins by opening all these old wounds?

She thought again about Chris. She was over him and had no reason to kill him. But of course, she had lied about that to the cops—and to herself—that she was over him, could so easily quit him.

She sighed.

It wasn't as if she were still in love with Christopher Thomas after all these years, but she still wasn't over what he had done to her. The man had taken something from her, and that loss had yet to be recouped.

But why celebrate Rosemary's death? What's the point of that?

She thought again about Nunn. Last she heard he was drinking himself to death and his wife had walked out on him and had married the Thomases' financial guru.

Why couldn't Nunn let it all die along with the Thomases? What if he didn't keep his word and she did go to jail?

She pulled into a Burger King and stopped at the drive-in microphone. She was suddenly starving and needed time to think. She needed to go over everything she could remember about the people who were in any way involved in Chris Thomas's death.

She ordered a number one without cheese and a Diet Coke. Ordering at Burger King made her feel even more as if she had fallen on hard times.

Chris Thomas's murder and Rosemary's subsequent execution had been a blight on the lives of any number of up-and-coming folks who were no longer so young or up-and-coming—including her. Especially her.

She parked on a side street and ate the burger, thinking about Christopher Thomas and the woman who she knew had come after her—Justine Olegard, his associate curator at the museum.

At least that bitch got a permanent job out of the deal, she thought bitterly.

What did I get?

Diary of Jon Nunn

ANDREW F. GULLI

Two days before the memorial, and I don't have much to go on, but I feel close to finding out the truth. Don't give a damn how I find it, all I know is that it won't be in a court room, the press won't be descending like vultures, and there won't be an ambitious DA, talking about how the state has to protect itself from the likes of Rosemary Thomas.

Years ago when the pain used to become too much, I'd go down to the subway and stand on the edge of the platform, wondering if I had the courage to take that final step as the train approached. It's the same reason I still go to bars. There's one about a block from where I live. Drab place, dark, mostly empty, smells weird. A big, tattooed black guy is always at the bar shining glasses—never says anything. I order a Jack Daniel's on the rocks, and take a whiff of that comfort brew and dare myself to take a drink. Before Tony rescued me, whenever I'd feel that emptiness that used to threaten to rip my soul apart, alcohol always helped numb me up.

Now, set against the shiny bar, moisture around the glass, the ice cubes glistening, it still looks good to me, but I won't touch it. I just stare at the drink, knowing that draining that six-ounce glass will take me back down a hole from which I'll never climb out.

Tonight I stared for a long time into the glass and saw a faint reflection of myself staring back. Usually the rest of the dancing ghosts join the show—all of them, Sarah, Rosemary, Tony, Chris Thomas—like actors taking their place on a stage.

Who would haunt me tonight?

You know whom I saw tonight? My dad. Saw him when he was my age, tired and on the roller coaster of addiction.

I got up, put my jacket on, and went out into the night.

When I got to my place, I walked past a bum and into the hallway that led to my tiny apartment. I never open windows, and as soon as I open the door, the stuffiness of times gone by is always there to greet me. I took off my shoes and lay on the sofa. The phone rang, I picked up.

"Jon Nunn?" I heard a tired voice say on the other end.

"Who is this?"

"It's Hank Zacharius."

I respected Zacharius, but I didn't know him well. "I left the SFPD years ago, so if this late-night call is about a story, I can't help you."

"That's not what it's about. Look, I need to talk to you. I need help, and I think I can help you."

"Are you drunk? Your voice sounds funny."

"My mouth's busted up, that's why."

"What happened?"

"I'll tell you when I see you." He gave me his address.

I had nothing to lose. Better this than another endless night remembering the execution, the day Sarah walked out on me, every mistake, every regret. I took a cab to Zacharius's place, a ramshackle, rent-controlled apartment that smelled like curry.

Zacharius wasn't at the door waiting for me, but the door was unlocked and I went in. He sat hunched over on a wingback chair, his face cut, eyes swollen.

"What happened to you?" Looking closely, I realized his nose was broken and had been packed. "Who did this?"

Zacharius took a gulp of his drink. "I don't know. He was wearing a mask."

"Was it a mugging?"

"I wouldn't call you if I'd been mugged, Nunn, I'd go directly to the police." He was breathing from his mouth and kept reaching for his drink.

"Okay, Hank, why did you call me?" I sat down on the sofa. Above the gas fireplace that looked as if it hadn't been used in years hung a large print portraying Che Guevara, and under that, a small Greek Orthodox cross. Zacharius took a moment to collect his thoughts.

"I got an invite to that memorial," he said at last.

"And?"

"You know she was innocent."

What else would Zacharius want to talk to me about? "I'm pretty sure she was—now."

"Now? Now that it can't help her? Why didn't you cooperate with me?"

"The evidence pointed to her. That's what I was called to testify about. That's what I did. And then everything went in one direction after that. I tried to stop it but I couldn't. I'm still paying for my mistake, Zacharius."

He didn't say anything.

"So what happened to you?" I asked.

"I've been asking questions again, about the case." He tried to smile. "I found this guy used to work security at the McFall at about the same time Chris Thomas disappeared. He used to be a cop at one time—Artie Ruby."

I'd heard of Ruby. He'd been kicked off the force for misconduct, but I hadn't known he'd worked at the McFall. So much for my investigative skills. "So the McFall Art Museum hired an ex–crooked cop to provide security. Didn't they do background checks back then?"

Zacharius shook his head. "Amazing, huh?"

"So who did this to you?"

"I don't know. Ruby wasn't happy with the questions I asked him, and about an hour later I was walking home and some guy wearing a mask beat the crap out of me."

"You think this Ruby had something to do with it?"

"I don't know." Zacharius leaned back in his chair. "You know Chris had all sorts of connections. The rumors were true, I'm pretty sure of it. Problem was, Chris never understood you don't fuck with those guys. They have a way of dealing with deadbeats."

"And Ruby's connection to all this . . . ?"

"That's for you to uncover, Detective."

My first instinct was to track down Artie, break an arm and a few ribs. I hate bullies, and I hate rogue cops. But there was more than one way to skin a cat.

I left a note in her hotel room and then drove to a Dunkin' Donuts and waited. She showed up an hour later. Haile hadn't changed too much in the last ten years, but her eyes were even more cynical than they were in her youth. She slid into the booth across from me.

"What do you want?" she asked.

"Typical call gal," I said with a smile. "Sorry about that note, but I thought it'd be better than sneaking up on you in your hotel room again. So how are you?"

"Tired of being blackmailed by a disgraced ex-cop whom the world has abandoned," she said with a sigh. "Excuse me, but I have to get a doughnut. Those sour creams are incredible. Want one?"

I admired her pluck. She came back a couple of minutes later with a cup of coffee and a doughnut.

"I've done my homework, Haile, and if you were going to spend a couple of years in jail for what you did the other day, I've managed to find some more stuff that will keep you in for a long time—the mail-fraud scheme in New Mexico; the old, wealthy trucker in Montana who died of a heart attack just a month after you married him; then we have your dealings with Chris Thomas, fencing off stolen artwork. I can go on and on."

She continued munching on the doughnut, then smiled and said, "You're going to have a hard time proving it though."

"Maybe I can't prove it, but I can make life very complicated for you." She didn't say anything, so I went on, "I need some info, Haile, and you're the only person I know who can get it for me. Unfortunately it'll probably involve screwing an older, greasy guy called—"

"You don't have to *blackmail* me to screw a smelly old shit." She paused. "I will of course charge my standard rate."

I dropped an envelope on the table that had $400 in it and said, "I come prepared."

would've turned it up. But I was wearing a black turtleneck. Sort of my uniform.

"Is that the best you can do?" Her voice was deep and throaty, a smoker's voice, but she didn't turn away.

"I'm a slow starter. But I finish well."

She lowered her eyelids and flashed a quick half smile.

She wore a designer suit, stylish. A navy-blue pinstripe number. Her legs crossed under the skirt. In the mirror, I saw the white blouse unbuttoned to reveal some skin.

Gave me a pang.

She set the glass down. It had her lip prints on it, a smear of red-brown.

I tried a smile while I studied her. Veronica Lake? Nicole Kidman? She had the looks and the moves, but something was missing.

Maybe I think that about *everyone.* My problem, right?

I slid down onto the stool next to her. Something about her was familiar, but maybe I think that about every woman I meet. Who knows? I motioned to her empty glass. "Buy you another one?"

She turned the green eyes on me. Green for *go?*

"You talked me into it," she said, rattling the cubes.

"Yeah, that's me. I've got a way with words."

Artie, don't sound bitter.

I waved to the bartender, a little blond number who looked about twelve.

That half smile again. "What else have you got a way with?"

I just laughed. It sounded strange to me. Guess I hadn't laughed in a long time.

So, okay, we had a few drinks. Maybe more than a few. I'm a Jameson guy too. Maybe the only classy thing about me.

We were there a couple hours. And what was I thinking? I was thinking maybe I didn't have enough to cover the tab. I was thinking about excusing myself to the little boys' room and then cutting out the back door.

So imagine my surprise when she leaned against me and pressed her face to my ear. She smelled like oranges and flowers. "Can we go to your place?"

I didn't move for a long moment. I wasn't expecting that. Most women can pick up right away on what a loser I am.

16

R. L. STINE

She looked so right on the barstool, as if she belonged there. As if she were *born* there.

I spotted her long red hair from the doorway. Saw the dip of her shoulders as she picked up her glass. I watched her rattle the ice cube. She took a sip. Her expression didn't change.

I realized she was eyeing me in the mirror behind the bar.

Artie, don't get involved, I told myself. I wasn't in the mood to be nice to anyone, or even pretend.

So why was I still there?

Why do I do anything?

I had that feeling of dread I wake up with every morning. You know. That cold, heavy rock in your chest that makes you pull the pillow over your head and scream into it until you can't breathe.

Or maybe you don't know that feeling.

Okay. She saw me watching her. I tried to study her reaction in the mirror. But the neon Sam Adams sign cast a flickering, blue glare over her face.

The drunk on the next stool bumped her arm. But she didn't spill a drop of her drink. She turned her green eyes on him. Gave him a stare I've seen a few times. He raised his shirt collar as if he were suddenly cold and moved away.

Time for more lies.

That's the way I approach the day.

What's my favorite film? *The Grifters.*

Not sure what made me think of it as I stepped on my half-smoked Marlboro and walked toward the bar and its neon glow.

"Hi. Is this seat taken?"

She turned, and her eyes were cold. If I had a collar, I

I squinted at her, trying to decide if maybe she was a pro.

She shivered. "Saturday night is the loneliest night of the week, right?"

"But it's Friday."

Her lips brushed my neck. "Let's pretend it's Saturday."

I don't need this, I was thinking. But I'm weak. I'll be the first to admit it. If a chick presses her face against mine, all soft perfume and whispers, what am I going to do? Say no?

And then we stepped out on Brannan Street and waved at a taxi.

As we climbed the stairs to my apartment, I was feeling a nice buzz, kind of warm and forgetful.

I closed the door behind us, clicked on the table lamp, and reached to take off her jacket. She glanced around. She was still in the shadows by the entryway, but I could see she wasn't smiling. And I knew the word she was thinking. *Shabby.*

"Artie, you said you had a condo on the Embarcadero."

"No lie," I said, raising my right hand. "It's being renovated."

"And so you took this walk-up dump on Mission? It looks pretty lived-in to me."

I forced a laugh. "Did we come up here to talk real estate?"

I tried to clear my head. I didn't like the way this was going. I shouldn't have had those drinks. I couldn't think straight. I took a few steps back. You know. To assess.

She took off her own jacket and folded it neatly over the back of my ragged armchair. "Is your name really Artie?" Her silver bracelets rattled. She had like six or seven of them. Her hands clasped and unclasped at her sides.

"Yeah. My name's Artie. Want me to show you my driver's license?"

She actually said yes.

So I did.

She studied my license like she was gonna be quizzed on it, said, "Arthur Ruby. It's got a ring to it."

I shrugged.

She shivered again. Not from the cold, I guess. She took a step, snuggled against me.

That's a little better, I thought. I wrapped my arms around her. She sighed as I raised my hands to her tits. And then . . . she started asking me questions!

And it's weird 'cause I heard myself answering even though I didn't want to, but I couldn't stop and the room was spinning.

Then we were in bed and we were having sex, but the whole time she was still quizzing me and the damn room wouldn't stop whirling.

So how was the sex? Not bad. I guess. I mean, sex with a total stranger is always good—right? Okay. Maybe I was a little distracted or even worse, but my head didn't feel right. But I was pretty sure she didn't notice.

It'd been so long since something good happened to me, I kept thinking about what it takes for luck to change. For something to fall your way.

Next thing I knew she was all dressed and brushing back her hair and putting on her jacket. And I was up, though shaky, moving to open the door, ready to offer a few tender good-byes. "I'll call you tomorrow" and all that.

But then her face changed and she didn't follow me to the door. She crossed her arms in front of her. Even in the dim light, I could see her face was flushed. Was that a shadow or a lipstick stain on her chin?

She stuck out her hand. "I want the bracelet back," she said softly.

I blinked a few times. "Bracelet?"

She rattled them on her arm. Like she was showing me what a bracelet is. "I was wearing six," she said. "I put them on your bed table when I got undressed. Did you think I can't count?"

I shrugged and wrinkled my forehead and did my innocent act. Like I couldn't follow what she was saying.

"Did you hide it while we were in bed? Just give it to me." And she turned the cold, green stare on me.

I squinted at her. "You think I'm a thief?"

I had that feeling I get, that sharp pain in my chest, my throat all tight. The first time, I thought I was having a heart attack. After that, I knew what it was. And I knew it was something I had to deal with.

"It's fucking Cartier. It's an antique Cartier bracelet. I'm not leaving without it."

"You're crazy. I don't have any bracelet." My heart pumped up a little. I pictured the bracelet where I slid it, between the mattress and the bed frame.

"Stop the bullshit," she said, and she sighed like a bad actress. "Do you think I won't call the police?"

I didn't think she would but I said, "Police?" An angry cry escaped my throat. The pain in my chest grew sharper, and I really felt my heartbeat race. "I'm not a thief."

She took two quick steps toward me. Her fists were tight at her sides. "I think you are. Give me the bracelet. Give it to me—*thief*."

She didn't make a sound when I slapped her face. Just blinked her eyes and worked her jaw up and down.

I was surprised how soft and warm her skin felt against the back of my hand.

I could breathe again but I was instantly sorry. My hand throbbed with pain, but that wasn't the worst of it. I knew I'd screwed up.

She rubbed her cheek, the green eyes accusing me. She still hadn't made a sound.

I kept hearing the slap.

"I'm sorry," I said. "I didn't mean it. I didn't mean to do that. Really. No lie."

"Are you fucking crazy?" she whispered

"Know what? Here. I'll get your bracelet. I'll give it back to you, and that'll be that. Everyone happy. No problem—okay?"

My hand shook as I pulled the bracelet from its hiding place. I gave it back to her.

She stared at it in her hand. Just stood there gawking at it. Like she never thought she'd see it again.

"No hard feelings," I said.

How dumb is that?

She glared at me one more time. Brushed her hair off her forehead. Pulled her jacket tighter around her and disappeared out the door.

I was breathing hard. Wheezing a little. I stared at the door as if I expected her to come back.

I rubbed my fist.

That was an example of how I lose it. It only took a second and there I went. But the whole thing was messed up. I knew I wasn't angry at her.

I knew who I'm really angry at. It's anger that's been in my chest for ten years. I can't get that Christopher Thomas job out of my head. It's there with me every morning. It's the dread. It's the cold dread.

I helped, did my job. And I expected to be paid fairly. Maybe I was naïve, but I thought those guys would spread it around like they said.

Naturally, they didn't. Not enough anyway.

When was I born? Yesterday? And here I was, twelve years later, stealing a bracelet from a woman in my bed. How low can you go? Finding yourself desperate like that can make a guy angry.

So, now I'm going to do something about it. That's what I decided, standing there looking at my bruised knuckles. That's what I decided. I'm going to get what is mine.

Then I started feeling shaky again like maybe I was gonna pass out, and I realized that bitch slipped me a roofie. *Jesus.* I've slipped a girl or two a roofie in my time, so it's, like, only fair, but, hell, why'd she do it?

I started remembering her asking me all those questions, but for the life of me I can't recall a single one or what I answered. *Shit.*

What'd I tell her? What the fuck did I tell her?

17

MARCIA TALLEY

Sarah Ballard plumped up her pillow and stared at the clock on her bedside table, watching the digital display quietly *snick-snick-snick* through the minutes as she relived the previous evening's events. She didn't need to turn over to know that her husband's side of the bed was empty. Eight twenty-three a.m. If Stan had returned home after walking out on her following yesterday's argument, CNN would already be blaring from the living room TV and the smell of fresh coffee would be teasing her nostrils. The house was silent. Rosemary Thomas's ghost was wrecking yet another of her marriages.

But whom was she fooling? Her marriage to Stan had been foundering for some time. An unlikely pairing—he, an up-and-coming estate lawyer, and she, a cop's wife. She thought about how they'd come together. It was the case, of course. The case she'd pushed Jon on—even when he'd told her he had a hunch the evidence was skewed. The case that ruined so many lives, but brought her and Stan together. He'd entered her life when she was vulnerable, showered her with love and attention, while Jon was disintegrating. Stan was ambitious, exciting, while Jon had always been a bit of a dreamer. But now she'd come to see those very qualities that had attracted her to Stan as nothing more than an example of his unmitigated selfishness.

She slipped out of bed. If Stan didn't want to go to Rosemary's memorial, she would. She owed it to herself, to Jon, to her previous life, the one she'd lost the day Rosemary Thomas was put to death.

It was noon. Jon Nunn usually got up around this time—he couldn't face the morning gloom. He got out of bed, headed to the kitchen and straight for the coffeemaker.

The doorbell sounded. He yawned as he made his way to the door and opened it. Sarah, his ex-wife, stood on his doorstep, stylish heels planted firmly on the mat that said GO AWAY. Sarah. Looking as beautiful as the day they were married. Before he fucked it all up. But he could tell from the swelling around her eyes that she'd been crying.

He massaged the sleep out of his eyes, half convinced that when he removed his fingers, she would have disappeared.

But Sarah was still there, smiling apologetically, and saying, "May I come in?"

Jon shrugged, stepping aside as she walked into his living room, suddenly embarrassingly shabby and small. "Coffee? I was just putting some on."

She raised a bag, holding it by its brown, string like handles. "Coffee. Two percent, three sugars, right?"

She'd remembered.

Jon took the coffee, thanked her, then pointed to the love seat, glad that he'd picked up his dirty laundry the night before. "I can't say I'm not happy to see you. But why are you here, Sarah?"

He took a sip of his coffee, waiting for the answer.

"A certain invitation."

Jon raised an eyebrow. "You got one too?"

"Not me, exactly. Stan."

"And what does Ballard say?" Jon asked, although he told himself he didn't give a shit what Ballard thought or said about anything.

She shrugged. "We don't see eye to eye on attending the memorial. He says we're too busy and that we should just send flowers." She stopped and, looking down at the floor, said, "But she was innocent, you know."

Jon laughed out loud. "That's ironic. Didn't you say I was obsessed? That I should be locked up in a rubber room, along with my goddamn briefcase and a gallon of Jim Beam?"

"I know what I said," she said quietly. "But I've had a long time to think about it."

"Have you?"

"Yes."

They stood there a long moment, looking at one another, Nunn not sure of what he should say or do.

"Since Tony Olsen's invitation came, I've been thinking about it even more, and . . ."

Nunn raised an eyebrow.

"Well, the invitation was for Stan and I don't care if he doesn't want to go. I was hoping I could go, that you would take me."

Another long moment, then Jon Nunn did what he'd wanted to do, had thought about doing for a long time. He took his ex-wife in his arms and tugged her toward him.

"Jon, no." She pressed her hand to his chest. "That's not why I came."

Nunn didn't say anything, just dropped his arms and turned away.

Later they had dinner at a intimate café, where brick oven-baked pizzas were served on proper white tablecloths, and copper pots and sailboats dangled from the ceiling. Talking. Laughing. Like old times. Only this time it didn't take booze to grease the wheels.

They were in bed by eleven. Separate beds. Sarah curled up on the double, hair spread out on the pillow, smudges of blue under her eyes, a bolster at her back and the duvet tucked under her chin. Nunn claimed the sofa and the remote control and fell asleep in the middle of *Leno*.

Seven a.m. now, and she'd hardly moved. Nunn got up, fetched his briefcase, then closed and locked the bathroom door. He perched on the toilet seat, balancing the briefcase on his knees. He eased open the catch, soundlessly, and began pawing through the contents, as familiar to him now as the deepening lines on his face when he studied himself in the mirror every morning.

A newspaper clipping, yellow with age, detailing Rosemary's trip to Mexico, where she told friends she knew that Chris would never be coming home. Stupid-ass thing to say, Nunn thought, like that crazy nurse in Maryland who'd offed her husband with succinylcholine chloride—on Valentine's Day no less—after telling colleagues exactly how she'd do it.

Nunn studied the black-and-white photos of the Thomas children, Leila and Ben, that accompanied the article. The same brown hair and inquisitive eyes as their mother, but where Rosemary's hair had been long, Leila's was cropped and curly, almost the same length as her older brother's. He wondered if they'd show up at their mother's memorial.

He exchanged the article for crime scene photos and a transcript of the trial, where he had testified for over two hours, the evidence he'd found in the back of Rosemary's closet—the blouse stained with

Christopher's blood and the missing button that had been inside the iron maiden; the strands of Rosemary's hair in Christopher's fist.

Damn.

Nunn slid an issue of *Vanity Fair* out of its protective plastic sleeve, the one he'd saved for over a decade, the one containing the pre-execution interview from death row at California's Valley State Prison for Women.

Nunn flipped to a picture of Rosemary wearing an orange jumpsuit and white sneakers. He skimmed the piece and reread a line here and there, Rosemary telling the world her story: how Christopher had asked her for a divorce; how they had fought at the museum; how she'd stormed out and how sad and desperate she'd felt. But that she had *not* killed him.

"So, your husband was a . . . whoremonger?" the interviewer had suggested.

And Rosemary, ever dignified, had refused to answer.

"So, how," the interviewer had asked, "did your husband's body end up in the *Eiserne Jungfrau,* the iron maiden that was on loan to the McFall?"

Rosemary claimed she had no idea.

"And all the evidence against you?"

Again, Rosemary could not supply the answer to a world waiting to hear a confession from one of the few women who was slated to die by lethal injection in the state of California.

Nunn closed his eyes and rested his head against the cool bathroom tiles. He remembered the exact moment he'd seen the magazine at a newsstand. By the time he got around to reading the article, it was two days after Rosemary Thomas was dead.

He put everything neatly away and closed the briefcase. He washed his face and shaved and eased into the same shirt and trousers he'd worn the day before, then gently shook Sarah by the shoulder.

"It's nine o'clock. You getting up anytime soon?"

Sarah moaned and pulled the duvet over her head. "Go away."

Nunn smiled. It suddenly felt as if they were an old married couple. "I'm going out for breakfast, a café just across the street. Want to join me?"

The duvet shrugged.

"I take that as a no."

"I'll be down soon." Muffled.

Nunn stared at her a moment, trying to decide what it was he felt. It was like some B-grade movie, his beautiful ex-wife asking him—not her current husband—to escort her to such an important event. But the ache he felt in his heart was all too real and definitely not part of a script.

Nunn settled into a chair with a cup of Italian-roast coffee and a copy of *USA Today*. He had read through the Life section and started on Sports, but he couldn't concentrate.

What did Sarah really want? Was her marriage to Ballard coming apart?

Nunn was picturing Sarah from the night before, fantasizing about whisking her off to someplace exotic such as Rio or Bali, when she finally made her appearance. She looked fresh and bright, her hair still damp from the shower. She laid a hand on his shoulder.

"I'm going shopping."

"For what?"

Sarah straightened, extended her arms. "I can't wear *this* to the memorial, now, can I?"

In Nunn's opinion, Sarah looked spectacular, her extraordinary body in a white, scoop-necked sweater and tight jeans. He raised an eyebrow. "I guess not. Coffee?" He indicated the chair opposite him.

She flapped a hand. "No, thanks. Gotta run." She executed a delicate about-face, waved, and was gone.

Nunn watched her disappear down the street.

He downed a second cup of coffee, then left the café, walking down North Point to the Embarcadero and wandering up to Grant near Pier 39. It was unusually quiet for this time of day, he thought, but the back of his neck prickled, as if he was being followed. He turned and thought he saw . . . something . . . but then there was no one, and he walked on.

A few blocks later he felt it again. This time when he turned, he was sure he caught the shadow of a man. He sprinted after it, but when he rounded the corner, the alley was empty.

Enough, Nunn thought, and headed back to his apartment. He still needed to tie up a few things before the memorial this evening.

He starts the car and follows the ex-wife.

When she goes into a department store, he parks, cuts across the street, makes his way past counters of women's perfume and makeup, men's underwear and cologne, keeping the ex-wife in his sights only yards ahead, a few shoppers between them, mostly women, and it's early, the store practically empty so he's got to be careful.

He almost swats the bottle of cologne out of the saleswoman's hand after she sprays him with something he thinks smells like rotten oranges, and she catches enough of the expression behind his metallic aviators to back away mumbling apologies.

Damn it, where is she? Has he lost her? He looks left, right.

There she is.

Half an escalator between them now.

As the ex-wife browses the dress department, he moves to a table of cashmere sweaters, head down, pats and caresses the soft wool as if it were flesh.

Three or four dresses draped over her arm, she disappears into the dressing room. He waits a minute, surveying his surroundings and, when he's sure no one is looking, darts in.

He spies her legs under a cubicle. She is the only one in the dressing room.

He stands in a room opposite, the door closed, and when she comes out wearing one of the dresses, a short silky number, and twirls in front of the mirror, he watches, holding his breath until she heads back into her room, then he bolts, pushes her forward, locks the door behind them, gets one hand over her mouth, another around her waist so hard the air goes out of her with a gasp, and he whispers in her ear, "Do not make a sound or I'll kill you."

A noise escapes her throat: neither scream nor gasp, just the smallest squeak, like a yelping puppy.

"You don't like the dress?" he whispers.

He gets a hand under the silky fabric, then pushes the straps off her shoulders and tugs the dress down till it puddles around her feet and she is in her panties, and he tightens his choke hold and feels her body tense and whispers so quietly it's little more than a breath, "Tell him to stay away from the memorial for Rosemary Thomas."

The ex-wife says nothing, trembles.

"Did you hear me?" His lips graze her ear.

She nods several times, even though his hand is still pressed tightly against her mouth.

"Tell him. Your *life* depends on it. Do you get that?" His breath in her ear causing more chills.

She nods emphatically.

"You'll tell the ex-cop to stop, won't you?"

"I need to hear you say yes," he rasps as he slightly eases his grip off her mouth and chin.

"Yes," she says.

"Good." His hand tightens against her throat and she smells his breath and feels his beard against her neck and tries to turn her head for one look at his face but can't move and he says, "You'll tell him."

Just then she hears women's voices and is about to call out when he pushes her to the floor and sprints out of the room and the women scream and then he's walking past shoppers and racks of clothes and pushing past people on the escalator and weaving around the makeup and perfume counters until the hot, damp air hits his face and he keeps walking not once looking back, and not until he is driving along the Embarcadero does he start breathing normally again.

18

THOMAS COOK

Some love-struck [...] had once called her hair a "curtain of flame." Haile had liked the phrase at the time and thought it so appropriate now, as she gazed at herself in the mirror, that she half expected her brush to throw off sparks. Her beauty drew attention, and most of the time she liked that attention. But not tonight. Tonight she'd prefer no eyes follow her once she arrived at the McFall Art Museum. Instead, she hoped to drift almost invisibly from room to room, a little ghost ship flying its red pennant. Tonight she had to be a huntress, and it would be better, safer, if she went about unnoticed, like some bejeweled old dowager, dripping diamonds and pearls, with a slack neck and smelling like a mixture of camphor oil and Chanel No. 5. She'd even briefly, and absurdly, contemplated wearing a disguise, then dismissed the idea because she knew the guest list would be small, and there'd be no crashing this event. But then, who'd want to crash a memorial service for a woman who'd been executed ten years before? No, she'd have to go as herself, Haile Patchett, flaming hair and all.

But once at the McFall, what then? She considered the options, the method. She'd have to mingle with people, pretend she was there for the same reason as everyone else, to remember poor dead Rosemary. She'd have to listen to stories of how great Rosemary had been, how smart, how clever, all of which, had, of course, made her grim end just that much more tragic. And grim it had certainly been, as Haile imagined it, strapped to a gurney, nameless people inserting needles, someone reading her death sentence in a low, mournful voice. She cringed at the thought of Rosemary's execution, and how someone would no doubt bring it up and she'd have to stand there, listening.

But at some point she'd drift away, and with any luck no one would find it particularly unusual that she walked from room to room. She'd have to stop and pretend to pay attention to whoever interrupted her ramble, but after a time she could pull away, and at those moments, just as she stepped back, she could allow her eyes to search for the room.

Briefly, she considered the information she had gotten out of Artie Ruby. That crazy cop, Nunn, had blackmailed her into sleeping with Ruby, hoping to uncover something about Chris's murder. Instead Ruby had pointed her to a bit of information that would prove useful to her. Apparently, she was not the only one of Christopher Thomas's lovers who had been involved in the stolen-art racket. The respectable curator of the McFall Art Museum, Justine Olegard, was another. Haile was willing to bet Justine didn't quit that lucrative little side business once Chris was murdered. It would take some nosing around, but Haile was sure she'd find something damaging in Justine's office, something that would put Justine exactly where she wanted her, and soon Haile would get the train wreck of her life back on track.

She glanced at the clock. Not much time left, and out the window, one of those dense San Francisco fogs had drifted in. That would slow traffic to a crawl, so she would need to hurry up if she wanted to get there early enough to look around a little before anyone spotted her and came over to talk. Hurriedly, she applied the last of her makeup. This had once been reassuring, but time was beginning to make it a lesson in the things she'd done wrong and now couldn't change—the thought that always returned to her when she noticed some new crack in her mirrored portrait.

At the McFall Art Museum, Justine Olegard reached for her drink the way others reach for a brass ring. She looked at the little painting that had hung in a dark corner of the gallery for ages, ten years at least. Tony Olsen had made a big deal of its installation, a last wish for Rosemary. Part of the museum's permanent collection, it was now installed behind a locked glass display case as if it were the *Mona Lisa*. Here it moldered in obscurity in this quiet room that didn't see much traffic. She knew the artist was a friend of Rosemary Thomas's, and the installation was a tribute to her friend, honoring her for all patrons to see.

Museums were haunted by such paintings. They were the naughty kids who were never introduced to guests, and this one now struck Justine as naughtier than most. Something about it was tense, gave off a disturbing little charge. Looking at the waves, you sensed something underneath them, a shadowy presence, silent, stalking, preparing to surge upward toward a pair of struggling white legs. Some paintings truly spoke, and this one did. Its true subject was the dark undercurrent of things, she thought, and the creatures that lurked there. She examined the signature.

B. McGuire.

Belle McGuire.

Rosemary's friend.

As this night had approached, a night Justine had been dreading, she thought about her time with Christopher. She recalled the many things they'd done together, the tightrope she'd walked between the personal and the professional, and even the legal and the illegal, and how, at certain moments, she'd quite helplessly fallen off. Christopher would have liked this little painting, she decided. He would have liked its deceit, the way it played the one-eyed Jack. He would have admired its skill for betrayal and misdirection, the way it turned the sea into a shadowy back alley. And what about Rosemary? Rosemary, who had always believed that something good could not have something evil at its core? Someone would probably say all of this about Rosemary during tonight's memorial service, and Justine knew that she would nod and agree while all the time imagining the world beneath the world that this dead woman had never glimpsed—or maybe she did.

Justine walked to the window and looked out over the city.

The white signature spire of the downtown San Francisco skyline was hung in fog.

Sheathed in fog like a knife.

Wrapped in it, like a shroud.

The McFall Art Museum was only a few blocks away now, and Tony Olsen knew that once his limo turned the corner, he'd be able to see its lit windows. The elegant place was also oddly playful in its overall design. The curl of the stairs that wound up to the exhibition floors was almost impish, and the bright colors painting the lobby were like a middle finger lifted at the old-lady interiors of the Uffizi and the Louvre. He had always loved to seed his philanthropy with a sense of mischief. He knew that the kid inside him was a nasty little bastard, and as his limousine turned the corner and the McFall swam into view, he could see his own nastiness on full display. How dark and amusingly impudent, he thought, to use an art museum to memorialize a woman put to death for murdering her husband. Sure, Rosemary had requested it in her last will and testament, but he took no pleasure in what he would normally have found a deliciously inappropriate juxtaposition. Something about Rosemary had actually penetrated his otherwise quite impenetrable character. He had played the mystery man all his life, and most of the time he had played it convincingly. Once a reporter had asked him how he wished to be remembered, and he'd replied, not without accuracy, "As a blur." But Rosemary had somehow seen through the illusion he had created and lived behind. It was as if she had drawn the cloth up from one corner of the masterwork, seen only that tiny bit of canvas, and yet, with stunning intuitiveness, had grasped the work as a whole.

The limousine stopped abruptly.

"Sorry, sir," the driver said. "A cat just ran in front of us."

Olsen glanced out the window and through the light mist saw the cat as it leaped onto the curb, then stopped and looked back at the black car it had so narrowly avoided. It was black with white feet like a dancer's shoes, and for a moment it stared directly into Olsen's eyes, haughtily, as if it had proved its point, defied the odds again. But how many escapes were now left to it, Olsen wondered, how many lives, before chance turned the tables at last?

Jon Nunn's gaze swept over everyone as they assembled in the room. They were like ornaments on some grim tree, each hanging from its own withered limb.

Sarah stood silently beside him. Why had she come? he wondered now. She had no relationship with either Rosemary or Christopher. He glanced over at her stunning, sphinxlike profile and thought of the last time they'd been here together, all those years ago at the fund-raiser for inner-city park programs. She seemed tense, more so than usual, but when he asked her about it, she shrugged it off. Perhaps she had come out of some weird nostalgia, since it was Rosemary's case that had broken up their marriage. Sarah had always been good at keeping old wounds open, and he supposed she was busy plucking at whatever scabs she'd since gotten from Stan. But Rosemary was a different story. Sarah had not even known her. He shrugged. Maybe she'd just needed a night away from Stan. Who wouldn't, after all?

19

DIANA GABALDON

The fog laid its frozen hand on the back of Haile Patchett's neck. The day had been a summer dream of sun and heady breezes, but the fog had rolled in just after sunset, and the air that rattled the palm fronds now was straight out of Neptune's bait locker, dank and cold, with a whiff of dead things. Ten thousand goose bumps were on her bare arms, her flimsy silk evening wrap no bar to the piercing, unexpected cold that so often rolled into San Francisco.

The museum's courtyard was scattered with rocks, each the size of a large ottoman, and in her rush to get inside Haile had barely avoided running into one. She cursed under her breath. She'd be on her ass if she wasn't careful.

She was outwardly cranky but could feel the excitement in her revving up like a Corvette at a stoplight. The invitation had said the gathering was to be held in the big observation room at the top of the tower, but the curator's office was tucked away, down a short corridor.

She thought she'd let the crowd get started, talking, drinking, before she slipped away.

Haile thought of her time with Christopher Thomas, what she'd expected, all their pillow talk that had amounted to nothing.

The fog glowed ahead, the light from the museum's entrance softened and diffused. Other people were coming up behind her, vague figures making their way through the courtyard; she could hear murmured snatches of disembodied conversation.

"Jesus, what are we in for?" a male voice said softly, but whoever he spoke to didn't answer.

The tower was barely visible through the fog, an unlikely lighthouse, shaped like an upside-down ziggurat of glass and concrete blocks. The fog was thick enough to shroud the lower part of the building, making the low, circular roof look as though it were floating.

Stan Ballard thought, *This is insane. I'm insane. What was I thinking?*

He stood just outside the museum, wreathed in fog. For one more moment he thought about leaving, then opened the door.

20

THOMAS COOK

One by one the snakes slithered in, and Jon Nunn found himself looking at each of them as if he were trying to pick a face from a line of mug shots. There was Justine Olegard, dressed in black, with a single strand of white pearls and spiked heels, but otherwise quite somber in her appearance. She was talking to two people he didn't know. Perhaps she knew them. Perhaps she didn't. It wouldn't matter to Justine. She was used to glad-handing strangers, talking up the museum, angling for a donation. It wouldn't surprise him if she managed to pass the cup a little even tonight. Something in Justine never quite turned off. She was like a candle that never sputtered out, though he'd never been able to figure out exactly what her light revealed.

Suddenly, as if summoned, Justine broke away from the two people. She'd probably gotten the message that they were of limited means, or indifferent to art, or had sunk their money into some hospital wing that bore their names and would thus not be making a contribution to the McFall. Whatever it was, it had caused Justine abruptly to lose interest.

Nunn glanced in the other direction, to where he could see Peter Heusen uncomfortably flanked by his niece and nephew, Rosemary's two children. Rosemary had been convicted when they were still young, and Nunn wondered how they'd fared beneath the burden of having their mother executed for the murder of their father. He couldn't imagine their uncle providing solace. Something about Peter Heusen added little knifepoints to the air. It was as if he made a tiny slit in everyone he met, which no doubt explained why Ben and Leila looked so uneasy at the moment, both of them glancing about in a way that showed just how quickly they wanted to get away from their uncle. There was something icy in the way they stood a little too far away from him for actual conversation, both quite stiff, though only Ben had his arms folded, the sure sign that he felt himself under attack. Leila's attitude was just as wary, it seemed to Nunn, so that she appeared less enclosed within a family circle than trapped in a steadily closing vise.

"Hello, Nunn."

Nunn turned, surprised to find Stan Ballard standing beside him.

"I didn't think you were coming," Nunn said.

"Well, a man has to be careful, don't you think?"

"Careful about what?"

"Leaving his wife on the arm of her ex-husband," Stan answered. "Old fires sometimes give off new sparks, right?"

Nunn shrugged.

Stan glanced around the room. "You must really be in your element, Nunn."

"In what way?"

"Oh, you know, everyone gathered together in one place. All the suspects in the parlor."

"Suspects?"

"Of murder most foul." Stan smiled. "Don't expect me to believe you're not thinking of Rosemary's case."

Of course Nunn had been thinking of nothing but the murder since his arrival at the museum. He'd never been able to get it out of his mind—it had spread over his life like a stain, and even now he could feel that stain still spreading. He thought of the way those old Cold War films used to show the red tide of Communism sweeping over Europe and Asia. Rosemary's crime and punishment was like that, he thought, a force that had engulfed his life.

"You must be reviewing the whole thing," Stan said lightly, so that Nunn thought he was being vaguely mocked, or if not that, then reduced to a prissy little parlor-mystery stereotype, or worse, a rumpled gumshoe going over yellowing case files while his life trickled away in futile reenactments and baseless surmises. He was thinking that neither of these unflattering visions of himself was wholly inaccurate, as he watched Belle and Don McGuire arrive. Belle as beautiful as ever, the perfect California girl, Don every inch the thuggish ex-con.

"So what are you thinking, Detective?" Stan asked with a laugh.

"Actually I was thinking that that guy there once beat the hell out of Christopher Thomas." It had come out at the trial, and briefly at the time Nunn had wondered if Don had been in some way connected to Christopher Thomas's murder.

Stan's gaze shifted over to the man Nunn indicated. "Who's the girl on his arm?"

"That's his wife, Belle," Nunn answered. "Rosemary tried very hard to help her rise in the art world here."

"And you think the husband might have felt that their relationship was a little too close?" Stan asked.

Nunn shook his head. "Who knows?" he answered impatiently, now tired of the little game Stan was still playing with him.

"The Shadow knows," Stan answered with a laugh. "But the question remains."

"What question?"

Stan's smile slithered into place. "Who is the Shadow?"

With that, Stan stepped away, then walked over to Sarah, took her arm, and placed it in his, a gesture of possession Nunn knew he was clearly meant to see, and one that Sarah just as clearly resented. As well she should, he thought, since it was as crude as a prospector staking a claim.

Still, he found Sarah's ultimate acceptance of the gesture somewhat painful, so that he turned from the scene and fixed his attention on Haile Patchett, who caught his eye and smiled. He'd wondered how much of anything she'd told him the other day was true.

Now in the museum she was drifting from place to place, sometimes stopping for conversation but clearly uninterested in engaging anyone for long. Something about her movements was odd, Nunn thought, purposeful, like a cat in an unfamiliar room, sniffing here, there, everywhere. Haile had always been something of a prowler, of course. Rosemary had certainly detested her, and for a moment Nunn could almost feel Rosemary at his side, watching with the same odd suspicion as Haile sauntered about. The tingling sense of Rosemary's presence beside him was strange, but then that was the way it worked with a haunting case: it was like a body that never cooled.

And Rosemary's never had.

The Shadow knows.

This time it was Rosemary's voice, rather than Stan's, and Jon felt an odd quiver because he had heard it so distinctly, a whisper, or perhaps a hiss, Rosemary's angry ghost.

For a moment, he surveyed the "shadows" that surrounded him and it occurred to him that Stan, arrogant bastard that he was, had been right. Jon *had* come to this service not to remember Rosemary in death but to return her to his life, not to memorialize but to resurrect her. Perhaps all the debts he'd incurred in pursuit of her were now demanding to be paid no less adamantly than Rosemary's ghost had suddenly demanded to be heard.

Without realizing it, he suddenly whispered her name: *Rosemary.*

In his imagination, all movement abruptly stopped, and slowly, as if controlled by invisible strings, each head turned to face him: Stan, Haile, Justine, Tony, Sarah, Belle, Don, even Rosemary's own children, all of them now peering at him coldly, with their lips tightly sealed.

21

DIANA GABALDON

The door of Justine's office opened with a loud click, but nobody was around to hear it. An attendant was guarding the roped-off ramp to the lower exhibit galleries, but Haile had gotten rid of him by telling him a locked car had its lights on in the parking lot—having made sure on her way in that there *was* a locked car with its lights on. By the time the attendant checked out the car for a license number, came in, went upstairs, and found the owner, she hoped to be done here and gone.

She could count on ten minutes clear, she thought, and with luck it would take no more than half that.

Justine, bless her heart, had left a small lamp on in her office. *Great! No fumbling around in the dark.*

Haile scanned the office, her fingers itching with acquisitiveness, trying to decide where to start. Her eyes fixed on Justine's desk. *As good a place as any.* She walked over noiselessly and carefully opened one of the side drawers. There had to be something here, something she could use to get what she wanted from Justine.

22

PETER JAMES

Away from the hubbub of conversation, the silence in this room felt intense, and the strong, sterile smell of polish was intense too. Haile's nerves were popping and she had a faint throbbing, like a pulse, in her ears; she was nervous as hell. But she was here, ready.

Then she heard voices approaching. She froze. It sounded as though they were just opposite the door to the office.

Jesus, who was it?

She held her breath.

She tried to calm herself. It was probably just a couple of guests who had slipped away from the reception in the observation room of the tower, giving themselves a tour. They must have been staring at a painting that she'd seen and thought it might have been hung upside down. She caught a snatch of their conversation.

"It's revisionist postmodernist," one of them said. "Definite juxta-position of Klimt and Chagall, you know what I'm saying, with a sur-realist—or is it closer to Dada?—overlay. You wouldn't perceive that in any visual context, but to me it's there like a kind of metaphorical palimpsest."

That old museum curator, Alex something-or-other. Haile remembered how much Christopher had resented him.

She waited until their voices drifted farther down the hallway, then took a deep breath and tried to focus on what she was doing, but her nerves were shot to hell, her eyes leaping erratically around the room. It was spare and minimalist, glass table, white furniture and blinds, bare wooden flooring. She looked at the prints and paintings hung on the walls, then the small, precious-looking objets d'art that sat on the flat surfaces. She looked down at the desk.

It had to be in here somewhere.

But where?

She noticed a tiny bronze statuette near the desk lamp and slipped it into her handbag—shit, this whole world could have been hers, a thought that kept recurring as she stood at Justine Olegard's desk.

A small vase of flowers sat on it, a framed photograph of Justine, ten years or so back when she looked a little like Whitney Houston, but she'd put on weight since then and her pretty face had filled out. It made Haile glad.

A neat leather blotter was on the desk, and a silver letter opener and an old, tired-looking computer terminal that was out of keeping with the rest of the modern décor. Again she pulled open each of the drawers in the desk, hastily rummaging through them before closing them again and turning her head back at the door every few seconds. That damn curator was out there *again,* pontificating over the painting. She remembered the way Christopher used to talk about the world of art to her, explaining images and themes and *schools* in paintings. Renaissance; Dutch; fête galante; impressionist; cubist; surrealist; Native American; the symbolists and precisionists such as Georgia O'Keeffe and Charles Sheeler, whom Christopher had particularly liked. He used to make her feel so good, made her feel intelligent, despite her lack of education, made her feel there might be a whole new, rich dimension to her life.

Then it was snatched away from her, and she went straight back to who she had always been, Haile Patchett, trailer trash from Brooksville, Florida—*Home of the Tangerine!* Only now she was a decade older, on a downward spiral, making money as an escort, pickpocketing her clients—her *tricks*—when she could, funding a constant and ever more expensive battle to keep her looks. How long would she be able to maintain the image before the cracks became too large to conceal?

She continued fishing through the desk's middle drawer. It was full of papers. For a successful woman, Justine was pretty disorganized. But underneath all that was a file. Haile pulled it out, placed it on top of the desk, and opened it.

Then she heard the creak of the door and a furious voice behind her. "Just what the hell do you think you are doing?"

Justine Olegard.

Shit!

Haile grabbed the file and held it to her chest.

"I asked you a question." Justine glared at her. "What are you doing in my office?"

"Nothing." Haile shrugged.

"Nothing? What's that in your hand?" Justine stepped forward and put out her hand. Haile held on to the file, refusing to let go. She couldn't let Justine have it. Not now, not after all she'd done.

Justine lurched forward, trying to grab it out of Haile's hand. "Give me that!"

Haile quickly moved back and stumbled, dropping the folder and its contents. She managed to avoid falling by grabbing the edge of the modernist coffee table, knocking over books and a small ceramic sculpture of a tall, thin, elongated man, which skidded to the floor and shattered.

Justine stood still for a moment, then said quietly "That was a Giacometti study. It's priceless."

She dropped to her knees and started picking up the broken shards, practically in tears. "Just get the hell out of here," she said, shaking her head.

Too many people here. Too much stuff. Too many memories banging around in her head and none of them good. Belle had been trying her best, but she didn't really do crowds; big gatherings made her nervous. She preferred the peace and quiet of her studio, the isolated life of an artist. She looked around: faces, so many of them familiar, but all of them were in little groups talking, and right now she didn't have the energy or the courage to interrupt them.

Belle drained her wine, put down the glass, and scanned the crowd for the one man she was looking for. Tony Olsen. She walked directly over to him and said, "Mr. Olsen, I need you to do something for me."

Olsen smiled. "Of course, Belle. Anything."

"I need you to open the case housing my painting . . . Rosemary's wishes."

"Why would you want me to do *that*?"

"Please, Mr. Olsen. I promise you'll understand as soon as you open the display case." He stood a moment as if considering what to do, then Belle watched as he located Alex Hultgren and walked out of the room with him. A few minutes later both men reappeared and together with Belle went to the small oval room where *Waves 27* hung.

Olsen unlocked the display case and opened the glass door.

"Please take the painting down, Mr. Olsen."

"But I promised Rosemary it would never come down. Would you mind telling me what this is about, Belle?"

"Please. I also made a promise to Rosemary. Please do as I ask."

Olsen carefully unhooked the painting from the wall. Belle pulled out a small Swiss Army knife, took hold of the painting, and before Olsen could object, sliced open the thick fabric backing of the frame. A Moleskine notebook fell from the interior.

"What is it?" Olsen asked.

Belle didn't answer. She handed him the painting and opened the notebook to the first page, her hands shaking so much she could barely hold it. Then she turned pages, staring at the handwriting of her friend Rosemary Thomas, crushing away tears with her lashes.

She wasn't even aware that Olsen had moved beside her watching as she flicked through the pages to the last entry. *August 22, 2000*. Ten years ago. The entry had been written the day before Belle had stood in the viewing room and had seen her friend laid out to die.

Belle had recently read that the death rows in U.S. prisons were known as cemeteries for the living. It was true. Rosemary had been dead for all of those months with the lethal-injection sentence hanging over her, as each of her appeals fell over, in turn.

Tony Olsen started making his way back to where the rest of the guests were assembled; Belle closed the notebook and followed. She couldn't stop the pictures in her mind. Seeing Rosemary strapped down, wrists and ankles and chest, and how they had opened the curtains so that the witnesses to the execution could watch the deadly injection being administered. All of it came back to Belle now in hideous detail, the botched first attempt, those curtains being opened and closed, opened and closed, and the look on Rosemary's face.

She could remember every moment of the long night before: Rosemary's last night.

Rosemary had always been composed, almost regal in her bearing, but the stress had lined her face and stooped her shoulders. She'd sat in her orange prison tunic and white sneakers in the small cell, with no window and the CCTV camera ever watching her, and despite it all maintained her dignity to the very end. Belle could see Rosemary now, working away in a frenzy on the diary, writing that last entry.

When she had finished, they spoke for a while and she had held Belle's hand, and finally she said, "Belle, let's not talk anymore. Just sit with me." And then: "Just make me one last promise. I want you to keep the diary. Those I've written about will know what it means. But I don't want any of it coming out until after Leila and Ben are old enough. Do you understand? In my will, I've asked for a memorial service on the tenth anniversary of my death. That's when I want you to read it, at the service, not before. Will you promise me that?"

Belle had promised.

Now she glanced at the diary, rubbed a finger over the leather cover and the pages as if to make sure it was real. She looked down again at the pages of that last entry. She remembered Rosemary cursing when her ballpoint pen ran out of ink and how Belle had to rummage in her purse to find another for her. Belle could see that place where it had happened, that change in color in the ink, from blue to black, now.

When she reached the reception area, she saw Tony Olsen going around the room, whispering into the ears of some of the guests. Silence took hold of the room as the chatter slowly died away. Eventually it seemed as if someone had hit a freeze-frame button on the event. Every single person in the room had stopped talking and was looking at her. Or, more accurately, at the object she was holding in her hand.

Belle looked over at her husband, Don, who was suddenly chewing the inside of his mouth, something he did only when something bothered him that he needed to think about.

Then she looked at Peter Heusen, Rosemary's brother. According to Rosemary, he'd been on the verge of bankruptcy before her death but would benefit handsomely from her estate. Why was he looking as if he'd just bitten into a lemon? Belle wondered.

Stan Ballard, Rosemary's lawyer and estate manager, had the face of a man who might not make it to the bathroom in time. He kept switching his weight from one leg to another, tugging his ear, dragging a hand through his hair, adjusting his tie.

Haile Patchett and Justine Olegard had taken up positions on opposite sides of the room. Olegard had her arms folded across her chest, face stern, a mask hiding any and all emotion. But Patchett's face seemed to have crumbled a bit, a weariness overtaking her features, mouth droopy, eyes sad, as if something inside her had let go and given up.

Belle looked from one person to another. It was like a painting, she thought, a group portrait.

Now she realized she was going to enjoy this. She felt a sudden surge of confidence. With a nod and a nervous smile she opened the diary to the pages Rosemary had written on the last night of her life.

23

TESS GERRITSEN

Belle could feel her heart thumping hard. What secrets lay inside? What Pandora's box was she about to open? "The last entry is from August twenty-second, 2000." She paused, looked up. "The day before she was executed."

"Read it," Olsen said.

Belle swallowed hard. And began to read.

I have become the invisible woman.

I don't know the precise moment when it happened, when I began to fade from view like the Cheshire cat, my face dimming until only the ghost of my smile remains. I think it must have started soon after Leila was born. That's when I first noticed that Christopher no longer seemed to look at me, but instead looked through me, as if I had turned transparent. Once your husband stops looking at you, you begin to feel that the rest of the world has stopped looking as well.

There was a time when I could catch a man's eye just by wearing a short skirt and high heels. I could walk into a gathering of staid historians and see the startled looks on their faces when they realized that the Arms and Armor curator was an attractive young woman. And I was attractive. The Rosemary who once was: confident and serene. Ready to love and be loved.

That woman is gone now. In her place is a woman whom no one seems to see, a woman who walks into rooms unnoticed and unacknowledged. In this, I am not alone. This is what the passage of time does to all women. It thickens our waists, streaks our hair with gray, crinkles the skin around our eyes.

But invisibility also has its uses.

I certainly found it useful that summer.

On this, my final evening on earth, I don't know why I should be focused on that particular memory. Over the past weeks I have been reviewing my life, remembering all my bad choices, all the points in time when a wiser decision could have sent me on a path toward a different and happier fate. But this is the fate I am now locked into. And I can't help thinking about one of those crucial points in time—that day in June when I walked into the lobby of the Coronado Hotel.

That was the day my future was sealed.

It was not my first visit to that grand old hotel. Years before, as a newlywed, I had strolled through the lobby in a sundress and had seen a bellman stare admiringly at my legs. But this time, when I walked in, no one looked at me. I was just a mousy, brown-haired matron in a shapeless shirt and slacks, scarcely worth a glance when there were other females to stare at, young females who still had the glow of youth. They hadn't lost their figures to motherhood. Their shoulders weren't bowed from the humiliations of marriage to Christopher Thomas.

It's as if I am there now. I watch one of those magnificent specimens walk past me in the lobby. She has shiny hair and perfect skin and the stride of a woman who knows she is beautiful. Enjoy it while you can, honey, I think. Because someday you'll be where I am. Exactly where I am. I hunch deep in a chair and the woman doesn't see me as she walks past, into the cocktail lounge. But I can see her perfectly. I see her glide across to the bar counter. I see her tap the shoulder of a man seated there. He turns, smiles at her, and reaches an arm around her waist to pat her ass. It is a gesture of easy familiarity, the way a man might greet his wife.

The problem is that man's wife is me.

I watch as the shiny-haired woman and Christopher leave the cocktail lounge and stroll hand in hand to the grand stairway. They are too wrapped up in their lust; they don't notice me follow them up the two flights of stairs into the historic section of the hotel. They head down a charming but creaky hallway and disappear into a guest room. The door closes, and I hear the privacy lock click shut.

I cannot help myself. I stand outside the room and imagine what is going on behind the closed door. I picture the clothes strewn on the floor, the naked bodies on the bed. I picture my husband's hands on that woman's silky young body, a body that has not given him two children and a decade of devotion.

Why did I torment myself that way? Why did I follow him when I already knew the purpose of his trip? Not business, as he'd claimed. No, it's never about business. After all the women I've had to suffer through, I knew exactly what he was up to whenever he'd disappear for a few days, or even for just a few hours.

Suddenly, standing outside the room, I can bear it no longer. I leave that closed door and walk out of the building, to the garden courtyard. There I call the only person I can call about this. I have little regard for him, but at least, in this case, his interests are aligned with mine.

"I have to find a way to divorce him, Peter. I can't deal with it any longer."

My brother, never one for sympathy, gives an impatient sigh. "This again? You always say it, and you never follow through."

"Because of the children."

"They'll get over a breakup. Kids always manage."

"No, it's not that. It's Chris. He'll fight me for them."

"Why? He doesn't give a damn about them."

"But he does give a damn about the money. He'll use them as a bargaining chip to squeeze every penny he can out of me."

Only then does my brother take me seriously. Money has that effect on him. "He can't do that," says Peter. "The money is from our family."

"But the children are his too. And if he gets custody of them—"

"He could get his hands on their trust fund," Peter says, finishing for me. Peter is clever when he wants to be.

"This could complicate your life too. It's all tied together, all our investments."

"What are you suggesting?"

"I don't know! I don't know what to do! I want to be rid of him. But at the same time . . ."

"What do you want me to do?"

"I don't know. I can't think straight. I just want the pain to be over with. I want to stop hurting"

Peter laughed. "Well, Rosie, you know Christopher, maybe one of his underworld connections will get sick of him one day and make a merry little widow out of you."

I didn't say anything to that because at times deep down I would have welcomed such an outcome. This was one of them.

"Peter, I'm asking for a little reassurance. I want to know that Ben and Leila will always be taken care of. That they'll be safe and comfortable, no matter what."

"Well, that much is assured. They've got generous trust funds."

"But will it stay *generous? Even if something happens to me?"*

"What could happen to you? And even if something did, I am their uncle. You think I'd let them be robbed blind?"

"You mean it, Peter? You would look after them?" Even as I ask this, I realize it is out of sheer desperation, that I have no one else to ask.

And of course Peter lets me down.

"Look, why don't you go get a stiff drink or something?" he says. "Take your mind off this. You're just working yourself up over nothing."

That's Peter's answer to everything: a stiff drink. But this time, maybe it's good advice. I hang up and go to the bar.

But two martinis later, my mind is still chewing over the image of my husband and that woman on the bed. I wonder who she is; I've never seen her before. When and where did he meet her? Does she know he's married? Does she know anything about him?

I'm feeling drunk and reckless as I go to the hotel's front desk. "Excuse me," I say. "I've lost my key. It's to room two fifteen. The last name is Thomas."

"I'm sorry, ma'am, but I'll need to see ID."

"Of course." I show him my driver's license. I'm gambling that Chris checked in under his real name.

The gamble pays off. He has taken a woman to our honeymoon hotel and has not bothered or cared enough to hide his identity.

"Here you go, Mrs. Thomas," the clerk says, and he hands me a key card.

I wait until Chris and his latest slut are dining in the restaurant, then I make my way to their room and let myself in. Inside I find rumpled bedsheets, damp towels on the floor. In the bathroom I find a woman's makeup bag, open it, and take out a vial of pills. The woman's name is printed clearly. All I know about her is that she takes sleeping pills and I know her name.

Haile Patchett.

Belle stopped reading and looked up, her eyes locking on Haile's. The room had gone absolutely silent, everyone staring at Haile.

Haile looked down at the floor, muttered, "Excuse me," and left the room.

"Go on," Nunn told Belle.

Belle cleared her throat and continued where she'd left off.

On that awful night when I saw her again at the Pollock opening after Chris had asked me for a divorce, it was just too much and I blew up. What a mistake that was. That's the moment I recall when my life began to spin out of control.

But Haile was just another conquest, another in a long string of women who were used and abandoned by Chris. There's only one woman I know of who had the courage and decency to stand up to him and refuse his advances. And he made certain she suffered for it.

Which is why I will always consider Belle McGuire my friend.

Belle stopped again, seemed to catch her breath before she continued.

But she was the one shining exception. The others were only too eager to be used. I've learned to feel sorry for them, to think of them as merely weak-willed victims. I write about them now only to explain what kind of man I've been married to. It's a poor defense, I know, but it's the one defense I can offer to my children, who will one day read these words.

This, my final entry, is for them.

Dearest Ben and Leila, I have asked my friend Belle to keep this diary until the appropriate moment. By the time you hear these words, you will both be adults and in full control of your own funds. You'll no longer need a protector. And you'll be ready to know the truth.

Sitting alone in my jail cell night after night, I have repeatedly wondered if my phone conversation with Peter that afternoon in the hotel sealed your father's fate. I've even wondered whether I am passively guilty. My brother's primary motivation in life has always been money and I've always known that. Did he panic when he heard me blow off at your father about the divorce? I cannot fathom my brother being capable of such a crime, let alone letting me die in his place.

Besides I have no evidence, and the law only considers evidence, and all the evidence somehow points to me.

You have been told that I am a murderer, that I killed your father. It may have been true that at times I wished him dead, but I did not kill him. I struck no blows, drew no blood. It's important to me that you both know this.

Now the day comes to a close, and tomorrow is my last. I love you both, my darlings, and will forever blow you kisses from heaven.

Always your mother,

Rosemary Heusen Thomas

Slowly Belle closed the diary and said softly, "Those were the last words she wrote."

"How do we know any of it's true?" Stan Ballard snapped.

"That diary is like a deathbed confession," said Hank Zacharius.

"She'd just finished writing this when she gave it to me," Belle said. "She had no reason to lie."

Nunn took a breath, looked directly at Peter Heusen, and said, "We have to assume that Rosemary *did* tell the truth. Which means that she did not kill her husband."

24

No, she didn't. But thanks to you, Detective, she's dead." It was Ben Thomas, Rosemary's son. Although at first glance the young man seemed to have an almost uncanny resemblance to his father, the eyes that now bored into Nunn's looked very much like Rosemary's. His sister was standing beside him looking at the floor, her rich brown hair partially covering her face. Few of the guests had seen the Thomas children since the trial. They'd been away at school and later college.

Ben walked over to Nunn, his demeanor cool. "So now you know what we've always known, that our mother did not kill our father. What did it have to take for you to realize that?"

Nunn was quiet. The entire room had gone quiet.

"What did it have to take for you to do your job and investigate our *dear uncle Peter*?" Ben turned around and glared at Peter Heusen.

Peter sighed impatiently. "Why would I want to kill your father?"

Leila Thomas looked up. "Why? Mom says why in the diary. Money. It's always been the only thing you've cared about. It's never been enough for you." She looked at her brother. "He used to dip into our trust funds before we were old enough to ask questions."

Peter polished off his drink and cleared his throat. "That's a lie!" he shrieked. Then he took a deep breath. "Listen, no one knew your mother better than I, and no one loved her more, and you know that. But Rosie had gone nuts in that jail cell, day after day, waiting to die. We can't take those ramblings of hers seriously." He looked at Stan Ballard. "She cracked up, remember?"

Ballard just nodded.

Leila had crossed the room and was standing across from her uncle, looking him directly in the face. "Don't you ever stop, Uncle Peter? Our mom was a wonderful and loving person, she was framed for a murder

she didn't commit, and she suffered so many disgraces in her life—"
Leila stopped, her gaze shifting to Justine, who looked down, avoiding
the younger woman's eyes. Leila turned to look at Peter again. "And
now *you're* disgracing her in her death."

She reached up and slapped him, hard, across the face.

Peter's eyes flashed with resentment. He stared at his niece for a
moment, then turned and left the room.

Ben Thomas moved over to stand beside his sister.

Tony Olsen came forward, took the diary from Belle, closed it with
care, and handed it to Ben. "This belongs to you, to both of you. It's a
living legacy, and your mother would want you to have it. You're its
rightful owners."

Ben accepted the diary.

Leila blinked away tears. "Thank you."

Tony walked over and rested a comforting hand on her shoulder.
"You know, I never believed your mother had anything to do with it."

"I know," Leila said.

"I was secretly hoping we'd expose a murderer, tonight. And we
might have," he whispered in her ear.

The girl looked up at him and nodded.

25

PHILLIP MARGOLIN

Nunn knew he had to get away for a few minutes. He needed to be alone, needed to mull over what had just happened, so he headed for the ramp to the lower exhibit gallery, and the exit. A guard had been stationed at the ramp but he was now gone. When Nunn got to the ground floor, he wandered through the darkened halls, preoccupied by his thoughts about what he'd just heard, until he found himself in the Arms and Armor Room.

He walked around the room, then stopped when he walked past one of the display cases. Something was wrong. The case contained daggers and swords. Each was labeled with information about the artifact. One of the labels read RONDELL DAGGER, FOURTEENTH CENTURY, but there was a space where the dagger should have been.

He was walking over to the case so he could examine it more closely when he heard a scream echoing through the marble halls of the museum.

Hank Zacharius could sense a news story when other reporters were oblivious to what was going on around them, but he didn't need any special instinct to know that a hideous scream at a museum was out of place.

He was off and running. He made the turn into the corridor and was surprised to see Tony Olsen walking down the hall toward him. Olsen's shoulder was even with the door to the ladies' room, and Hank thought he saw the door closing, but he couldn't be certain.

"Did you hear a scream?" Olsen asked.

"Yeah, I thought it came from this hall," said Zacharius.

"I already passed the offices," Olsen said, pointing to the rooms on the other side of the hall from the restrooms, "and there's no one in any of them."

"That leaves the bathrooms." Hank pushed open the door to the men's room, which was empty.

"In here," Olsen shouted from the ladies' room.

Hank got his cell phone and darted inside.

Haile Patchett lay crumpled on the floor.

Hank snapped a quick photo of the young woman and a close-up of the blood that was coming from a nasty gash on the back of her head.

"What the hell do you think you're doing?" Olsen shouted.

Hank took a step closer to Haile but Olsen pushed him away.

"Go outside and keep everyone away from here," said Olsen. "And get someone to call the police."

Everyone was huddled around the door to the ladies' room.

Nunn pushed his way inside.

He found Tony Olsen and a horrified Haile Patchett, who was seated on the floor with her back pressed against the wall. Haile had a hand to the back of her head and blood was seeping between the matted strands of her red hair.

"What happened?" Nunn asked.

"I, I don't know," Haile said. "I was fixing my lipstick when I saw a shadow across the mirror. The next thing I remember is opening my eyes and seeing him." She pointed at Tony Olsen.

Olsen looked up at Nunn. "I was with Zacharius when I found her."

Nunn nodded. "Do you think the attacker was already in here when you came in or do you think whoever it was followed you in?"

Haile just shook her head.

Two policemen rushed up the ramp toward the ladies' room, and a few minutes later, Haile Patchett came out, a bandage on the back of her head.

"I'm fine," she announced to a confused and worried crowd. "It's just a scratch." She was embarrassed everyone was staring at her.

Hank Zacharius had rejoined the group but hung back, whispering on his cell, calling the story in.

26

JEFFERY DEAVER

"Crazy night, huh?" the crime scene officer, who'd just come, said to the security guard sitting behind the massive desk in the front lobby of the museum.

"Rates as one of the strangest," the guard answered the cop, who along with his partner was assembling their gear. The two police officers who'd initially responded to the call had left, but not before asking him a few questions. The poor lady with the cut on her head had also left the museum, but in an ambulance. The guard glanced up at the crime scene officers again. They were wearing those outfits—jumpsuits and bootees and hats and masks—that made them look more like surgeons than cops. They'd come in to *process the scene*—he knew that was the term they used because he watched *CSI*.

The guard looked outside and noticed the crime scene van parked on the curb. Beside it another ambulance that had responded to the call.

"What's with the second ambulance?" the guard asked the taller of the crime scene cops.

"That's how it is sometimes, more than one ambulance shows up. Are they having a party in there?"

"It's a memorial."

"What's your piece?" The first cop was nodding at the pistol on the security guard's hip.

"Oh, just a Colt. Thirty-eight. They don't let us carry automatics here. I don't know why."

"How 'bout that. I've got a thirty-eight as my backup." He glanced down at his ankle. "Nice weapon."

"Totally dependable," the guard said proudly, pleased a cop had liked his choice of gun.

"*You* have a backup?"

"Me?" the guard replied with a laugh. "Not hardly."

"Ah. Good."

"Good?" the guard asked uncertainly, wondering why it was good. Then his mind did a leap and it occurred to him that it made no sense for crime scene officers to be here. That only made sense if—

"Tell you what," the taller cop said. "Lift your hands out to your sides."

"Oh, no," the guard said miserably as he felt the other officer behind him touch a gun to his skull. "This is . . . shit, this is all a setup, isn't it? You're not cops. You're hitting the place, aren't you?"

"Hands," the first one repeated.

The guard lifted his hands. He felt like crying. "You're not going to hurt me, are you?"

The second cop—well, *fake* cop—pulled the .38 from the guard's holster. His wallet too.

The first one asked, "What's your half of the code to the special exhibit room, the one in the tower?"

The room that contained a traveling exhibition of some small but important Renaissance drawings and prints. It had taken a year to get the Vatican to agree to lend the masterpieces, and they only did it because the museum installed a special security system that required two people to open it.

"Oh, they don't tell us that."

A voice behind him: "Who's the little girl in the picture?"

The guard whirled around and saw the second fake cop looking through his wallet.

"Your daughter, right? Is she at home now?"

The guard started to cry. "I only know half the code."

"That's all I asked for," was the calm reply.

"One seven seven A M K question mark eight three one; the letters are caps. It's case sensitive," the guard blurted out breathlessly. "Please, I'll do anything. . . ."

The first cop jotted the code. "If this's right, you don't need to do anything else." A nod, and in a moment the guard was duct taped and being dragged into the cloakroom nearby.

As they left, they shut the lights off, leaving him in darkness to consider how careless he'd been in not following the strictest security protocols. And to consider what kind of nightmare was about to unfold in the tower room.

They went by the names Bob and Frank, names that were short but, more important, distinct, so if they were working with a third person, there'd be no confusion as to who was being summoned.

The men were professional thieves. Killers too, though there'd been a major decrease in the market for hit men lately—because that job was relatively easy. Quality guns and explosives were cheap and easily available. But good thieves were hard to come by—a trace-free B and E required a lot of technical skill—so they'd reaped a windfall in fees over the past few years.

After dumping the guard in the cloakroom, they'd returned to the lobby. They were still in the crime scene outfits that had allowed them access into the museum. They wore these as often as they could on a job because the outfits protected them from sloughing off trace evidence as efficiently as they prevented cops from contaminating crime scenes.

Bob now walked to the front door of the museum, looked out, and unlocked it. He waved to their accomplices—the men posing as paramedics in the fake ambulance. One of the fake medics looked up. Bob called, "Ten minutes. We'll secure the room and let you know when it's clear."

"We're all set."

Frank and Bob climbed the stairs toward the large room at the top of the tower. At the top, they paused only long enough to double-check their Beretta pistols and make sure the silencers were properly mounted.

Then they glanced at each other, nodded, and turned the corner, walking into the room where the guests were still assembled, talking among themselves about what had already happened that night, downing drinks to calm their nerves.

The attendees didn't at first notice the intrusion. But then somebody gasped, somebody else cried out, and the rest of the crowd turned.

"Wait!"

"Who're you?"

"What're you doing here?"

Other pointless questions and screams. Emotion . . . such a waste of time and energy, Bob thought.

"No one touch a cell phone," he called in a calm voice. "I want everybody on your knees, and lace your hands behind your head. If you don't, you'll get shot."

No one did anything for a moment—which was typical—and then a bulky man, an older guy in a suit, strode his way. "I don't know what this—"

Bob shot him in the head twice, blood flecking the wall and the clothes of those standing near. More screams and gasps.

A pretty, dark-haired teenage girl in a dark blue dress, horror on her face, ran toward the body.

Bob raised his pistol to shoot her too, but she controlled herself, dropped to her knees, then put her hands behind her neck.

Crying, gasping, begging, everyone else followed her lead.

Bob then did a fast head count. *Hell . . .* two of the guests were missing. Frank noticed the same. Bob pointed his gun at the girl again. "Where are the others?" he called to the crowd. "Tell me or I shoot her in five seconds."

But no more bloodletting was necessary.

Just then two men turned the corner from a dark corridor leading off the tower and froze at the sight of the two intruders. Frank, the closer of the robbers, trained his weapon on them.

One of the men, whom the robber took to be in better shape than his friend, glanced at the body, then at Frank, then at Bob. They got the impression the man was quickly analyzing the scene. Bob would need to keep a special eye on him.

When the two new guests were on their knees and Bob was covering them all, Frank carefully frisked everyone. When he identified Justine Olegard, he said, "I need the second half of the code to the special exhibit room—I have the first half. The wall alarm codes too."

"But—"

"We showed you we have no problem killing anybody. I want the code now, or I'll kill . . . her." He stepped forward and pointed the gun at an attractive thirtysomething, blond and pretty.

"No!" cried the burly man beside her.

"Don, don't say anything to him," she said. "Don't make him mad."

The guy with her, Don apparently, shouted to Justine, "Give him the code! Please!"

Justine nodded. Bob pulled her to her feet and walked her to the door of the special exhibit room. He stopped her at the keypad and typed in the first half of the code. Then she typed in the rest. A faint buzz and they pushed the double doors open, then stepped into the exhibit hall. She flicked the lights on. The place was filled with old sketches and prints that Bob knew must have been worth millions.

The crop was free for the harvest; it was time to earn his $500,000 fee.

Bob pulled a walkie-talkie off his belt and hit the transmit button. "We're secure," he radioed the fake paramedics.

A moment later a crackling answer: "Roger, we're on our way."

Bob led Justine back into the main room. He deposited her back on her knees. Then he caught a glimpse of that man he'd noticed earlier, the big guy. Bob walked up to him. "What's your name?"

"Jon Nunn."

Bob stared down coldly at him but Nunn held his eyes without a problem. In fact he was looking back in a funny way, studying him, it seemed. With the shower hat, the bootees, the face mask, and the jumpsuit, there was no chance of getting a description. But Bob had an odd feeling that this Nunn was committing some kind of a description to memory, looking for attributes that could later be used in an investigation or at trial: how Bob walked, how he stood, left hand versus right hand, height, weight.

Time to kill this prick.

He lifted the gun. Started to pull the trigger.

Then the elevator door opened and the paramedics walked into the room.

Bob frowned. Shit, hadn't they gotten the instructions right? They were supposed to bring the carts in to haul out the art. Time was at a premium; as it was, they'd still have to load the artwork into the ambulance and fake crime scene van.

He started, "We need the carts—" but his voice froze.

These weren't the men he'd hired! And they were clearly wearing body armor under their uniforms.

Police! Shit!

With a slam in his gut he understood that he'd been outsmarted. Somebody had figured out that a robbery was going down and called the police. The cops had arrived silently, found the phony paramedics outside, overpowered them, then dressed two officers in medic overalls as point men for a takedown team.

Which would of course be sprinting up the stairs right now.

The two cops crouched, weapons drawn.

"Shoot, shoot, shoot!" Bob cried to his partner, who started firing toward the two officers, the ring of brass on the stone floor nearly as loud as the silenced report of his Beretta.

Bob's strategy was to wound as many in the crowd as he could, forcing the tactical team to stop and give them aid. He could get out through the back, via an emergency route he'd planned earlier. Frank too, if he was able, but that was up to him.

The cop closest to him had his back turned, aiming at Frank. Bob lifted his gun to shoot the cop in the spine, but as he did, he heard a slap of feet behind him. And thought, *Oh, hell* . . .

An instant later he was tumbling to the floor after a shoulder caught him low and hard, right in the kidneys. A flash of yellow light burst in his eyes, an explosion of pain. Bob gasped, breath completely knocked out of him.

Nunn—of course it was Nunn—ripped the pistol from his hand. As Bob, writhing on the floor, reached desperately for the weapon, Nunn delivered an elbow to his nose. He collapsed, stunned and groaning in pain, blood spewing from his nose. Frank noticed him and spun around, shooting, but his aim was wild and he missed his target, instead shooting his partner, Bob, in the chest.

Nunn stood his ground, drew a target, and dropped Frank with three well-placed rounds. Then he immediately spun back to cover Bob, but Bob was already dead.

Being a cop is more about talking than shooting or chasing down criminals.

Well, not just talking: asking questions.

The next day, Jon Nunn was at the museum again. Captain Harvey Meyer, who was leading the investigation into the previous night's attempted robbery, had called him earlier in the afternoon. The two men had known each other back when Nunn was still at the SFPD, and when Meyer heard Nunn had been there last night during the attempted robbery, he asked Nunn to be present while he questioned Justine Olegard at her office in the museum. Nunn knew from his time on the force that Meyer had a reputation for the unconventional and didn't bother to question why Meyer would want an ex-cop there, he just showed up.

Justine, it seemed, had called both Tony Olsen and, to Nunn's surprise and dismay, Stan Ballard to her meeting with Meyer. Justine explained Ballard's presence by saying he was the only lawyer she knew. She hadn't been accused of anything per se, but the number of felonies that had gone down in the tower yesterday meant that there were plenty of penal-code violations to go around for everyone. Nunn hadn't even been aware that Justine and Ballard knew each other and realized it must have been from her time with Christopher Thomas. Still it was odd that Ballard, an estate lawyer, would agree to be there and not refer her to someone else. But Nunn suspected Ballard was there for Ballard only.

Justine was going out of her way to be cooperative, but there didn't seem to be anything she could add to what Meyer already knew.

"I'm sorry," Justine said. "I spent all night looking through security tapes and poring over reports about, you know, people casing out the museum over the past few months. I couldn't find any pictures or descriptions of them." Her voice was soft, eyes distant, and Nunn knew it was because she'd had to use as references the pictures shot last night of the dead thieves. Her boss, Alex Hultgren, had also been killed.

"Who called the police?" she asked Meyer.

Meyer pointed to Nunn.

Nunn explained how he'd been near the staircase after Haile had been hurt and looked down into the lobby and thought it was odd to have crime scene officers there. Then he heard the screams in the tower room and realized the museum was being hit.

Meyer asked Justine, "Are you sure you've never seen those men before?"

"I don't think so. I've looked at those pictures so many times I can't be sure of anything anymore."

Meyer looked at Nunn questioningly, but Nunn's mind was elsewhere. He kept thinking about the text message he'd received earlier in the day. It didn't seem possible.

His BlackBerry buzzed, Nunn picked it up, then he looked at Meyer. "Can I talk to you outside for a second?"

They stepped out into the hallway. "Look, on my way over here I got a text from a friend which gave me a new theory about what happened here last night. "

"And?" Meyer asked.

"You're going to think I'm nuts, Harvey."

"Tell me."

"My friend's down in the lobby. I'm going to have him come up here. I'll let him tell you. It's quite a story."

27

KATHY REICHS

S taccato footsteps clicked across marble.

Everyone's eyes swung toward a figure framing up in the door.

The man wore a Duke sweatshirt and cargo pants tucked into plat-form boots. His left hand gripped a leather briefcase that looked as if it left Spain before the civil war.

Nunn made introductions. "Gentlemen, Justine—may I present Dr. Ignatius McGee."

McGee was leading-man handsome, with a square jaw, blue eyes, and hair that left Brosnan in the styling-gel dust. Only one unfortunate base-pair sequence barred him from a star on the Hollywood walk. If he stood ramrod straight, which he was, Ignatius McGee was no more than four foot six. Two of those inches belonged to the boots.

Palms were pressed, then the group sat. McGee too, left ankle crossed onto opposite knee, right foot not quite touching the floor.

Everyone dragged chairs into a semicircle, grad-seminar style, except for Stan Ballard, who was leaning against the wall, stone-faced.

Nunn got right to the point.

"Dr. McGee is a forensic anthropologist. Everyone clear on what that is?"

"Bones," Justine Olegard said. "But not old ones."

Nunn swept an upturned palm in McGee's direction. "Take it away."

"The answer's spot-on," said McGee. "I'm a specialist in the human skeleton." The accent was blue-collar Boston, the voice surprisingly deep for a man McGee's size. "I work the dead too far gone for a Y incision—the burned, mummified, decomposed, dismembered, mutilated, and skeletonized. I dig 'em up, ID 'em, determine how they bought it and when."

Olsen rocketed forward, fingers squeezing his armrests. "You exhumed Christopher Thomas."

McGee studied him, then slid his eyes left.

"An exhumation wasn't possible," Nunn explained. "At my request, Dr. McGee analyzed the dossier compiled at the time of Thomas's death."

"Wasn't everything written in German?" Olsen asked.

"I had the reports translated," McGee said.

"And you found proof of Rosemary's innocence!" Olsen said.

Irritation filed the edge of McGee's rich baritone. "Who else thinks he knows how my movie ends?"

Olsen flicked an angry glance at Nunn. *Who the hell is this guy?*

Nunn raised two placating palms. "Let Dr. McGee walk us through his findings without interruption. Then you can ask all the questions you want, okay?"

Face locked into neutral, Olsen settled back.

Twisting sideways, McGee swung his case to the desktop and withdrew two folders, one brown and battered, the other bright pink and OfficeMax new. Setting the former aside, he flipped the cover on the latter.

"The original paperwork is here if anyone *sprecht Deutsche*. My comments will focus on my interpretation of the evidence."

Not pausing to gauge reaction, McGee pulled a multipage document from the folder.

"According to the pathologist"—he flipped to the back—"one Bruno Muntz, the remains were soup and bones, rendering visual identification impossible. Most of the teeth were toast."

McGee's gaze crawled the faces of those fanned out before him. Frowning, he ran a hand across his perfectly formed jaw. "Muntz was unable to determine cause of death. Understandable. Due to decomp and damage inflicted by the maiden, the body was hamburger. No Germanic pun intended."

The corners of McGee's mouth twitched in what might have been a grin.

No one smiled back.

"Where Muntz erred big-time was in failing to solicit the opinion of a specialist. In going solo on the anthro he jumped into dung way over his head."

McGee took a mustard-colored envelope from his briefcase, unwound the string, and fanned out a dozen autopsy photos onto the desktop.

Four chairs scooted forward as one.

"Fortunately, Muntz had a kick-ass photographer. This is a close-up showing what remained of the victim's left hand. Missing from each digit is the distal phalange, the little arrow-shaped bugger that underlies the fingertip."

McGee rotated a print for the benefit of those opposite. "Anything strike you as odd?"

No one ventured an opinion.

Snatching up a pen, McGee pointed to the tubular bones that had once formed fingers. "Look at the first four sets of phalanges."

Everyone did.

McGee rotated another photo, this one showing the bones of a single digit.

"These are the bones of the left fifth finger after removal of the soft tissue. Again, look at the phalanges."

"The fingertip is present," said Olsen.

"Yes. This was the digit that yielded the one partial print. What else?"

"These bones seem skinnier and smoother than the ones in the other fingers. And they flare out more at the ends," said Justine.

"Head of the class, little lady."

Normally, Olegard would have bristled at the "little lady" endearment. Given McGee's stature, she let it slide.

"What does it mean?" Olsen asked, eyes glued to the photos.

McGee ignored him and produced a magnifying lens from the briefcase. He handed it to Justine, along with the first autopsy shot of digits one through four.

"Note there are tiny slashes at the ends of each of the first four middle phalanges."

Leaning forward, McGee reached out and shifted his pen from thumb, to pointer, to middle, to ring man. Justine followed its progress with the lens.

"The horizontal lines?" she asked.

"Yes. Those are cut marks created by a nonserrated blade. The marks are absent on the *middle* phalange of the pinkie but present on its *proximal* phalange, the one at the near end. Cut marks are also present on the fifth metacarpal, adjacent to where the finger articulates with the hand."

"So the left pinkie was the only digit to retain its tip and to have no cut marks at that end?" Justine said. She addressed no one in particular, as though sifting data in her mind. "The left pinkie was also the only digit to have cut marks at the end where the finger joined the hand."

"Again, the little lady nailed it."

The little lady handed the photo and lens to Olsen.

"May I hypothesize?" Justine asked, encouraged by McGee's smile in her direction.

McGee dipped his chin.

Justine took it as assent. "The fingertips were removed from every digit but the left pinkie. That finger was severed intact."

"Bravo."

Meyer performed an eye roll directed at Nunn. *Are you believing this lunatic?* "You're saying the killer hacked off nine of Thomas's fingertips but cut off his left pinkie and left it intact?"

"No," McGee said. "I am not."

Meyer's brows reached for his hairline.

"Moving on. Muntz based his positive ID on three things." McGee raised a hand and moved a stumpy thumb from finger to finger. "First, the presence of a belt buckle belonging to Christopher Thomas. Second, a match to a partial print taken from a left fifth finger. Third, consistency between the skeletal profile obtained from the remains and Christopher Thomas's known age, sex, race, and height."

McGee replaced the hand-bone shots with views of the skull. As before, he pen-pointed at features in the photo.

"Short, globular head shape. Wide face, flaring cheekbones. Broad palate and nasal opening. Complicated zigzag suture pattern. Accessory bone at the back of the skull. To me that configuration screams Mongoloid."

Blank looks.

"Those traits indicate Asian or Native American ancestry." Slowly, teacher to dull pupils.

"You saying Thomas was Asian?" Tony Olsen made no effort to mask his skepticism.

McGee ignored the interruption. "Muntz made another error. In calculating stature he relied on only one bone, the femur. He then chose an inappropriate formula for performing a regression equation and misinterpreted the statistical significance of the estimate that equation generated. I remeasured leg-bone lengths, using the scale provided in the photographs, and recalculated stature applying statistics appropriate to Asians. My height estimate for the decedent is 162 to 168 centimeters. Christopher Thomas measured 183 centimeters."

"What about the print?" Tiny vessels had blossomed in Tony Olsen's cheeks. "Fingerprints don't lie."

"I have to admit that bothered me too. 'Iggy,' I said to myself, 'it doesn't add up. Or does it? What's the pattern? You got a boatload of dots, now link them together.'"

Again, a stumpy thumb worked stumpy fingers, ticking off points.

"Dot: the vic is supposed to be a tall white guy, but his skull says he's Asian and his leg bones say he's too short.

"Dot: the left-fifth-finger bones look different from all the other finger bones, smoother and more gracile in the shafts and broader at the ends.

"Dot: every fingertip was removed but the one on the left fifth finger.

"Dot: nine digits were reduced to bone, but the left fifth finger retained its soft tissue."

McGee did his best at crossing his arms on his chest. It didn't go well.

"Then I remembered. The glycerin."

Mystified looks all around.

McGee scanned the text, then read aloud from Muntz's autopsy report: "'One digit was deeply embedded in the femoroacetabular junction.'"

Not a single *Aha!* expression.

Scooching forward with an alternating cheek-to-cheek maneuver, McGee teased a photo from the assortment cascading over the desktop, grabbed the lens, and gestured everyone close.

"The bone in this shot forms the left half of the pelvis. That deep, round hole below the blade is where the head of the thighbone sits. The joint is called the femoroacetabular junction. That socket is protected by very thick muscle. Soft tissue is often preserved there long after the rest of the flesh sloughs. You with me?"

Nods all around.

Satisfied, McGee positioned the lens over the pelvic photo.

"What do you see circling the hip socket?"

"Cut marks," said Olsen.

"Exactly."

McGee laid down the lens. Justine picked it up and drew her nose and the glass to within inches of the print. The others assumed listening postures.

"Here's my take. Bruno Muntz screwed up the ID. The man in the iron maiden was *not* Christopher Thomas. The victim was an Asian male of roughly Thomas's age and size but slightly shorter in stature. The man's teeth were destroyed to prevent dental identification. His fingertips were removed to eliminate prints. His left fifth finger was replaced by that of someone else. Incisions were made into the gluteal mass of the Asian victim, rather clumsy ones, I might add. Thomas's finger was coated with glycerin and fat to retard decomposition, then jammed through the muscle deep into the dead man's hip socket."

"And Muntz blew this whole phalange-bone thing?" Tony Olsen flapped a hand at the photos. "The missing fingertips?"

"Distal phalanges are tiny, often missed in recovery. If he noticed their absence, which I doubt, the good doctor probably thought they'd gotten lost. Perhaps he didn't bother to sift through all the sludge in the maiden. Thomas's belt, with recognizable buckle, was placed on the victim. The body, *sans* fingertips but *cum* Thomas's pinkie, was sealed inside the iron maiden. The apparatus was crated and shipped. The rest is history."

"The mismatched bones? The cut marks?" Tony Olsen's cheeks were now the color of raspberry sherbet.

"Muntz was a pathologist, not an anthropologist. The man overstepped his abilities."

"But—" Justine sat forward. "One of Christopher Thomas's teeth was found inside the iron maiden, wasn't it? And that was proved."

"Right again, little lady." McGee gave her an odd, lopsided smile. "It *was* Christopher Thomas's tooth. And it surely did *not* come out of the Asian man's mouth."

Silence.

Olsen was the first to break it. "If you're right, someone took brutal measures to ensure that the victim would be misidentified as Christopher Thomas."

McGee nodded.

"Who?" Tony Olsen.

"Why?" Meyer.

McGee's shoulders rose and dropped. *Beats me.*

All eyes turned to Jon Nunn.

But Nunn was looking at Stan Ballard.

It was Olsen who voiced the question on everyone's mind: "Then where the hell is Christopher Thomas?"

28

R. L. STINE

know where to find them. I know more about *everything* than all of them.

I found Peter Heusen easily. No prob. Rented a rubber dinghy with a putt-putt motor and sailed out to his cabin cruiser moored near the St. Francis Yacht Club.

Typical San Francisco day, foggy and damp, the water choppy, blue-brown under the clouds. I could see the Golden Gate Bridge off to my right, but I didn't come for sightseeing.

Twelve years later, and I knew how happy Heusen would be to see me.

Peter must be in his fifties now, I figured. And richer than God. Thanks in part to me.

As I came closer, I saw him seated by himself at a table on the back deck. He had a wineglass in his hand. He stood up when he saw me and stepped to the rail.

"Remember me?" I shouted. He didn't look much older. Money'll do that for you. He was in a white admiral's jacket. He had a blue yacht-ing cap pulled down on his head. What *was* this? Halloween?

I couldn't see if he still had his hair. But he looked tanned and fit.

Of course he recognized me. He began waving his arms in front of him, like signaling an alarm. "Ruby? I don't want to see you!" he shouted. "Turn around! Go back! You're not welcome here."

Of *course* he didn't want to see me. I scrambled onto the deck and tied the dinghy to the side. The sun came out for a moment, and every-thing started to gleam. Like a spotlight shining on me. Time for my close-up.

I thought maybe he had some flunkies who would come push me off the yacht. But he appeared to be alone.

"I have nothing to say to you," he said as I stepped up to his table. "You're not welcome here. Why have you come?"

"Peter, come on. I thought you'd be more friendly." I couldn't keep a smile off my face. "I mean, I did a very big favor for you."

Beneath the cap, his forehead creased. His pale eyes narrowed. "Favor for me? I don't know what you're talking about. I know who you are. But you never did anything for me."

"Why, just the other day, some guy finds me, starts asking me questions about the favor I did for you."

"What?" Peter squealed.

"Don't worry, I had him taken care of."

Peter looked worried now.

"Did you really think that lousy ten K was going to last me forever?" I sat down at the table. I picked up his wineglass and took a long sip. "Is this a Chablis?"

"I can call the harbor police. I've had intruders before."

I picked up a biscuit from the silver bread basket. Still warm. I took a bite. "Are you really going to pretend you don't know anything?"

He stood over me. His lips began to twitch. "I don't have to pretend. I didn't have anything to do with it."

"Amnesia? Let me help you." I decided to go for it. "The body in the iron maiden?"

Heusen swallowed. But he didn't blink. "Excuse me? Are you insane?"

"Jeez, how long you going to keep up this charade?"

"I'm going to call the patrol now."

"Oh, I know who you're going to call—and it won't be no police."

He made a move toward the cabin, but I grabbed his arm. "Just sit down. Let's be civilized, Peter. Tell you what. I'll tell you a story, and you sit there and pretend you don't already know it." I had to pull him down to the chair.

"I'll give you five minutes," he said, still playacting, but he was sweating. "What's your story?"

"Yeah, let's say it's a story," I said. "Let's pretend it's not all total truth."

He stared at the wineglass in my hand. I tilted it to my mouth and drank the rest.

"Peter, let's say there was once an iron maiden in a museum in

San Francisco. Let's say it was built hundreds of years ago, but used recently—"

"I'm not a history buff," Heusen interrupted, shaking his head. "You're wasting your time."

"Well, I did my homework—*after* the fact." I ran my finger around the rim of the empty wineglass.

Heusen started to his feet. "You're out of here."

I pushed him back down. I had to be a little rough. I could see a flash of fear on his face. His tan had disappeared.

"Let's say there was a dead man stuffed inside the thing?"

"That's very old news," Heusen muttered. "Why did you come here?"

I brought my face up close to his. "Is it old news, Peter? What if I told the story—the whole story? What if I call the police?"

That got to him. I saw two red circles blossom on his cheeks. "Why would you do that, Artie?" His eyes danced around. As if he were look-ing for a way to escape. "It, it was a lot of years ago. Why would you go to the police now?"

"Do I look desperate to you?" I asked, leaning close to him again. "Well, I am. I *am* desperate. I know what you think. You think I'm a piece of low-life scum who crawled onto your big yacht like a cock-roach. But I know some pretty big words for a cockroach. Like *accessory.* You know, like in *accessory to murder?*"

Heusen was breathing hard. Under the admiral's jacket, his chest heaved up and down. "You wouldn't dare," he whispered. "You would turn yourself in? Admit to murder? And drag me down with you?"

I nodded. I was enjoying this. "I told you. I'm desperate."

Heusen's shoulders slumped. He narrowed his eyes until they were thin slits. "What do you want, Artie? Money?"

"Yes. Good guess. I want money. A lot of it."

"Okay. Okay. Money. And then you'll go away?"

That went very well.

Now I had one more call I wanted to make. One more call before I left town for good. I had a fat wad of money from Heusen. But I wanted more. A lot more.

I needed to make the call. Call it closure. Or call it my sadistic streak. Or maybe a victory lap. Ha-ha. And more money.

I had gotten the number out of that cowardly worm Peter.

I punched it in eagerly.

"Hello?" I recognized the voice right away.

"I have information on Christopher Thomas."

A silence. Then: "Who?"

"Don't you recognize my voice?"

"You—you have the wrong number."

"I don't think so," I said.

"I'm sorry. You have the wrong number." He hung up.

I laughed. It felt good to laugh.

"Call you back later," I said into the silent phone.

I pulled on a jacket and headed out.

29

JEFFERY DEAVER

With his four-fingered hand, Christopher Thomas poured ancient Rémy Martin cognac into a glass obviously bought at Wal-Mart. The Trompe l'Oeil Hotel, a good one, had scrimped on a few details. Still, it made sense. It was logical. *Nice booze, cheap delivery.*

He glanced into the large window at his own reflection. Even after nearly ten years with his new appearance, he was never completely used to this version of himself. Not that he disliked what he saw; the plastic surgeon had been an artist.

Dr. 90210 . . .

A zip code, he reflected, whose numbers represented about one-third of the doctor's bill.

Now he looked past his image and gazed through the early-evening dusk.

He was angry and he was troubled. He'd heard on the news, of course, about the bungled robbery at the museum last night and had gotten brief text messages from Peter Heusen about the debacle. The sloppy keyboarding suggested the man had been drinking.

Thomas sighed. The theft had been so perfectly planned, the haul so astonishing . . . When Heusen had heard that Tony Olsen was putting together a memorial for Rosemary, Christopher and Heusen had immediately put together a plan that would allow them to snag one of the biggest troves in the history of art: works by da Vinci and Michelangelo, mostly, but also by Rembrandt, Watteau, Rubens, Tiepolo, and de La Tour. Christopher had buyers for virtually all of the pieces in place, and the net to him, after expenses, would have been millions.

But it'd all turned to dust. . . .

And topping off the tragedy, just today he'd received that phone call.

"I have information on Christopher Thomas. . . ."

Information? Christopher Thomas had been murdered by his wife and stuffed into an iron maiden. Christopher Thomas was dead and buried. Christopher Thomas was a faded memory—a despised or hated or, in a few cases, envied memory. That's all the information he wanted anyone to have.

But he knew the caller.

A noise behind him intruded. He swiveled around to see Tanya— no, her name was *Taylor,* right?—pulling her tiny dress back on. When he'd yanked the handful of Lycra off her an hour ago and flung it to the floor, he'd been focusing on her supple body and trying to forget about the failed heist. The sex was supposed to distract him from the loss; it had zero effect, and he blamed her for that.

"Oooh," she said, eyeing his cognac, "I wanna cosmo."

"No. Leave."

She blinked. "Well, you're not very nice." In a little girl's singsong tone.

He walked away, ignoring her. He heard her pull together her things and leave, sighing loudly.

Who cared? There'd be more Tanyas. Wait . . . *Taylors.*

He called Heusen again, using the untraceable, prepaid mobiles that they relied on in their operations.

Finally an answering click.

"Hello?" said the slurred voice.

"You haven't been answering me," Thomas snapped.

"The police've been taking statements from everybody."

"You've been drinking. Now is not the time to get drunk. What's going on? Do they suspect anything?"

"About us? I don't know. I didn't hang around at the museum to find out."

"Where are you? What're you doing now?"

"Sitting on the boat and getting drunk."

"Well," Thomas said slowly, "I think we'll be fine. There's been no personal contact?"

"Absolutely no connection."

"How'd they figure it out?"

"I don't know."

Heusen was a snake and a drunk, but he wasn't fundamentally stu- pid. After all, the two men had been stealing art for the past decade and had managed to avoid the smartest cops and insurance investigators in the business. Thomas said, "I think everything'll be fine. We'll let the dust settle. Lay low for a while."

"Yeah, lay low."

Thomas disconnected, resisting the urge to pitch his glass against the wall. He sat down and stared out the window.

Thinking back to the days when Christopher Thomas had an ever-growing need for money and mistresses. And all the while Rosemary had been growing more and more impatient with him, less willing to dole out her family money to him.

So Thomas began to reconsider his future. As a curator, he'd forged connections with shady businessmen and criminals around the world and had learned about the huge market for private art collectors.

Tidy couple this, that.

People thought that some paintings were so famous that they were safe from theft. Ah, but they didn't know about men—always men, it seemed—in Saudi Arabia, Jordan, Iran, China, Japan, Malaysia, and India with limitless funds and a lust for owning genius. They never showed the art in public; sometimes they didn't show it at all. The passion was about possessing what someone else could not.

And so Thomas came up with his idea, inspired by the iron maiden. He and Heusen, with the help of Artie Ruby, who worked for Christopher, would fake his death and slip another body into the device, and Ruby would arrange to have the maiden shipped to Germany. In a bit of medical trickery, Christopher had to break off one of his teeth *and* cut off his own finger, placing it strategically in the dead guy's thigh so the body would be identified as his. Hell, what was one finger and a chipped tooth compared to escape from his debtors and billions? Besides if he hadn't taken such elaborate measures to ensure his own safety, he'd probably have been killed years ago by one of his "connections."

But framing Rosemary had been Peter's idea. Thomas went along with it reluctantly because he had to. He needed Peter. Even now, twelve years later, the memory of how he'd smeared her blouse with his blood and torn a button off and placed it with the dead body disturbed him occasionally. Still, better Rosemary should die than he. That's probably how she would have wanted it anyhow. That was always the problem with her in the first place, the more she gave him, the more he despised her. She'd never understood that. *Poor Rosemary.*

And so Peter Heusen, the tipsy socialite, and Christopher Thomas, the former curator with an eye for the art market and connections, made a perfect team. They despised each other, of course. But so did half the Allied commanders during World War II (Thomas loved his history). Over the past decade they'd stolen hundreds of millions' worth of art and artifacts and placed them privately overseas—generally one or two pieces at a time: a Renoir from a university museum in upstate New York, a jewel-encrusted medieval chalice from a fashion magnate in Milan, a Picasso from a foundation in Barcelona, a Manet from the secret pied-à-terre that a philanthropist kept for his mistress (no police reports on *that* one, unsurprisingly).

And there were more to come.

But right now he had one thing on his mind: escape. As fast as he could. Jon Nunn was no longer a cop, but he was still nosing around. After the botched heist it was only a matter of time before Nunn learned of Heusen's involvement, and the path would lead to Thomas himself, if it hadn't already.

Then there was the phone call.

A fast, clean escape wasn't as difficult, or unanticipated, as it seemed. Christopher Thomas had always known that he risked being found out and that he might have to bail at any moment. He had an escape plan, millions in cash, gold in international banks, his safe house in Brazil.

He placed a call to his private charter service and had them stand by.

Thomas now strode into his bedroom and pulled the American Touristers out from under the bed. (Vuitton? He didn't even own any. What is somebody going to steal, a suitcase from Macy's or a $1,000 one? *Why are people such idiots?*)

In five minutes he'd packed all his clothes. He'd drive himself to the Oakland airport, leave the rental car in long-term parking, where it wouldn't be noticed for two or three months.

Thomas looked around the hotel room. Where was that other suitcase?

The doorbell rang.

He looked through the peephole. Grimacing, he opened the door.

Artie Ruby stood there, hip cocked, looking . . . *jaunty* was the word that came to mind. The man was wearing a rumpled suit that he might've owned when they'd first met more than a decade ago. He blinked uncertainly as he gazed at Thomas. Then his eyes took in the deformed hand. "Chris! It *is* you!"

A sigh. "And you're the one who called, Artie."

"Holy moley. I never saw the new face. You look . . . Jesus, what'd they do, move bones around or something?"

Thomas looked over the man's shoulder.

"Don't worry. I wasn't followed. Took me hours 'cause I doubled back three times."

Satisfied, Thomas muttered, "How did you find me?"

"Little bird sang."

"What the fuck does that mean?"

"I went to see Peter. He was drunk and he let slip where he thought you were. Relax! I see that look. I didn't tell nobody! I've kept every-thing a secret all these years." Artie snickered. "That Peter, just can't keep his mouth shut."

"No, he can't. That's true."

Artie was looking around, impressed. The hotel room was twice the size of Artie's entire apartment. His shabby shoes left mud stains on the carpet.

"So?" Thomas asked because the script called for it.

"We're adults, right, Chris? Businessmen?"

"No. I am, and you're nothing. Now get to the point."

"Ha. Funny. Okay, I know that some shit is going to hit the fan pretty soon. I want to get out of the country."

"And you want the number for the airport shuttle."

Artie's face hardened. "You know what I'm here about."

"Money, of course. So you're blackmailing me."

Artie paused, as if offended. "I just want to be compensated, like everybody else."

"You already have been."

"But not enough." Artie grinned, cocky.

"How much?"

"Enough to live on for the rest of my life."

"That could be pocket change."

Artie's eyes widened and he blurted, "If you hurt me, there's a letter I've written and given to . . . to somebody. If anything happens, it gets delivered. It's got everything in it, Chris—faking your death, getting the body into the iron maiden, shipping it off to Germany."

"Well, I'm not in the mood to argue with you. How much are you talking?"

People invariably underbid themselves.

"Five million."

Thomas adamantly shook his head. "You're crazy. I could do one, maybe."

"Three."

"Two."

Artie grumbled, "Okay. But cash."

"I can get it."

"No way, José. I mean *now*."

"Why do you use all those clichés? 'José'?"

"Huh?"

"Never mind. Um, Artie, I mean, I can *get* the money from the other room. Now."

The man blinked.

Thomas added, "But the problem is this letter you were mentioning. You spend the two million and you're going to come back for more."

"No, I won't."

"You say that but *of course* you would." A frown. "Wait. Here's a thought. I'll pay you two million now. Then when you're safe somewhere, I'll meet this guy who has the letter—your brother-in-law or lawyer or . . . whoever—"

"Yeah, yeah, it's . . . a lawyer I know."

"I'll meet him, and if he gives me the letter unopened, I'll give him another million for you. How's that sound?"

"Yeah?" Artie rubbed his face and looked like a kid who'd just been told school was canceled for the day. "Deal." He stuck out an unclean hand.

Thomas ignored the gesture. Walking into the bedroom, he heard Artie say, "Man, that's one kick-ass bar. You mind if I help myself to a short one?"

"Go right ahead."

Christopher Thomas *did* have several million dollars in the bedroom—an amount that probably weighed more than scrawny Artie was able to lift, let alone cart off. But instead of the money, Thomas walked to his dresser and withdrew a Colt Python .357 Magnum. Though the diameter of the bullet was smaller than a .38, .44, or .45, the load was massive, and the hollow-point slug would mushroom instantly upon hitting human flesh and fling the victim to the floor as if struck by a car.

Hand at his side, he returned to the living room, where he found

Artie not with a "short one" but with a glass full to the rim with single-malt scotch that cost $800 a bottle. He was slavering like a spaniel.

"For a dead man, you got some nice shit here—" Artie gasped as he saw the gun. The glass crashed to the floor. "No! Don't shoot me!"

"I've often said people should die just because they're stupid. . . . Blackmailing *me,* Artie?"

"The letter! I'm not kidding. It tells everything!"

Thomas could only laugh. A minute ago Artie had told him how to find the letter—if there even *was* a letter. And later in the night, before anybody noticed Artie was missing and Thomas was long gone, he would have some of his minders comb through Artie's apartment and get the name of every lawyer he'd ever had contact with. The muscle would make sure the letter, if it existed, was recovered unopened.

Or maybe they'd just kill the shyster.

Either way . . .

Thomas drew back the hammer of the weapon with a click and aimed.

"No! Please!"

He began to pull the trigger.

30

JEFF ABBOTT

The gathering last night had felt haunted by the restless ghosts of Rosemary and Christopher Thomas. Now the forensic anthropologist's words had shoved one of those ghosts from shadow into light, dissolving him. Because Christopher Thomas might well still walk the earth.

Jon Nunn felt breath surge back into his chest. The numbness that had clutched him since he'd realized Rosemary could well have been innocent began to ease its awful grip.

But if Christopher Thomas wasn't dead, where was he?

The meeting had now broken up, and everyone had begun to drift away, and Nunn knew that too many questions and uncertainties clouded their minds. He watched them go, not wanting to talk to anyone. No one spoke to him, no one met his gaze. What kind of detective was he that he could have been fooled? Never mind the evidence. He'd always doubted Rosemary's guilt, but he'd ignored the doubts. Full speed ahead to conviction, to make everyone except himself—and Rosemary, tragically—content and certain that justice had been served.

A hot, sudden anger at the waste of it all tore through him and he leaned against the wall. He closed his eyes, then opened them again.

A painting hung to his left, a wild, modernist smear of blue and orange and white in a chaotic tango. A painting, a creation, with a meaning and a pattern he didn't understand.

Creation. Pattern. Death. Rosemary's death, and the death of his own marriage and career, that extraordinary lie had been someone's creation, crafted with the careful touch of an artist, with an underlying pattern, a foundation, that he'd failed to see.

Why?

A framing of this sort implied cold calculation, not passion. And for such a crime, he had one rule that he should always have obeyed with unbending focus: follow the money.

In this case, the money took the form of one sodden, rotten Peter Heusen.

Nunn stepped away from the chaotic modernist painting. He looked around, everyone was gone: the living and the ghosts of the twisted, lying past. Maybe everyone had fled from him, the cop who had built the case against Rosemary, the cop who had been so wrong. He must smell of failure and regret and incompetence. A wave of nausea surged through him and he thought, *I am going to find out the truth.* An ember suddenly fanned into flame in his heart. *I am going to find out the truth.*

Maybe Rosemary was innocent. Maybe Rosemary had killed the person the world assumed was Christopher.

He wanted to know.

Follow the money. He wanted to talk to Peter.

His footsteps echoed in the emptiness. The painting watched him as though measuring his resolve. He nodded at the security guard waiting for him to leave. He exited the McFall, out into the damp, foggy blanket of night. The wet chill cut through him. The glowing stars were smears behind the clouds.

He saw a figure in the shadows of the looming art museum. Along the deserted sidewalk, walking with a momentary unsteadiness: Peter?

Nunn hurried forward, walking on the balls of his feet, silently.

The fog parted, cut by a knife of streetlight, and he saw it wasn't Peter, it was Stan Ballard, reaching into his pocket for a cell phone, bringing it up to his face.

Maybe Sarah is calling him, Nunn thought. Sarah preferred a liar and a scumbag like Stan Ballard over him. *What's wrong with me?* Nunn thought. *What's wrong with her?* Their marriage seemed like one of those modern paintings, the foundation lost in the wild chaos. Had Sarah ever loved him?

Ballard turned into an alleyway, eschewing the warm comforts of a café and a bar another block down the fogged street.

Ballard wanted privacy in the wake of the shocking revelations. Interesting.

Nunn stopped at the corner, risked a glance down the alleyway. Dumpsters and crates from the café lined the pavement. He could see Ballard, moving behind a Dumpster, and Nunn hurried forward, his hand going to his gun, the relic of the cop he used to be. Odd that the urge to wear a sidearm and bring handcuffs to the museum had taken him: the visible proof that he still thought himself a police officer, although he wasn't. But he was grateful for his idiosyncrasy now.

Ballard's voice made a low hiss into the phone: "It's all going to come out, what we did to make money off the estate." Panic touching the words, poisoning them. He sensed the presence behind him and turned, so Nunn simply stuck his service piece into Ballard's cheek.

Ballard froze, pale with shock.

Nunn put a finger to his lips. Ballard stayed mute. Nunn snapped fingers at the phone. Ballard handed it over.

Nunn put the phone to his ears. The rant blurted into his ear: "Shut up, shut *up* about it." Peter Heusen, slurring words in a whiskey drawl.

Nunn made a noise of assent.

"I don't care, Stan. We're safe, we're fine, we're, best of all, we're cool. We're beyond cool. We're icy. We are non-globally warmed." Peter's voice cracked into hard, brittle laughter. "It doesn't matter whatever you say that CSI guy said. It doesn't matter. Because we can't be caught. The money is yours, mine, and ours."

Nunn grunted, and as Peter launched into another drunken tirade of reassurance, Nunn covered the phone and whispered to Ballard. "Tell him to stay put. Tell him you want to come to see him. Now. Don't take no for an answer."

"You won't . . ." Ballard's gaze darted to the gun against his cheek.

"I will," Nunn whispered. "Nothing to lose, man. You made sure of that. You're the one with everything to lose, Stan. Do as I say." Nunn put the phone back up to Ballard's face.

"Yes, Peter, I'm here." Ballard's voice was steady. The lawyer in him kicked in. He would not show he was rattled, not to an audience. Or to an accomplice. "I want to see you. Now." A pause. "No, not at a bar. Stay on your boat. You're not in any condition to be in public again tonight. I'll be there shortly. . . . All right. . . . Yes, Peter. Good-bye."

Nunn clicked off the phone. "If only I had a tape recorder so I could prove to the world what a complete waste of skin you are."

Ballard risked a half smile. "You just assaulted me and listened in on a private conversation. I'll sue you into complete financial oblivion unless you just turn around and walk away. You think you hit bottom after Sarah dumped you? You're still a mile above bottom, but I will crash you, Nunn."

"Crashing is my hobby," Nunn said. "I'm in Olympic training for hitting bottom, Stan. Seriously. I'm impressed with the level of jackass-ery you've managed. You helped Peter bilk the Thomas kids out of millions after their mother, his own sister, was executed. If only they gave medals for class and integrity."

Ballard's mouth worked and decided on a frown. "You're making a huge assumption."

"No, that's what I used to do. Assume. No more. Show me your wallet and your car keys, Stan."

Ballard fished out his wallet and keys. A Mercedes logo gleamed on the key chain. Nunn thumbed through the thick wallet. "You're living so much larger than when Rosemary marched off to the death chamber. You and Peter raiding the family funds? It's hard for a dead woman to ask for an audit."

Ballard didn't move. Didn't answer.

"Peter's a jerk, but he's also a drunk and not exactly a guy you'd entrust with a plan," Nunn said. The need to twist the knife in Ballard ran deep through Nunn's bones. Part of him, wrongly he knew, wanted to pull the trigger and make Ballard's usually sneering face disappear; but then he thought of Sarah. Did she really love this man? Did she even *know* him?

"What?" Ballard, usually so sharp, didn't see Nunn's meaning.

"Someone hatched a plan to put a body in that iron maiden and frame Rosemary. It is a crime that required a great deal of forethought and planning."

"You sound like a textbook."

"You're sleeping with my wife, and I have a gun, so mocking me wouldn't be a smart strategy."

Ballard said, "Your *ex*-wife—"

Nunn cut him off. "The candidate pool is thin, Stan. You're smarter than Peter, and your motive isn't so obvious as Peter's would be. If Peter profits, you profit."

Ballard's mouth twitched, moved, turned into a frown of disbelief. "You only say that because of Sarah. Because you want to believe the worst of me."

"I don't *want*. I *do* believe the worst of you. Tell me what you and Peter did."

"This wasn't my plan."

Nunn shoved the gun harder into Ballard's cheek. The flesh went red in the dim light. "Whose plan?"

Ballard didn't answer.

"You think I won't kill you?"

"You won't. You love Sarah too much to kill me."

The awful truth of Ballard's words, the blunt truth coming from a man he knew to be a liar, burned into Nunn's brain. He pictured Sarah in Ballard's arms. He didn't know if he loved her or hated her. But he kept his voice steady and calm. "I won't be the one hurting Sarah. You helped frame an innocent woman for murder. I guarantee that is a marriage ender for Sarah."

Ballard narrowed his stare. "What do you want? Money? I can raise your standard of living."

"That money is Rosemary's money. Her kids' money."

"Rosemary is dead and that's your fault, Nunn."

Nunn's finger squeezed on the trigger. Ever so slightly. Ballard saw the flexing of the vein on the back of Nunn's hand and made a sudden, low moan in his throat. "I'm sorry, I'm sorry, I'm sorry, don't—"

"What did Peter mean, they won't know?"

"Peter's drunk. He's just blathering."

"Is Christopher Thomas alive?"

"I don't know."

"Has he touched any of the money since Rosemary died? Is he part of your scheme?"

"I told you, I don't know if he's alive or dead. You know as much as I do."

"You thought he was dead?"

"Until twenty minutes ago."

"You're lying. You engineered all of this with Peter."

"No."

"If I killed you right now, Stan, the scales would even out." Nunn wanted to scare Ballard, banish the smirk from his face. "You stole Rosemary's life. You ruined mine."

"You're not going to shoot me."

"I am. I am going to shoot you, Stan. More than once. First the ears. Then the nose. Then the knees. Then, when the pain is more than you can bear, I'll shoot you in the brain that cooked up all this misery."

"You're bluffing."

Nunn pushed the gun past Ballard's ear and fired. The blast boomed down the alleyway. Ballard screamed and dropped, clutching at his uninjured head as though blood fountained from a wound. He screamed like a man trying to determine if he was alive or dead.

Nunn grabbed him, flung him against the brick wall. *Did anyone hear the blast?* Nunn wondered. He had maybe a few minutes before the police arrived, if anyone reported a gunshot.

"You're fine, crybaby," Nunn said.

"The money . . . it was Peter's idea . . . all his idea . . ."

"But you helped him, right?"

Ballard made a noise in between a sob and a grunt. Nunn took it for agreement. "You know Peter will spill every detail, Stan. You want to talk first, trust me; you want to be the police's golden boy right now. You tell the police everything about what you know, Stan. Everything."

Ballard, cringing, didn't look Nunn in the face.

Nunn reholstered the gun in the small of his back. He made Ballard stand up and hustled him out of the alleyway. In the front of the museum, the same security guard who'd nodded earlier as Nunn left stood watching, listening. Apparently the sound of the shot had brought the man out of the building. The guard was a big guy, six-six, heavy. He looked as if he could handle Ballard.

"I heard a shot," the guard said.

"Car backfiring, I think," Nunn said. "This gentleman has information for the police regarding the woman who was honored at the memorial service at the museum last night."

The guard glanced at Ballard. "Um, I can't detain him or arrest him."

"Neither can I. But Mr. Ballard is going to be a good boy. Just call the police and Mr. Ballard will detain himself until they arrive." Nunn released his grip on Ballard's arm. "Look at me, Stan."

Ballard looked up finally, blinking, as though he'd stepped into a new world where legal strategies and filings and easy assurances did not carry their usual weight. It was a different reality for him.

"I'm going to go talk to Peter. So if you want to make a good deal with the police, before Peter does, I suggest you start talking as soon as they arrive."

"Peter . . . , " Ballard started, then stopped. Then he didn't say any more as Nunn hurried into the fog-choked night.

The St. Francis Yacht Club was at the Marina. The fog lay low over the water, like a cloud come to rest. Nunn had taken Ballard's Mercedes and told the security guard at the parking lot that he was Stan Ballard, expected by Peter Heusen. The guard spoke to Heusen on the phone, nodded, and waved Nunn through into the lot.

Nunn parked and hurried down the dock. Despite being in a marina named after a saint who embraced poverty, St. Francis's sailboats and yachts were grand, beautiful ladies. Heusen's was a seventy-two-footer named *Désirée*. Beyond the boat Nunn could see the rising majesty of the Golden Gate Bridge, solidity in the drapery of fog. The dock was quiet; most people didn't live on their boats, but Peter Heusen did. From the *Désirée* Nunn heard the shattering of a glass.

He stepped onto the deck, walked across, went to the galley.

Peter Heusen knelt on the floor. A broken cocktail glass glittered on the tile, lying in a puddle of whiskey. Peter picked up the biggest fragment of glass and glanced up at Nunn.

Then Peter laughed. "The memorial is over, Detective Nunn." He snapped the word, *dee-teck-tive,* into three hard, snotty syllables. "But you're not a dee-teck-tive anymore, are you?"

"Yeah, actually, I am, Peter. I have every reason to be now."

"Look, that, um, science dude, from what I hear, saying the body wasn't Christopher's, that's just ridiculous. He's just some attention-seeking nerd. We'll find out tomorrow"—here Peter stood up, awkwardly, dropping the glass fragment to the floor—"that he's been hired by one of those tabloid websites, and he was wrong." Peter leaned back against the counter and circled an aiming finger at Nunn. "Now. You got onto private property by lying to the guard, and I'm going to call him, and you're going to jail for trespassing."

Peter reached for the phone and Nunn walked through the broken glass and shoved him down to the floor.

"Uh, you can't do that," Peter blustered. He was well into his drink now, and when he tried to stand up again quickly, Nunn pushed him back down. "Get the hell off my boat. Now."

"Why?"

"Why what?"

"I don't even know where to start with you, Peter. Why have every advantage in the world and drink it away? Why let your sister die? Why steal from your own blood?"

"Why . . . don't you get the hell off my boat?" Peter laughed.

"You and I both know that the forensics is telling the truth." Nunn crossed his arms. "Ballard is talking to the police right now."

"If Ballard is talking to police, it's going to be about charges against you, trespassing, and incompetence. If my sister's dead, that's *your* fault, not mine." Peter shook a finger at Nunn, then dragged a hand across his own mouth.

"Ballard is talking because he's going to do what it takes to salvage his career. He's cutting a deal. Now. Who do you think will negotiate the smarter terms, Peter? A seasoned estate lawyer or a drunk trust-fund baby?" Nunn glanced at his watch. "You and Ballard stole Rosemary's money from her kids. He'll get disbarred. You'll get prison. Maybe you can give your fellow inmates sailing tips to pass the years."

"You're lying." Peter's voice rose. "You can't touch me. You can't come in here and threaten me. I take good care of those brats. You're incompetent. Do you honestly think anyone will believe you?"

"Honestly, Peter? Yes, because Ballard is talking. He's with the police now. The only way you'll get leniency is if you confess to bilking your nieces and nephews. Or the *brats,* to use your pet name for them."

"You can't prove anything."

"The body isn't Chris's. The case will be reopened. A mother was executed. The press, the public, will go nuts."

"Fat lot of good that will do for my sister."

"As if you care."

Peter stood up and stared at Nunn, then he got another cocktail glass and poured an inch of whiskey into it. He looked at the glass and added a second inch. He took a long sip. "You think I hated my own sister? Maybe. But maybe I loved her too." And for one awful moment Nunn thought Peter would cry into his whiskey. A huge, shuddering breath rocked him.

"Where is Christopher, Peter?"

Peter drank the top inch of whiskey in a long, hard swallow. "He's dead. Rosemary killed him."

"It's not Chris's body."

"He's dead. He's dead." Peter backed away along the galley counter. "He's dead and locked in the maiden."

"Peter. Where. Is. Christopher?"

Peter threw the glass at Nunn's face. Nunn ducked, the splash of whiskey burning his eyes, the crystal slamming against his forehead.

Peter tried to run past Nunn, and Nunn closed his fist around Peter's collar. Peter might once have been an athlete, but the liquor had bled too much of his muscle and will away.

Nunn, gripping Peter's collar, blinked away the sharp sting. He yanked Peter down to the floor, dragged him toward the glittering shards of the broken cocktail glass. He seized Peter's thinning hair, forced his face above the sharp fragments.

"Tell me. Tell me where Christopher is."

"No, no. No!"

"Peter. Think of it this way. If you stole from the kids, and you can give them their father back, then the judge is going to like you way better than Dallard. Maybe he'll even let you keep the boat."

"The boat," Peter repeated.

"The boat. Tell me. Or I'll dust up the broken glass using your face as my broom. It will hurt."

Peter Heusen took three ragged breaths while Nunn counted silently to ten. When Peter stayed quiet, Nunn shoved his face toward the glass.

Peter screamed. Nunn stopped. "The Trompe l'Oeil Hotel! He's at the Trompe l'Oeil Hotel. I mean, I think he is."

Nunn knew the hotel, a four-star, not far from Union Square. "Don't lie to me, Peter."

"I'm not but—"

"But what?"

"You won't recognize him. His face—"

"Got himself some plastic surgery, did he?"

Peter nodded. "So he says. He obviously won't be using his real name there. And I don't know what he looks like now, I haven't seen him in a decade. That was our agreement."

"But you've talked to him."

"Yes. And yesterday he called me. I thought he was gone from San Francisco but he's been here." Peter almost sounded afraid.

"How do you know he's at the Trompe l'Oeil? Did he tell you?"

"No. But when he called me . . . I could hear background noise. Music. A jazz singer. It sounded like the singer they've had at the Trompe's lounge for years, a very throaty alto. I drink there. So I think that's where he is. . . ."

Peter, Nunn thought, was a good detective as long as all the clues involved a bar.

"Why would he call you?" Then it sank in. "You helped him hide. You helped him run." Nunn took a step back from Peter.

"You think I'm so bad?" Peter sobbed.

Then Peter cracked. Guilt or booze finally loosened his grip, and in a low voice he confessed how he had helped Christopher fake his death and vanish.

"Christopher came up with the plan," he said. "A replacement body. He killed an errand boy, some Chinese guy, who supplied him with hash and coke, a nobody. He stuffed his body inside the maiden."

"Name?"

Peter thought. "He had a nickname like a James Bond character . . . Odd Job, or something."

Odd Body.

"Christopher sliced off his own finger, left it in place of the dead guy's. Did it here on the boat. I had to cauterize the wound, bandage it up for him." Peter made a gagging sound. "Then he broke off a piece of his own tooth, put it in the guy's shirt pocket."

Nunn felt ill, remembering the nearly unidentifiable body. He remembered the tooth and what the forensics guy, McGee, had said about the one intact finger.

"Then you helped frame your own sister."

"It was Christopher's idea—every bit of it!" Peter screamed.

"Go on."

"He had one of her blouses—he stained it with his blood after he cut off his finger. It was like he was painting it, I remember. Then he took hair from her hairbrush and put it in there with the body. And later, we had someone put hash and coke in her office for the police to find. . . ."

Nunn listened to the murmured, slurred words with an unforgiving silence.

Then Nunn released Peter, who staggered away from him, collapsing by the sink, fingers testing his face for glass. Only a slight scrape, barely bloodied, lay along his cheek, and he almost hummed in relief.

Nunn pulled out handcuffs from the kit in the small of his back and he latched one onto Peter's wrist, cuffing the other one to the oven handle.

"You're not a cop anymore, you can't handcuff me!" Peter screamed.

"Ballard had a reason to stay put. You're on a boat that could be in international waters in short order. I'm not trusting you."

"Nunn, please. Let me go. I told you. I'll pay you."

"Second bribe I've been offered in an hour," Nunn said. He took the whiskey bottle and stuck it between Peter's legs. "I'm going to call the police for you, Peter."

Peter made a noise between a cough and a snuffle.

Nunn jumped off the *Désirée* and ran down the dock.

Christopher Thomas, alive, and within reach. He could finally solve the case. Maybe he could get real justice for Rosemary. Maybe he would get his job back.

And maybe, Nunn thought, he could get himself back.

31

MARCUS SAKEY

"I'm afraid I can't understand you." Christopher set the duct tape on the bar beside the Colt. "You really should work on your enunciation. It separates one from the lower classes." He picked Artie's glass off the plush carpeted floor, washed and dried it, then poured himself a couple of neat fingers of the same single malt. "That and money, of course."

Artie whimpered. His face was pale. Sweat dripped off his chin as he tried to crawl. It was impressive, actually. As Christopher watched, the man fought to lift one arm and flop it forward a scant couple of inches. He looked like a man possessed, as if agony were a razor-clawed demon inside his skin.

The blood that pumped from his stomach was dark against the white weave of the carpet. Almost black.

Christopher took another swallow, savored the burn. He felt alive in a way that he usually associated with sex. Not orgasm, which had a vulnerability, a giving of himself. But that perfect instant when the next Taylor—or Haile or Justine—surrendered herself. The flicker of submission in her eyes before the clothes ever came off. The moment she let go.

Only Artie wasn't letting go, and that just stretched it out more sweetly.

Christopher watched for another moment, then turned, walked to the bedroom. Snapped on the light and looked around. One gunshot, even from a .357, would be written off as street noise, a bottle rocket, or a backfiring truck or even what it was, gunfire. No one would believe that it had come from inside a $4,000-a-night suite.

Still, best to get moving. Besides, he'd had about all the fun San Francisco was likely to afford him. Tailing Ballard, holding a knife to Belle's pale throat, stalking the cop and Ballard's gorgeous wife, creeping up on her like that in the dressing room, seeing her quivering in her panties, had been a kick. His only regret was that he hadn't gotten the chance to see his children, Leila and Ben—even from a distance. Artie had ruined that with his second-rate scheming. Ah, well. Rio called.

Christopher took down a suitcase from the closet, unzipped it. Opened the room safe and began to haul out bundles of money. When he'd filled the first suitcase, he took down a second, packed it as well. From one of the American Touristers he took out a fresh shirt, patterned white cotton and French cuffs, and traded it for the rumpled one he wore. He stood in front of the mirror. A little . . . staid. He popped the cuff links, then shook his wrists to loosen the fabric. There. At once elegant and rakish.

He picked up his bags—it was amazing how much real money weighed, even in high denominations—and walked back into the living room.

Artie had made it almost six feet. A smear of dark blood marked his progress. His hands were coated with the stuff.

"I have to say, Arthur, you're smarter than you look." Christopher dropped the bags, sauntered over. "Going for the phone, very clever. I'd have guessed you would try for the door." He raised one foot, put the arch of his dress shoe against the man's shoulder, and pushed.

Artie toppled like a lamp. Even muffled by the gag, his scream was raw and sharp.

"But then, what would you have said if you did reach the phone?" Christopher went to the bar, picked up the heavy revolver. "Plm-mmphhmmpphmmeph?" He dropped to one knee beside the onetime security guard, careful not to dip his pants in blood. "Can you hear me?"

Artie's eyes were huge. His pupils were pinned as if he were staring at something bright and close. He made no response. Christopher leaned in and flicked the man's stomach just above where the bullet had torn it open.

Artie responded.

"I said, can you hear me?"

The man nodded feverishly.

"You've probably already guessed that you're going to die. Shuffle off this mortal coil, as it were. But how fast you shuffle is up to me. Remember that when I take your gag out. Yes?"

Again the nod.

"Excellent." Christopher ripped off the tape and pulled Taylor's abandoned panties out of Artie's mouth. Christopher tossed them aside, then wiped his hands on a clean spot on Artie's shirt. "Now." He put the barrel of the gun against the man's crotch, cocked the hammer back. "About that letter."

Tired. So tired.

Jon Nunn's shoulders were clenched like knuckles. Eyes grainy and dry. When he raised a hand to rub them, the fingers were trembling. As if he'd been running for days.

Not days. Years. Twelve long years.

Twelve years of pain and guilt about his marriage—about Sarah.

Twelve years of believing that Christopher Thomas might be a snake and a climber, but that he was also a murder victim.

Twelve years since his testimony sent Rosemary Thomas to her death for a murder that never happened.

Twelve years of letting things happen around him. Of drink and despair and weakness. Of second-guessing himself and squandering time. Passively watching the world go by and wishing it were different.

Years when Christopher Thomas lived his dream while Jon Nunn was trapped in the drabbest of nightmares.

And now, that it should all end here, in this hotel of all places. TROMPE L'OEIL the sign read. Trompe l'oeil, "tricks the eye," if he remembered high school French.

Just fucking perfect.

Nunn flipped on the hazards, stepped out of the Mercedes. The valet made a move in his direction, but he shook his head. "I won't be long."

The lobby doors parted soundlessly, revealing a broad expanse of marble and subtle lighting. The air had the sweetness of a pear two days past perfection. The heels of his shoes clicked as he wove through brokers and lawyers and doctors in overstuffed chairs. The wall behind reception was lined with trees. Not until he was standing at the desk did he realize they had been painted on, the perspective rendered so carefully that it seemed he could reach out and touch them.

"Welcome to Trompe l'Oeil, sir. How may I help you?"

"I'm looking for someone. A guest."

The woman—her name tag read CLAIRE—barely looked up from her keyboard. "What's your party's name, please."

He grimaced, pulled the old photo out of his pocket. "This is him. Do you recognize him?"

"I'm sorry, what is this—"

"I'm a cop." No reason to start playing by the rules now.

"Still, I'm sorry, but I can't . . . I could call my manager, perhaps he—"

"Listen to me." Nunn leaned into the counter. "This man is a killer. Get me? He's dangerous. Please. Think. Have you seen him?"

Claire licked her lips nervously. "I don't know."

A muted boom. Somewhere indistinct. It wasn't loud. The investment banker in the lobby bar didn't stop running his game on the model, and she didn't stop touching her hair and cocking her hips. Conversations continued, the low murmur of wealth and influence.

But Jon Nunn knew the sound, even through however many insulated floors.

The woman behind the counter said, "What *is* that? I heard it just a few minutes ago."

He turned back to her. "Think. Have you seen him?"

"I—"

"Yes or no."

"No." Her voice strained.

"Anyone else?"

"What do you mean?"

"Is there anyone else who might have seen him?"

She shook her head. "Usually there are two of us, but Jonathan met this curly-haired boy, and I told him—" Claire shrugged. "Do you want me to call my manager at home?"

Nunn was already walking away. That noise had been gunfire, something with muscle, a .45 or even a .357. What was Thomas shooting at?

Not what. Who.

Nunn clenched and unclenched his fingers. Every instinct developed in a lifetime spent protecting people told him that Christopher Thomas was here. That he was armed. That he had probably just shot someone.

And none of it made any difference. What was he going to do, knock on doors? Call SWAT and cordon off the building? He wasn't a cop anymore. He couldn't call for help. Couldn't explain what he was doing there or how he had gotten the information in the first place. Couldn't flash the badge he didn't have.

Besides, Peter Heusen had said that Christopher had had surgery. A brand-new face. There was no way to be sure Nunn would recognize him even if they passed in the hall.

Yes, you will. He can't change the eyes. His arrogant, certain eyes, always the same across a dozen case-file photographs.

Nunn paced the lobby in short, angry laps, feeling time ticking away. There wasn't time to delay, but there wasn't time to make the wrong call, either.

Sure. Hesitate again. Just let it happen around you. Like you did for the last twelve years.

An expensively dressed blond guy was crossing the lobby towing two suitcases behind him. He was slender, and his walk was smug and swift, almost a sway.

Nunn broke into a sprint. He bolted between two leather chairs, leaped the outstretched legs of a man reading *The Wall Street Journal*. There was a shout from behind as he knocked over someone's drink. Two more seconds brought Nunn up behind the blond, who started to turn. Nunn grabbed his shoulder, yanked him around, and cocked his right arm back.

A woman with boyishly close-cropped hair stared back at him, eyes wide and terrified, mouth falling open. "What the—"

Nunn held the punch he'd been about to throw. "I'm sorry, I thought—"

"Help!"

Shit.

He turned. Throughout the lobby, people were frozen. Staring. Nunn looked from one to the next. Behind the desk, Claire had a phone in one hand and was looking at him as she spoke. Calling the police?

A sudden sharp pain and a quick jerk of the world. He heard the slap after he felt it. The blond woman. She was winding up for another. He caught her arm. "Lady, listen—"

"Hey. Buddy. Back off." The doorman, starting this way. Nunn looked around, saw that the lobby was back in motion, most of them coming toward him. The elevator on the near wall had opened, and the man inside hesitated, the scene not what he'd expected.

Nunn whirled from person to person. Everyone was staring at him. He had a flash of school-yard paranoia, the feeling of being singled out. "I'm a police officer," he said, using his cop voice. "Everyone calm down."

It was enough to freeze people. In that silence, across the span of marble and wealth, framed by gilded metal doors, Nunn saw them. Time seemed to stop.

Then, as Nunn pushed himself into motion, two things happened.

The elevator doors began to close.

And behind them, a stranger with Christopher Thomas's eyes winked at him.

Well. That had been bracing. Peter must have given him up. Something to deal with later.

The moment the elevator doors opened on the parking garage, Christopher set off at a jog, dragging his suitcases behind, the wheels skittering and bouncing. The light was yellow and soulless. The Colt was heavy in his pocket.

Christopher didn't know a great deal about cars, but beauty he knew, and his rented Aston Martin DB9 was beautiful. The woman who'd shown it had blathered about horsepower and V-12 engines and rack-and-pinion steering, and he'd just smiled and nodded and imagined bending her over the hood of it, fucking her with the engine throbbing beneath.

He beeped open the car, threw in the suitcases. Quickly now, quickly. Poor, broken Jon Nunn would be on his way. He cranked the engine, shifted into first, and sped toward the exit. The tires clung to the pavement. The car hummed with power. Christopher rounded the corner, turned up the ramp. All he had to do was get clear of the hotel. Let the ex-cop try to catch him in this—

Jon Nunn stood at the top, framed against the purple mist of a San Francisco night, a gun in one hand.

The car was silver and expensive and hurtling toward him.

His arm moved on its own, the gun lifting as though it were immune to gravity. Decades of habit had him sighting down it, his left hand coming over to steady the automatic, finger sliding inside the trigger guard as the car bore down.

You can do this. Just aim and squeeze and aim and squeeze. You'll hit him, and then his car will hit you, and the two of you will go out together, and maybe that's how it's meant to be.

He locked eyes with the man behind the wheel. A man who believed he was above everything. Who wrecked the lives of those around him with a solipsistic abandon.

No. A tie isn't good enough. You need to beat him. For Sarah. For Rosemary.

For yourself.

He dove aside. The car was huge and breathing hot as it blew past. He hit the ground on his shoulder, managed to hold on to the gun. Brakes squealed as Thomas fought against his own velocity. The Aston Martin slid sideways, skidded, knocked trash cans like dominoes. Then the transmission ground, an ugly sound, and the car lurched forward.

Nunn was on his feet and running for the Mercedes.

He hauled himself in, tossed the gun on the seat, started up the car, and slammed the accelerator to the floor. The valet stood frozen as the Mercedes smashed through a brass luggage cart, sending designer bags flying. A horn screamed from behind. Nunn ignored it, yanked the wheel back to fight the fishtail. Ahead of him, Thomas streaked between two cars.

Now what?

The Aston Martin was probably faster than the Mercedes Nunn had stolen.

Then find another way.

Union Square was a shopping district, the lanes wide, the intersections marked in clean paint and smooth pavement. Logos blurred outside his windows, Urban Outfitters and Apple and Diesel. The sidewalks were almost as wide as the—

Wait a second, think about this before you—

Nunn jumped the curb, took the Mercedes up on the sidewalk. Beat out a warning on his horn without taking his foot off the gas. Late shoppers stared with cow eyes. Rich women clutched bags that held his month's salary. A longhair in a dashiki leaped aside, yelling curses. Nunn gritted his teeth and rode the edge, made it to the corner, blasted off the sidewalk, spinning the car as he went, south on Fourth now. Ahead, the Aston Martin wove between cars, the traffic slowing it. Until he got a clean run, Christopher Thomas's expensive toy wasn't going to help him much.

So he'll be going for a clean run. You need to beat him there.

But how?

As he crossed Mission, he saw the answer.

When Christopher had seen the ex-cop at the top of the garage ramp, he'd thought for a moment it was all over. Artie's body was flopped on the floor of a hotel room with his fingerprints all over it—no explaining that. But good old Jon Nunn remained as predictable as he had been when he'd worked the case. Instead of coming with an army of police, he was here alone on some sort of revenge mission. Still underestimating Christopher, still not realizing whom he was playing against. No, it didn't matter that he'd let Nunn live. The man wouldn't be a concern. Christopher just had to get a little space. Then to the Oakland airport, where a private jet waited, creamy leather upholstery and chilled champagne and a phone to begin arranging his final disappearance.

A Volkswagen Beetle stopped dead in front of him for no discernible reason. Christopher jerked the wheel, managed to squeeze the Aston Martin between the Beetle and a utility truck parked halfway up the curb. Stupid sheep with their stupid little cars. Ridiculous vehicle. He had to get some space. But where? The next street was Howard, five or six lanes running one way the wrong way, and after that another slow block. . . .

There comes a moment in the work of any painter when he stops thinking and begins to operate on instinct. When he goes with his impulses. It's the thing that turns a good artist into a great one.

Christopher turned left onto Howard, found himself staring at staggered headlights like accusing eyes. His heart beat harder, and he was conscious of the feel of the steering wheel in his palm, of the cool of the air-conditioning. A movie theater rushed by his side window. He swerved to miss a delivery truck. *Let's see that son of a bitch keep up with this.* He smiled, wove the Aston Martin to one side, then the other, the howl of horns almost symphonic. Yerba Buena Gardens on his left, trees and tourists, and—

No. It couldn't be.

Those lights smearing across the park, weaving between the trees, getting larger, they couldn't be—

Nunn squinted out the window, concentration whitening his knuckles. Driving right through Yerba goddamn Buena, he must be losing it, it was crazy, he could hurt someone—

How's this for not passively letting things happen around you?

Someone shrieked. His headlights caught nightmare images, young lovers leaping aside, a juggler staring as his bowling pins plummeted, a family pushing a stroller, *Fuck*, Nunn swung hard the other way, an oak forty feet tall, he pulled back, the side of the Mercedes scraping against the trunk, the side mirror snapping off with a pop, and then sidewalk, the tires gripping hard—*What now, Jon?*—and the staircase opening up like an answered curse; he grit his teeth and held down the horn and hurtled down the steps and saw the Aston Martin tear by, Christopher Thomas's eyes no longer arrogant and certain.

Nunn whooped, forced the Mercedes left to follow. One car length behind, maybe two. Thomas wove back and forth across the lanes, the oncoming traffic keeping him from opening the car up, and Nunn rode him down, closing the distance an inch at a time. Thomas went right and gained himself a quick twenty feet, until Nunn cut across the corner and took it back. He felt his lips curling in a smile unlike any he'd known in ten years.

Until the Aston Martin made another turn, and Nunn realized where Thomas was going.

No, no, no!

Nunn held the accelerator down, rocked back and forth in his seat, willing the car to go faster. He had to catch the man. Had to catch him soon.

The Bay Bridge was straight and broad and four and a half miles long. Thomas's pretty little car would practically set it on fire.

Come on, come on.

Thomas hit Essex, spun the car hard, and started up the bridge. He began to widen the distance immediately, the roar of his engine louder even than Nunn's heart.

No. It couldn't be, not now. Not after all of this. It wasn't fair.

Fair? Ask Rosemary about fair.

Because just like her, he was going to lose.

Christopher thrilled at the sound the engine made, the way the Aston Martin responded to his command. He dodged between cars, easier now that he was going the right direction. When the RPM needle was deep in the red, he upshifted, felt the car leap ahead.

Something in the moment was quite lovely. For years he and Nunn had been collaborators of a sort. True, the cop hadn't known he was alive, but even so, together they had created a work of art. The canvas had been spun of human lives, the paint mixed of blood and tears and semen, the subject wealth and desire and betrayal. And now it ended.

Collaborations don't last, Jon. One man is always the greater artist.

Christopher felt something tighten deep in his belly, a feeling that reminded him of the one he'd had as Artie crawled across his carpet. That sweet, stretched feeling of complete victory. He grinned, brushed his hair back from his eyes. Looked into the rearview mirror, savoring the image of Nunn's car shrinking. What the man must be feeling! It might be Christopher's masterpiece, even better than Rosemary. To take so much from a man, not just his marriage, but his career, his faith in justice, even his hope, then simply leave him behind, powerless to do anything but watch, it was—

Bright fire bloomed in the Aston Martin. The light seemed to flare right in front of Christopher, as though he were snapping a lighter.

A metallic *thunk,* meaty and clean.

Another flash from behind, and his rear window spiderwebbed.

What is—he's—is he—

Something shoved his shoulder. It felt like a punch, the kind of rough gesture men in pubs gave one another. Christopher glanced down and saw a hole in the Egyptian cotton of his shirt, then red, red— *What? No.*

He couldn't believe it.

The pain surfed the wave of comprehension, *suddenstabbingburning,* and he gasped. Tried to move his arm and fire spread down it. A scream of horn jerked his eyes back to the road. He was feet from the back end of a semi. Panic overwhelmed pain as he spun the wheel, yanked it right. The car fought to respond. The tires shrieked, loud and embarrassing. The car cleared the end of the semi, but the spin had it now, chaos taking control. For a terrible second he thought it might roll, but it just kept turning, the heavy guardrails of the bridge, open sky beyond, then the front of the car was facing the wrong way, traffic racing toward him, cars struggling to stop, and then he saw the battered Mercedes headed right for him, and through its broken windshield he thought he saw Jon Nunn's face.

Then the car slammed into the Aston Martin and ground and sky switched places.

Jon Nunn felt as if he'd been punched by a giant's fist.

The impact had slammed him against his seat belt, sent his body rocking forward, but before his head could hit the wheel the air bag had exploded, a confusion of white and gray and the smell of gunpowder and a wallop to his chest and face.

For a moment there was only the feel of it against his cheek, and pain.

Slowly the drone of a horn penetrated. The world was dark, then he realized his eyes were closed.

When he opened them, he was staring over the deflating air bag, through the splintered windshield, at the graceful sweep of a bridge cable two feet thick. The barrier rail was crumpled and torn.

And atop it, upside down, a car that had once been beautiful rocked like a seesaw.

Nunn shook his head, regretted it immediately. Pain sloshed in his skull.

He fumbled for his seat belt. Pushed the air bag away, opened the door. Dropped out, catching himself on the window frame.

The night was cool and burnished with mist. The glowing bridge lights were fairy lamps. A passing car began to slow. Jon gestured them on, didn't realize he still had the gun in his hand until the driver roared away.

Somewhere far off, sirens rose.

Jon took a tentative step, then another. Everything hurt, but nothing seemed broken.

The engine of the Aston Martin ticked. Something metal creaked. The roof of the car was crumpled by the concrete barrier. As he watched, something gave, and the car slipped an inch farther toward the abyss.

"Help me."

The voice was thin. Jon followed it until he could see Christopher Thomas. The face was different. It wasn't just that he hung upside down, or the blood streaming from his nose, or the ragged mess of muscle and tissue that was his shoulder. It was the eyes. The cocksure certainty was gone. In its place was a raw and animal panic.

Nunn stared at those eyes for a long moment. Then, slowly, he tucked the gun back into his holster.

Thomas's right hand still clutched the steering wheel, but the fingers were shaking. "You can't do this."

"What?"

The breeze off the water smelled vibrant and alive. The car groaned as the wind whistled over it.

"You can't kill me."

Jon shrugged. "I'm not killing you."

"Then help me."

"Help yourself."

Thomas stared with a 100-proof hate. Slowly he took his hand off the wheel and fumbled for the door. Nunn watched. The man was pale and shaky. He got a grip on the handle and tugged it. The angle of the car caused the door to swing open wide, pitching the balance of the car. There was a sound of sickening friction. The hood tilted down. Christopher threw himself back in his seat and turned to stone.

Jon Nunn thought of Rosemary after the injections, the way her skin had faded almost immediately. The sirens drew closer. More than one of them, and coming fast.

"You're not a cop anymore." Christopher was laying a veneer of reason over a wobble of panic. "You can't do those things. Shoot at people. Chase them."

"I did them anyway."

"Get me out of here." The wind sighed, and the car slipped again. "Get me out and I'll tell them it was just an accident."

Nunn didn't move.

"I've got money. In the back. Millions."

Nunn didn't move.

"It won't change anything, you know. Killing me. It won't bring Rosemary back." The man's voice was rational, not quite pleading. "The dead stay dead. You'll just have one more ghost. Can you handle that, Jon? Another ghost?"

"I don't know," Nunn said, surprised to realize he meant it. He was tired, so very tired, and Thomas was right. You didn't have to work homicide long to realize that vengeance did nothing to decrease the sum total of pain in the world. Not only that, but there would be consequences for his actions tonight. Everything he'd done since leaving the museum had been beyond the law. If he could produce a murderer, banged up but alive, it would go a lot easier on him.

Christopher was just trying to save his own tiny life; Nunn knew that. But that didn't make him wrong. If Nunn let this happen, he would pay penalties—and possibly they were more than he could bear.

He realized that, took a moment to acknowledge it. Then he said, "I don't know if I can handle another ghost, Christopher. But you know what?" Jon Nunn smiled. "I don't care."

The man's mask of reason disintegrated. "Goddamnit, get me out of here! Do you know who I am? Do you?"

"Yes." Nunn took a moment to think of Rosemary, and to pray that she forgave him. "You were Christopher Thomas."

Then Nunn turned and walked back to the Mercedes. A huddle of cars had stopped, people half in and half out. They froze when they saw him. Nunn ignored them. Carefully, he took the gun from his holster. He locked the safety, bent to set it on the ground. He could see the police cars now, two of them, lights flashing bright against the night, and behind them an ambulance. Nunn put his hands on his head and laced the fingers together. The first of the police cars jerked to a stop, two beat cops boiling out. Slowly, painfully, he eased himself down to his knees.

And as he touched the cold ground, as the police surged toward him and the breeze blew soft, as the lights of San Francisco twinkled through the fog, he heard a sound. A slow, metal creak like the yawn of some great beast, and a rush of air, and mixed with it, something that might have been a scream.

But not until he heard the splash did he let himself smile.

Diary of Jon Nunn, Last Entry

JONATHAN SANTLOFER AND ANDREW F. GULLI

I was detained for a couple of days. The cops asked me a hundred questions. Then they asked me a hundred more. I didn't have all the answers, but I had enough. I knew that Christopher Thomas had faked his death. That Peter Heusen had helped him. That Artie Ruby had aided and abetted by shipping the iron maiden off to Germany. That Stan Ballard had worked with Peter to make both of them multimillionaires while cheating the Thomas children.

And I knew something else—none of it really mattered. Rosemary Thomas was still dead.

Tony Olsen spoke on my behalf. He had more than a little influence with the SFPD, and a few of my old colleagues spoke for me too. Then Tony gathered up everyone one more time and got them to tell what they knew, or thought they knew.

Belle McGuire described how an unknown man, who she now believed had to have been Christopher Thomas, had assaulted her in her studio and displayed the red mark that was still on her neck where he'd drawn a palette knife across it. Her husband, Don, corroborated her story and even put in a good word for me. I'm not sure why. Probably because he'd wanted to hunt down Christopher himself and my doing it was the next best thing.

Peter confessed that he and Christopher had been selling stolen art in Europe and Asia for the past decade while everyone thought Christopher was dead. Greed knows no boundaries. He also admitted that he and Christopher had planned the museum break-in and that he was the one who attacked Haile Patchett at the memorial that night to create a diversion to get the fake police inside. Of course he blamed everything on Christopher and said he was forced into it. I won't even honor that by asking how you can force someone into committing such heinous acts. He also said that I'd come aboard his boat and threatened him with a gun, which he thought would get me in trouble. It did—for a minute—but it also helped establish that he'd told me where Christopher was staying and that I'd gone after him.

Peter's trial has been delayed now for more than a year. His lawyer is arguing that the evidence against his client was gotten by force—by *me,* an ex-cop with a grudge. I'm sure to be called as a witness, and I won't deny what I did, but I sure as hell hope the DA is tough enough to make Peter's words stick to him.

Hank Zacharius got himself a new story.

INNOCENT WOMAN EXECUTED

That headline appeared in newspapers across the country and with Rosemary's public, exoneration, the state of California was not only shamed but also forced to pay the Thomas children undisclosed millions in damages. It was exoneration for Hank, too, and from what I hear, he's got a seven-figure book deal to write the whole story, but when he called to interview me, I turned him down. He understood.

Stan Ballard was disbarred and is awaiting trial, and he and Sarah separated.

Sarah.

She told the police how she'd been attacked in a department store dressing room and how she'd realized, too late, that her attacker had to have been Christopher Thomas. I was furious she'd never told me.

Eventually the cops let me go. They didn't have much to hold me on other than reckless driving and swinging my gun around like a cowboy, and Christopher Thomas's fatal splash into the bay was finally ruled an accident.

Maybe it's poetic justice that he died painfully. Maybe not. Maybe it would have been better if he had to grow old in prison and live with what he'd done, although he'd need a conscience for that and clearly didn't have one. Still, a part of me feels robbed that I lived with pain for more than a decade and Christopher Thomas got off so easily. Again, my fault. I might have saved him if I was thinking straight at the time.

But I don't regret it. You could say the old Jon Nunn died that night too and I'm the guy who took his place. I was wrong—the phoenix does rise from ashes.

After everything settled down, I left San Francisco and bought a little ranch in Wyoming that was in foreclosure, nothing special, a dozen acres, a couple of old horses. The house was a mess, rotten floors and broken windows, but I've been fixing it up slowly and it doesn't look half bad. Tony Olsen and I speak from time to time and he always asks me to come to San Francisco. But I'm not going back. I've tried too hard to get away from it all and forget. But then, you never forget, you just build a layer of scar tissue over the wounds and keep going.

Just the other day I got a little painting in the mail, an ocean scene, from Belle McGuire. No note, just the picture. I stared at it a long time and it brought everything back to me—the case, the trial, the ten years of sorrow and frustration, and the reckoning that finally arrived. I hung the painting in the living room as a reminder of all that had happened, but especially of Rosemary.

Afterward, I called Sarah.

She was surprised by my call. I told her I was more surprised. She laughed and it cut right through me. She asked how I was doing, and I turned the question around, and she said she was okay, but I think she was lying. I told her to come out to Wyoming for a visit sometime and she said maybe, so who knows . . .

Nowadays, I pay the bills doing some consulting for a security firm, and I've been lecturing on criminology at a community college, more to keep myself busy than anything else. But today I'm home. Next to the painting Belle sent me is a window, and in the distance I can make out the pointy, jagged tops of Cathedral Ridge, part of the Rocky Mountain range that I pretend belongs to me alone. Above it, the sky is bright blue with choppy, white clouds and looks to me like a landscape by van Gogh—vibrant, childlike, unbroken.

Appendix: Additional Police Reports

KATHY REICHS

I. THE FORENSIC ENTOMOLOGY REPORT

FORENSIC ENTOMOLOGY SERVICES

C/O DR. PETER M. GERBER

OSTENDERSTRASSE 129–162

13353 BERLIN

030 532 77 43

FESB # 0236   31 AUGUST 1998

NMB 03–79

CONTACT: DR. GERBER

Subject: Specimens were submitted hand to hand, from the Institute of Legal Medicine, arriving at Forensic Entomology Services of Berlin on 27 August 1998 at 1330 hours. Samples were in three specimen jars, no preservatives. One jar contained multiple puparial casings. A second jar contained multiple dead specimens. Label indicated specimens collected on 26 August 1998. The third jar contained preserved maggots preserved in 70% ETOH. A fourth jar contained a single dead specimen. 70% ETOH added to jar containing multiple dead specimens at 1400 hours, 27 August 1998.

EVIDENCE SUBMITTED

1. Specimen jar containing multiple puparial casings. No data on outside or inside of jar.
2. Specimen jar containing multiple dead insects. Labeled NMBa 03–73; collect: 26-8-98.

3. Specimen jar containing preserved maggots. Labeled NMB 03-73b; collect 26-8-98
4. Specimen jar containing a single dead insect. No data on outside or inside of jar.

IDENTIFICATIONS

1. Diptera: Calliphoridae: *Chrysomya rufifacies*—23 empty pupae
2. Diptera: Calliphoridae: *Chrysomya rufifacies*—23 adults
3. Diptera: Piophilidae: *Piophila casei*—3rd instar larvae
4. Coleoptera: Cerambycidae: *Dihammus szechuanus*

ESTIMATED MINIMUM PERIOD OF INSECT ACTIVITY

18 to 30 days prior to collection on 26 August 1998.

This estimate is based on the presence of late third instar larvae of *Piphilia casei*. These maggots arrive typically around day 15 in decomposition and complete their development by day 36. The maggots in the collections here are consistent with development of approximately 30 days. The empty puparial cases of *C. rufifacies,* while not definitive, are consistent with this time frame. During decomposition studies conducted at 26°C, empty puparial cases of *C. rufifacies* were first reported on day 14. The presence of *C. rufifacies* suggests exposure of the body outside or near a window prior to or during shipping. Depending on available food materials, degree of exposure, and temperature ranges, the estimate of 18 to 30 days must be considered a minimum and a longer postmortem interval is possible.

II. THE RADIOLOGY REPORT

Document Identifier: C1998073042
Name: Unknown (presumed, Thomas, Christopher, DOB 19 09 52)
Analysis: Radiologic observation, skull, torso, upper and lower limbs
Request By: Dr. Bruno Muntz, ILM

Received From: Hand to hand, Mette Brinkman
Date of Exam: 20/07/1998
Time of Exam: 1100 hours
Place of Exam: Institute of Legal Medicine, Berlin

DECEDENT

Decomposed human adult found at German Historical Museum 18-7-1998

CRANIAL

The skull is complete and that of an adult. Bone quality is good. No antemortem healed or healing fractures are present. No congenital abnormalities or anomalies are present.

POSTCRANIAL

The skeleton is complete and that of an adult. Bone quality is good. Moderate remodeling is present in the right and left acromioclavicular and in the left tibiofemoral joint. No antemortem healed or healing fractures are present. No congenital abnormalities or anomalies are present.

A total of twenty-five (25) fractures and perforations are present in the following locations:

    2—right humerus
    3—right radius
    2—right ulnas
    2—left radius
    1—right clavicle
    1—left clavicle
    1—sternum
    5—ribs
    6—vertebrae (4 thoracic, 2 lumbar)
    1—right innominate
    1—right femur

DENTAL

Thirty-two (32) permanent teeth are present at the time of death. All maxillary and mandibular roots are fully formed. Only fragmentary crowns remain, rendering observation impossible. (See odontology report.)

SUMMARY

The decedent is an adult male whose bones exhibit no congenital anomalies or deformities, no evidence of disease, and no healed fractures or surgical modifications. Perimortem blunt and sharp force trauma has caused extensive damage to the dentition, skull, torso, and long bones of the lower and upper extremities.

Hanne L. Windman, M.D.   *20 July 1998*
Hanne Windman, MD   20 July 1998

III. THE FORENSIC ODONTOLOGY REPORT

FORENSIC ODONTOLOGY:

POSTMORTEM ORIENTATION AND RECONSTITUTION

AUTOPSY: 20-07-1998

DECEDENT: THOMAS, CHRISTOPHER (PRESUMED),

DOB 1952-09-19

ODONTOLOGICAL ANALYSIS: 20-07-1998

ILM: 2000-43271-CO01

MORGUE: 32885

POLICE INCIDENT REPORT: BPD 08443

ME: DR. BRUNO MUNTZ

At the request of Dr. Muntz, I examined, at the Institute of Legal Medicine in Berlin, radiographs of the jaws and teeth of human remains found in the German Historical

Museum in an apparatus called an iron maiden. The body was identified as ILM 2000-43271-CO01. See appendix 2.

- The victim had at least 32 permanent teeth present in the jaws at death;
- The victim had 32 teeth present when postmortem radiographs were taken;
- All crowns had been destroyed by blunt force trauma, leaving only roots embedded in the alveoli.
- Second lower left molar broken off and discovered in victim's shirt pocket (sent to U.S. lab for further testing)

INDIVIDUATING FACTORS

Age is estimated at 35 to 50 years based on the following observations: full formation of the wisdom tooth roots, very large pulp chambers, minimal periodontal resorption.

CONCLUSIONS

The remains designated 2000-43271-CO01 are those of an adult aged 35 to 50 years at the time of death. No crowns remain for observation. All crowns appear to have been destroyed by blunt force trauma. No antemortem dental records exist for comparison.

Hermine Kettgen, DDS   20 July 1998

Hermine Kettgen, DDS.
Forensic Odontologist

IV. THE FINGERPRINT COMPARISON REPORT

Report: 01-32432
Latent Examiner: Liesl Schwede #2766
Case Title: BNM
Comparison Date: July 20, 1998
Victim: Unknown
Location: German Historical Museum
INKED IMPRESSIONS
Print(s) of: Unknown

Print(s) taken by: Bruno Muntz, MD

Date print(s) taken: July 20, 1998

Total number of print(s): 1

Location of print(s): left fifth digit, hand

Condition of print(s): partial

Comparison requested by: Bruno Muntz, MD, Institute of Legal Medicine, Berlin

Dossier supplied by: San Francisco PD (USA), via Bruno Muntz, MD

RESULTS OF EXAMINATION

Lift 1: Positive identification to left fifth finger of THOMAS, CHRISTOPHER, DOB 09/19/52

OTHER SUBJECTS COMPARED WHO WERE

NOT IDENTIFIED

None

Acknowledgments

It is impossible to thank everyone who has been a part of this enormous project. The first person I have to thank is my sister Lamia. I can't think of a better person to collaborate with, and were it not for her attention to detail, her foresight, and vision, I doubt this book would be as gripping a read as it is today.

When I first embarked on this project, I approached some of the writers I knew well and asked them if they wanted to participate. Jonathan Santlofer, John Lescroart, and Tess Gerritsen agreed without asking how much they were getting paid or even receiving many details about the project. Participation from other writers snowballed from there.

As originally conceived, this book would have been an anthology had it not been for my late friend Les Pockell. An experienced hand in publishing and a vice president at Grand Central Publishing, Les possessed a mind that was as sharp as Sherlock Holmes. We became good friends and whenever I visited New York we had lunch or drinks with another friend, Susan Richman. One day, over drinks, Les suddenly paused when he heard about my plans to publish an anthology and donate the money to cancer charities. "If you want sales, Andrew, turn this into a novel in chapters," he said. "I read one of those when I was a kid and it had a huge impact on me." Then he picked up his credit card from the table and with raincoat in hand said good-bye. Susan Richman turned to me and said, "What a genius." Sadly, cancer took the life of Les last summer; during rocky times with this project I've often felt Les's invisible hand guiding me along.

The wonderful thing about an endeavor of this sort is that I've become very good friends with several of the contributors and my friendship has been strengthened with writers whom I had previously known only casually. A special thanks goes to Jeffery Deaver, that man for all seasons. He played a huge part in finding loose ends and tying them all together with a sleight of hand that David Blaine would admire. Jonathan Santlofer, one of the smartest minds around, also played a critical role in strengthening the book and writing the watcher scenes—though I have to admit that he and I did want to kill each other a few times. Thankfully our homicidal thoughts never interfered with our friendship. John Lescroart provided a lot of support and helped us find even more writers for this project and was always there to chew on any ideas that we had. And of course the great David Baldacci who wrote that great introduction; David is one of the true gentleman in the literary world and it was a pleasure to work with him. Alexander McCall Smith helped with exploring the depths of Christopher Thomas's manipulative character.

I would also like to thank my brother Farris for his support and wisdom and enduring presence in the process of bouncing ideas; Lisa Gallagher, one of the sweetest and most supportive people I know; Nancy Yost, who from the start was a guiding light; Joe Finder, who became our oracle; Doug McEvoy, who no matter how busy he was, always found time to give me his sage advice; and the Touchstone team of Stacy Creamer, David Falk, and Michelle Howry, whose faith in this project never wavered.

Some of the other people who were instrumental in helping get this project off the ground were Alice Martel, Alan Jacobson, Lukas Ortiz, Christian Lewis, Ben M., Lesley Winton, Louise, and Nick Ellison.

Also, I must thank both my parents for always encouraging me to read and write when they were alive. My dad spared no expense in buying me hundreds of books and giving me tons of confidence. When I was a scrawny little eight-year-old, writing stories on scraps of paper, my mom was always there to encourage me, and until her last few months on earth, she patiently read all my stories and was the gentlest yet sharpest critic I've ever come across.

This has been a three-year marathon. I learned a lot, felt frustration, suffered some sleepless nights, had that great feeling of anticipation every time I opened an e-mail with a new chapter, and now I revel in the exhilaration of a job well done. But above all, I'm humbled to know that were it not for the tremendous effort and dedication of all the people who played a part, I would not be writing this.

—Andrew F. Gulli

Putting together a cohesive novel written by twenty-six different authors is certainly not a two-person job. Andrew and I learned that—the hard way. *No Rest for the Dead* would not have been possible without the help of our publishers and so many friends; family members; agents; editors; colleagues; and, of course, the writers, whose work I was very privileged to edit.

First and foremost, I'd like to thank my brother Andrew for including me in this, although I must admit there were times (the all-nighters come to mind) when I hated him for it. Also a very big thank-you to my brother Farris. During some of my most frantic moments working on the book Farris was *always* there listening patiently and giving sound advice. He helped resolve plot problems, pointed out logical inconsistencies, and as a physician was always on hand to answer medical/forensics questions that came up. Many thanks also to Christian Lewis, who on very short notice took time out of his schedule to read the book and use his excellent editing and research skills to resolve several key issues in the novel.

Special thanks to Jonathan Santlofer for his help editing, for bringing in additional writers, and for so many of his obvious and less obvious contributions to this book. Also many thanks to Jeffery Deaver, who was always on hand to read large excerpts, offer advice, and even contribute to the editing, and to Kathy Reichs for her detailed and timely responses to all our forensics questions. I'd also like to thank Joseph Finder and Doug McEvoy for their support and invaluable advice, as well as Lisa Gallagher, Nancy Yost, Tess Gerritsen, John Lescroart, Peter James, Michael Palmer, T. Jefferson Parker, Alexander McCall Smith, Diana Gabaldon, Louise Ihm, Alison Jasonides, Marnie Fender, and Lisa Scottoline.

Thanks to everyone at Touchstone, including Stacy Creamer for her excellent editorial advice and for giving Andrew and me the time to make *No Rest* a better book; Michelle Howry for her help editing and for being so patient; and David Falk for deciding to look at the manuscript in the first place.

Lastly, I'd like to thank all of the contributors for their excellent work and for their patience and understanding of the editing process involved in putting together a serial novel. All of the contributors were extremely gracious about edits made to their individual chapters in order for the book to come together as a whole. Without this fantastic lineup of authors this book would not have been possible.

The idea for the book was dreamed up by Andrew as a means to raise funds for cancer charities—except for funds allocated to author payments, all of our profits from *No Rest for the Dead* are going to the Leukemia & Lymphoma Society. According to LLS, each day approximately 148 people in the United States alone die from blood cancer—one person every ten minutes. We're hoping that in some small way our contribution will help make that a smaller number. The Leukemia & Lymphoma Society funds potentially lifesaving research around the world. If you'd like more information about LLS, or to make a donation, please visit their website, www.lls.org.

—Lamia J. Gulli